Til' Death Do Us Part

Also by Franklin White

CUP OF LOVE

FED UP WITH THE FANNY

Til' Death Do Us Part

A collection of stories by

Franklin White

Atlanta, GA

Copyright©1999 by Franklin White

BLUE/BLACK Press is a trademark of A&W Communications

Cover& Book Designed by- A&W Communications
Cover Photo ©The Stock Market/Matthias Kulka

Library of Congress Cataloging-in-Publication Data
White, Franklin
Til' Death Do Us Part/Franklin White.
p.   cm.
CIP99096557
ISBN 0-965-2827-9-1

Manufactured in the United States of America

Dedication

To loyalty in all forms.

Stories

Foreword

Lately I've wondered if the bold challenge of beating death-defying odds, is the driving force of those who've attempted to see if they could stay committed in relationships, no matter what the circumstances? Let it be marriage, a long- term commitment between lovers, or a playground pact between young unknowing souls.

Everyone knows the divorce rate is at an all time high. And the rate of failing relationships, without going through the formalities of a marriage, is on the same level of divorce or higher. Still we try. But what makes us do it? What makes people think they can live together, love together and be together for the rest of their lives, after they've given their oath of commitment? Be it in front of a chapel full of family and friends, the justice of the peace downtown at city hall, or in front of a flaming fire, uttering words of commitment into a lover's ear. What makes us think we can beat the odds and not fall prey to its staggering numbers?

Making the commitment has always been the easy part. But staying true to those words is another story all together. There are way too many obstacles that seem determined to make us all eat our words and call it quits. Deep obstacles, some of which I've captured in this collection of stories that cause drama and heartache for everyone involved. Money, trust, selfishness, loneliness, sex and greed are just a few of the problems, that always seem to find their way in our paths of thriving relationships.

Til' Death Do Us Part, captures the good, bad and ugly of relationships, with entertaining situations of inviting characters who go through many of the tough problems of everyday life struggles to keep their word of commitment to the ones they love. One thing is for sure; you'll be able to relate.

Lockdown

"**I'll never understand** the love you have for that man, but I'm going to stick by you regardless," Teresa sided. She was my best friend in the world. Teresa and I went back as far as friends could go. From time to time, we even played the sister game and after all these years, some around Columbia, South Carolina still think we're sisters.

We'd just finished talking about Keith. Keith Anderson- my husband, and the reason he'd been locked up in the State Penitentiary doing a mandatory fifteen to twenty years, for some crazy ass off the wall foolishness that I didn't fully understand. I can honestly say one thing, his doings were completely under my nose- for a while anyway. I really don't like talking about it, because it hurts so much. The more I keep the details under wraps, what I've found out to be true about Keith, the more it helps me to control my anger and disappointment of having a husband who's in prison making license plates sixteen hours a day. But I will say this. Keith was locked up for pushing drugs and having illegal contact

11

with some fast ass little high school hoes who went to the high school down the street from our house. I even see them little fast ass bitches from time to time, walk past my house and cutting their eyes up towards my place, to see if by chance Keith had been miraculously released. And I really don't mean to call them out their name-but if they only knew what they've done to my life and entire family.

They say it was four of them that Keith was involved with. Keith admitted to giving drugs to only two of them. Then he became their drug contact, by selling drugs to them and at the same time taking them to hotel rooms on the weekends or during school hours to fuck'em. A couple of times with both girls together, but that wasn't his fault, Keith explained. Keith said those out of control little heifers were so bent out of shape in fulfilling their notorious MTV and BET visions of balling and living the lifestyle of high rollers, they'd do anything to fulfill their fantasies and –for the record- they approached him. Keith told me they wanted the life of those little fake ass girl's in the videos, who sweat those punk ass rappers who lie about how much sex they get. If you ask me ninety-eight percent of them punks could never get 'any' if they weren't on television every damn time you turn it on.

That's what me and Teresa were talking about mostly on the phone. Then she began to touch on things she knew I didn't want to hear from her, because I had already made up my mind about keeping Keith in my life, even though he was in prison. He was my man and he needed me in his life more than ever before.

"Kye," Teresa lashed out. It's what everyone called me since I was younger because it's short for Kiesha. "I just think you and the kids would be better off if you started all over. Get you another man or something. Listen, you don't even need a man. Get things back together on your own," she told me.

"That would be all well and good if I had a job, Teresa," I reminded her. I had quit my job, like a fool one week before Keith got caught up in his mess.

"I wish you hadn't done that, Kye."

"Me, too. But you know how long Keith was on me to quit my job. So I did, I wasn't thinking straight."

"You're still not thinking straight."

"So you don't think I should ask Keith about the money he mentioned to me?"

"They're about to cut off your phone, right?"

"Um...hmm," I replied.

"You need money in your pocket, don't you?"

"Um..hmmm."

"You have to feed them kids, I'm sure?"

"You ain't never lied about that," I told her.

"Then hell yeah-you better go see about that money. How much did you say it was again?"

"Three hundred thousand."

"Girl, I don't know what you're waiting on-you better go get yourself paid!" she advised me. "And after you get your money, I want you and your kids to start your lives all over again. It should only be about you and them. Keith has lots of time to figure out what he's going to do with the rest of his life."

I could really see her point. Teresa thought I should've been mad as hell at Keith for even making me and the kids go through all of our changes. The reality of my situation really didn't hit me, until the government seized our joint bank account. I tried to sit down and explain to the FBI that the money in the account was mine, and all they had to do was check all of my bank statements against how much I made at the gas company. But they said to me, in other words, "fuck off." They said if I wouldn't have been spending the money Keith was bringing home, I wouldn't have had the fifty-thousand I saved in the year and a-half that I started putting away. So they kept every dime of it. And I was left broke and in a position where I might have had to do some crazy stuff myself to get some money 'cause I needed it in the worse way.

There was no way I was going to go to my mother and father about my situation. That was out the question. They applauded, when the judge sentenced Keith to all those years, and called him nothing but scum. I couldn't believe they did that-and right in front of my face. They sat on the opposite side of the court room and looked down their noses at the whole proceedings, like they lived on mountain high and never had any problems of their own. I guess they didn't. Not like these.

Drug and rape charges? At one point, Keith even accused them of blowing the whistle on him. And when he started that mess, I told him to shut the hell up because, even though they didn't like him, they wouldn't want to be responsible for taking my kids father away from them. I realized Keith messed up on his own and we were stuck, loving him but hating our situation. So I took Teresa's advice. I was going to go get our money. But I wasn't leaving Keith. He was my man and I loved him. He was the father of my childern and there was no way I was going to look my kids in the eyes, when it became time for them to marry and tell them to "make sure they were ready because their commitment would be to the death," and not keep my end of the bargain. I couldn't let them see me turn my back on their father. So I was going to stay beside my man and do everything he told me, even though that big ass ugly 'can' they were keeping him in, was keeping us apart.

Before I got off the phone, I said to Teresa, "Thank you for being concerned about me."

Teresa chuckled. "Oh, girl, you're welcome. We go back too far and you know how I am anyway. I'm only going to tell you what you need to hear no matter how you feel about it. Call me later, when you find out what's going on with the money, okay?"

That's just the thing. I didn't know what was going on with the money. Keith had just told me about everything two days before and he couldn't talk long, because I heard someone tell him to hurry up and get off the phone. He said it was a prison guard. But I wasn't too sure, unless the guards call you punk-ass up in there.

When Keith was sentenced, I couldn't believe the expression on his face. His laid back, care free attitude he was showing during the trial instantly turned into wide eyes and nervous glances. He'd already been in jail, since they arrested him, because he was being held without bail. But after those big prison guards came in from behind him and nudged him against the table and hemmed him up to slap on the handcuffs, he seemed as though all of his life had been taken from him.

Teresa tried to tell me about what goes on in state pens in South Carolina. She had first hand hearsay about the matter. Her brother had done five years. She was told, if you didn't go into the pen with a horrible record- I mean some horrible nonsense like killing a cop or some insane mess like that- and weren't at least six-eight and two-hundred and ninety pounds of pure muscle, you were going to be tried by some rickety insane fool who wanted to show the rest of the cell block how much of a punk you were.

Keith assured me not one person had said anything to him in his first three months there. But I still don't think it was a guard hollering at him to get off the phone. I just hoped he wasn't in there as somebody's bitch or something, because I knew he would hate that. Keith was a take charge kind of guy. He took care of everything around here and that's how he'd always been with me. But then again, he was in prison now- where everyone wanted to be king. Teresa reassured me not to get alarmed, but after hearing the story of the guy who was put in for statutory rape, like Keith had been, and thrown to the floor by about four or five guys and beaten and raped because he wouldn't let them smell his dick to see if it still had the scent of the young girl's nature on it, it shook me up really bad. And I'm sure her story is going to give me some gray hair-thinking about the possibilities of something similar happening to Keith.

I worried so much because Keith wasn't really in any great shape. And those guys in the pen work out all the time. In the past, if Keith had got into a confrontation, he'd always talked about pulling out his pistol, instead of actually fighting, and everyone knew he would. Keith was barely five-nine, hundred seventy pounds and I know he was doing anything possible to keep those wild ass fools away from him. He kept telling me. "Kye...Kye.... I can handle myself." But if handling himself stood for being paraded around the prison like a bitch or being owned by someone, I know he would crack inside that place.

That's why I wouldn't take Pam and Keith Jr. to see their daddy up in there. Keith Jr. was shell shocked his daddy was in prison. One thing I can say about Keith. He loved his kids and did anything for them. That's what got him locked up in the first place, trying to give them anything they wanted under the sun, instead of giving them what they really needed, which was his love and undivided attention. He wasn't able to give them that 'cause he was always out in the street. So the only thing left for me to do was wait by the phone and hope to God my phone wouldn't be turned off before he called me back, with the information about the money. He eventually called.

"Hey you," Keith said to me. "See, what did I tell you? The phone would still be working," he boasted.

"Probably 'cause it's the weekend, Keith. Hurry up and talk to me about this money, before you have to get off the phone again." I heard him huff. "Keith are you sure you're okay in there?"

"Yes, Kye....I'm fine. Now this is what I want you to do."

Keith stayed on the phone this time long enough for me to get all of his instructions on people to talk to and people not to talk to, in order to get the money he was owed. My first question was simple.

"Is this dangerous?"

"Come'on, Kye, have I every put you in danger before? The money belongs to me -all you have to do is go and pick it up."

Keith had to be extra careful on the phone, but what I already knew about everything made it easy for me to understand Keith talking in code the way he did. The plan was to go see a roughneck that Keith hung out with from time to time, named Ranel. For the record, they were together, the day Keith was picked up by police. Keith and Ranel slung around crack, powder cocaine, weed and some heroin for some big baller' from Virginia named Calvin. They went to settle the score and take their cut on what they sold. Both of them ended up with three hundred thousand a piece, but Keith had an appointment downtown afterwards to pick up another large sum of cash the same day. Ranel dropped him off and understood that Keith would hook up with him later, for his half of the money, because he didn't feel safe carrying a stash that size. It just so happened that Keith never made it back to get his money. One of the tramp high school hoes he got involved with, turned 'states' on him, when her mother found out she'd been fuckin' and smoking weed with my husband on the regular.

When I called and told Teresa the deal, at the top of her voice, she said, "He wants you to do what? Oh...hell no! That shit there is too crazy, Kye!"

"Look, Teresa, I didn't call to get your approval. I just called to let you know what's going on, like I promised."

"Well, I wouldn't do it. Hell no," she snapped.

"Why?"

"At first I thought getting the money would be easy. But, Ranel? He's crazy. He has a bad reputation. If I were you, I'd forget about that damn money and go find me a man, until you can get things back to normal on your end."

"Not that again Teresa, I told you I'm still married. How would bringing a man into my house look to the kids?"

"It's going to look like you got some good damn sense, Kye, that's what."

"Uh..uh. I told you, I'm going to show them what true love is all about and stay true to Keith."

"True love?" Teresa laughed. "You need to get a divorce, 'cause to me Keith is no better for you than a dead man."

"Whatever," I shot back.

"What can he do for you, Kye?" I wasn't listening to her. "He can't touch you when you want? He can't talk to you when he want to? He ain't going to be nothin' but another bill for you once he gets out in the next...FIFTEEN to TWENTY years and if he does get out-who the hell's going to hire his old ass in the year 2020? Things are going to be done changed by then, girl. And lawd' have mercy, I know you ain't going to let him stick his thing in you when he gets back, with all the nasty things going on inside of them prison walls...If, he wants to stick you at all." She was so sarcastic.

"I told you what I was going to do, Teresa. I'll just talk to you later, because you're making me mad."

My car was out of gas and I be damned if I was going

to put what little money I had left in the car, when my kids needed to be fed. I gathered up sixty cents and got my ass on the bus and went to the other side of town to look for Ranel and get Keith's money. I looked around at a couple of places that Keith told me I could probably find Ranel. The people at the car wash, where he sometimes hung out and the restaurant, where he loved to eat, hadn't seen him. A waitress told me that Ranel didn't come in there too much anymore. She said that Ranel all of sudden was walking around the East Side like he was now the man and if he ordered from the restaurant he would have someone bring it over to him in his new condo. I had to beg her to give me the address and finally she did. We happened to have the same hairdresser, so when we found that out, we kind of meshed and sista' girl gave up the info.

Ranel was living large. He was living in a condo complex that had all white stucco structures, swimming pool, an outdoor fitness center and there were all types of nice cars parked under their individual lofts. I went to the address the restaurant had for him. Number three. I stood for a brief second, before I knocked on the door. Right before I knocked, the door was opened. And the guy inside looked at me and nodded his head upward. He was dark skinned with wavy hair and had on baggy shorts and his shoe laces on his sneakers were untied.

"Who you?" He sounded like a country thug.

"Kye," I stumbled. "My name is Kye."

"Kye?"

"That's right."

He started to look me up and down. I had on blue

jeans and a short fitting Fubu shirt. I cut my eyes at him."So what you want, Kye-with those sexy dimples and all that body?"

"I came to see Ranel," I told him. Then this guy looks back into the condo and smiles-showing me at least three gold teeth.

"Ranel got enough company already. Come back, like next week," he ordered. Then he looked down at my feet. There was a newspaper laying on the ground. "Could you hand me that?"

I bent down and I could feel the fool imagining I was giving him head or something. When I raised back up, he had moved a step closer to me. I handed him the paper. "Thanks," he kind of snarled then he shut the door.

I stood in my exact spot, frozen-still for about twenty seconds, and went over what just happened and I realized I'd just been played like a cheap trick. I was tired and had been looking for Ranel's ass all day. I wasn't going back home without talking to him. I knocked again.

'Fool' answered again and had the nerve to say, after he licked his lips, "So I guess you want to get with me now huh, since Ranel is busy?" He began to chuckle. "Anything to get a hit off that pipe- you bitches are wild."

'Fool' laughed in my face and I reached the end of my wick and exploded. "Muthafucka', bein' high wouldn't make me want to fuck your ugly ass. So what does that tell you? Tell Ranel, Keith's wife, Kye, is out here to see him."

'Fool's' eye's enlarged a bit, then he gave me a fake smile. This time I could only see half of his golden grill. I wished like hell he'd put his hand over his mouth.

"Hold up," he mumbled. Thirty seconds later I was inside, with a cool drink in my hands, sitting across from Ranel and all of his young hoes who happened to be there.

Ranel's place was nice inside. I only saw one room. I guess it was the den. But everything in it was white. White carpet, white leather furnature, white curtain shades, white table, white shelves, the little young girl's sitting around getting high had on white, even Ranel's black ass had on white but the entire atmosphere was far from heaven.

Ranel noticed me checking out his place. He thought he was so fly, sitting there with his bug eyes, trying to look like Puff Daddy or some damn body, beleive me, he wasn't. "So you like what you see?" he asked me and I nodded at him. "So what can I do for you, Kye? It's been a long time. Oh yeah, I almost forgot? How's Keith?"

I knew that bastard knew what I came for. I could see it in his eyes. "He's locked up," I told him.

"Oh..yeah....that's right. So what brings you out?"

I took a sip of my drink, because what Keith told me to ask for seemed like it was a whole lot easier to do before I sat down in front of this punk nigga'.

"Keith told me to come by and pick up what he never had a chance to get, before he was picked up and thrown in the pen."

Ranel's eyebrows raised and he calmly asked me while he was looking over his girls, "Did he tell you what it was?"

"Yeah, his money."

Ranel acted like he didn't hear what I said, because another one of his young hoes came into the room in a thong and bra and sat down on the arm of his chair. I looked through all of the make-up and the wig this young girl had on and it was the same heifer who took the stand and turned 'states' on my Keith. She bent down and gave Ranel a kiss, then turned and looked at me and smiled.

"Fuck Luke, ya'll! He ain't got nothin' on me!" Ranel shouted to all five girls laying around half ass naked. "Come on, smoke this weed up!" All the girls started to giggle like it was recess or some shit. At·that point Ranel looked at.me hard, "Money, you say?"

"That's right. Three-hundred thousand, Ranel. Keith told me you had it for him?"

Ranel began to laugh, then all of a sudden he stopped. "Bitch, I don't have no damn three-hundred thousand dollars for your ass!" he said. The little girls, all except 'Hoe' sitting on the arm of his chair left the room. Everything was silent for a moment. "Look, Kye. I've known you for a long time now. Why would you come over here and ask for some shit like that? If you need a couple of dollars, I can do that for you because you cool."

Ranel went into his pocket and took out what looked to be like six one-hundred dollar bills and gave it to 'Hoe' and nodded towards me. She looked at me like she was scared to get up. "Now that should help you out a little, Kye. And if you need more, I'm sure you and me can work something out." Ranel's eyes traveled my body and he licked his lips, then shifted his eyes to 'Hoe's' ass as she strutted over to me in her high heel shoes and thong. She was such a nasty little thing. Her titties were barely in her bra and the entire front of her stuff could be seen through the front of her thong. She held out the money. I looked her up and down.

"Ranel, you know Keith got locked up for messin' with this young stupid bitch, don't you?"

Ranel was just about to take a hit off his blunt, but stopped. "Yeah, I know. It's a shame he couldn't wait to get fucked 'cause she eighteen now and I'm hittin' it. To be truthful, you disturbing her birthday party," he said. Then I looked at 'Hoe' still holding the money in my face. Damn right I took it.

I tried my best to make ends meet, with the money Ranel gave to me. It turned out to be eight-hundred dollars, so I was able to pay my phone bill, get a whole lot of oatmeal, peanut butter and soup for the kids. Then I filled up the tank in the car and put about two hundred of it away. One thing I was grateful for. Keith paid off the house about a year and a half ago and I didn't have to worry about a mortgage, because if I did we would've been long gone into the streets.

I don't know why but it took three weeks before Keith called back. It was strange, because usually he called every week, sometimes three times a week. That's why my phone bill was so high, because he called collect. I started to worry, but I remember Keith telling me if the authorities didn't contact me, saying something was wrong with him, then he was okay. I needed to talk to him though. There was no doubt in my mind Ranel knew about the money. He was just playing stupid and trying to play me. I could see it right through his slick ass eyes. His pretending not to know anything about it really pissed me off and I know, if Keith was on the street, he would've just gave me the shit, no questions asked, and never called me a bitch. Because he knew if Keith was on the block and he would've said that crap- he would've been shot and laid to rest.

    I finally talked with Keith, but he was short and hurried. He asked me how things went and I told him as best as I could, but he didn't have time to react. He was rushed off the phone and it left me hanging wondering what to do next. I started remembering what Keith told me about Ranel and him hating to be loud talked and his business laid out in the street. All Ranel had was his rep' and if people started to hear how he was treating me with Keith's money, they would begin to have second thoughts in dealing with him and his drug business would suffer. I decided that if I could get into a couple of his contacts' ears about the situation, he would hear about it- then do right by me and Keith. I waited around a couple of more days and sat by the phone, hoping that Keith would call, but he didn't. Deep down inside I started to feel like a hustler, because that's exactly what I'd been doing since Keith had been locked up. Hustlin' to keep food and clothes on my kids back. I didn't worry too much about my needs. All those weekly trips to the beauty shop and shit was a thing of the past. I started to do my own hair and if it didn't turn out right -just plop a baseball hat on top and put on my earrings and I could still make it through the day. One thing about hustlin' though, it sure does put ideas in your head, especially when you're on the brink of having nothing at all. A time or two I had seriously thought about laying on my back, just to get some extra cash. I didn't want to go out in the street and sell my stuff. I still knew a couple of nigga's who were interested. Some nigga's who would still, from time to time, shoot game at me, even when Keith was on the block, who would happily give me money to sleep with me. All I had to do was pick up the phone and I decided that if my plan for Ranel didn't work, it was going to be the very next thing I would do because things were getting tight.

There was no way I was going to travel on the bus this time to begin putting salt in Ranel's game. His contacts' were too spread out. I got in my car and started hitting every drug corner where I knew Keith and Ranel's contacts' were located. After my first couple of stops, I realized what I was doing was a good idea, because it seemed that Ranel had taken over everything that Keith left behind. The best thing about that was, every single soul had love for Keith and they were listening to what I had to say.

"Hey, Kye! Kye, is that you?" I heard a raspy voice from behind me call out, as soon as I began walking through the outside flea market, looking for some of Keiths soldiers.

"Casper?" He was a friend of me and Keith's, who'd gone to prison years ago.

"Yeah, baby, it's me. It- is me!" Casper pulled me close to him and gave me a hug.

"When did you get out?" I wanted to know.

"About three weeks ago. I been on the low-low, trying to get acclimated to being back on the streets. You know it's a hard thing to do."

"I bet it is."

"So what you doing out this way?"

I didn't answer back right away. My mind and eyes were trying to determine how much Casper had changed since he'd been in prison. He looked much lighter than I remembered and his beard was ridiculously long. I mean, so long that it was twisted in locks and touched him at the midpoint of his chest.

"I see you checkin' out the beard, baby girl?" Casper ran his hand down the length of it. "It was my strength inside that hell hole, you hear me?"

I smiled at him, that's when I noticed all the tiny moles on his face. "I hear you," I told him.

"So what you doing out here?" he asked again.

"Just looking to talk to some people."

It was almost like he'd forgotten and he touched my arm, "Hey, I saw Keith on the inside."

"You did?"

"Yeah. I saw him. A couple times. He was on my block for a week, then I got moved to release block."

"Did you get to talk to him? How was he doing?"

"He was doing okay- as good as you can do in that place. He was telling me what happened and how he and Ranel had things tied up out here."

I shook my head. "That's why I'm out here now, Casper." He didn't understand, the look on Casper's face told me so. "Ranel's trying to do Keith for some money he owes him and I'm out here broke, with two kids and bills to pay, while my man is locked up."

"No shit?"

"Ummm.hmmm. Right before Keith got picked up he asked Ranel to hold some money for him. But Ranel is acting real fucked up about the whole situation. I guess he thinks the money is his."

Casper squinted his eye's, "Naww', that money ain't his. That's family money," Casper said. "So what you trying

27

to do about it?"

"I'm out here puttin' out the word on Ranel's ass."

Casper looked around, "You spreadin' hate, Kye?"

"I have to. What else am I going to do?"

"Kye, you tryin' to get yourself killed? Come on, let's talk about this."

Casper sat with me in my car for about two hours. At first, I didn't understand why he took such an interest in my well being. He told me it was because he'd seen too many people since the early eighties get killed over drugs. Even fools in prison, who would fight over a hit off a joint. One thing I realized about prison, when I was talking to Casper, was how deep and complicated it was. He told me more in the first hour than Keith had ever revealed to me.

"What's on ya' mind?" Casper wanted to know. He could probably tell I was agitated.

"Trying to figure out why Keith hasn't told me all of this stuff that goes on in prison, that's all." Casper laughed at me.

"Think about it, Kye? Why would he? Prison is hard, especially if you never really thought you would end up in that bitch. Let me tell you something. When you go up in there, looking like a bitch, all scared and shit, that's what you're made and it don't take long from them crazy fools to notice who's scared. I've seen niggas' come up in there and within hours are holding on to muthafuka's' pockets or walking behind a nigga wit' they head down, following every step of a hard ass who's already turned him out and beat the shit out of him, until he admits he's a bitch. Do you know what it means to a man, to submit and be another's bitch? It's sick-I'm telling you, sick."

I didn't want to ask, but I had to. "So how did Keith look?"

Casper didn't answer me right back. He thought about it for a minute. "I never talk about anyone specifically in the joint, Kye. That shit is too shaky and whatever a man have to do to survive, a man do. I know that's your man and I have to respect what you two have going on...you know?"

"I understand," I said back to him.

Casper noticed my disappointment. "But I can tell you this. He was holdin' his own, he was holdin' his own," he repeated as though he was reflecting.

I was relieved to hear it and I noticed Casper smile. "What?"

"I'm only going to tell you this Kye because I can see the pain and anxiety all over your face and shit."

"Tell me what?"

"I can tell Keith got you caught up in the game."

"Game? What game?"

"The game that's necessary for a con when he's locked up. Look, it's a must that a con control his lady who's out on the street. It's like this. If a convict can make you feel good while he's inside, he's got it made. Personally, I never did any shit like that. I don't fuck with people's emotions."

"What are you talking about?"

"I'm talking about the emotions of a woman. Ninety percent of cons want to make you feel like you're the only thing they have left in the world. I mean they lay it on thick too." Casper laughed and pretended to spread peanut butter on a slice of bread, "Baby, I love you. Baby you're all that I need in my life, even these walls can't stop the penetration of our love. They can't lock up our love. They can throw away the key, baby, 'cause when it comes to you it just don't matter." Casper chuckled again. "And that shit works more times than you would believe. But three fourths of the time, when a convict gets out? He go running to someone else. That's the game. That-is-the-game-I-know."

We talked for a while longer and Casper said that he would go with me to see Ranel again. While we rode over to Ranel's place, I thought about what he said and I realized that I did feel good about being all that Keith had left in the world. It was the exact feeling I was looking for, while he was on the outside, touching on those girls. But it never materialized. I got mad for a minute, 'cause I felt like a fool, because it was the same thing Teresa was trying to tell me. But coming from Casper, who'd lived the life, made it hit home that much more. Soon we were at Ranel's. When we pulled up, he was washing his car. When Ranel recognized me, he began to shake his head and laugh. We got out of the car.

"Something told me you would be back."

"You were right," I told him.

"Casper? Whaz-up my brutha'." Casper walked over and embraced Ranel.

"Good to see you back on the block," Ranel told him.

"Good to be seen," Casper said flat out.

There was a brief pause. Everyone's eyes were on Ranel's car.

"New?" Casper asked.

Ranel puckered his lips at Casper.

"Must have cost you around fifty-sixty thousand?" The words came out of me uncontrollably.

"So, what's this visit all about?" Ranel asked.

"Ranel, I came out here with Kye to talk to you."

"Talk to me? Talk to me about what?"

"About my money," I snapped. Casper raised his hand up and motioned for me to calm down.

"Look, Ranel. Keith told Kye to come by and pick up the money he left with you. He left money with you, righ'?" I guess Ranel knew about Caspers kick ass ways, so he respected him and told him the truth. Ranel looked like his big brown ass was eating those weights in the pen and his six-foot-five frame gave him that straight crazy ghetto ass look.

"Yeah. We had dealings."

"So where's the money?" Casper asked.

"Not that it's any of your business. I reinvested it."

"What kind of shit is that, Ranel? You don't put nothing away that ain't yours," Casper told him.

"Look. Me and Keith were partners. Not me, Keith and Kye. My bidness' partner got swallowed the fuck up, so I have to keep rollin'."

"Well, he was my partner, too," I told him. "So give me my fuckin' money, Ranel."

"Listen bitch. You don't come over here demanding shit."

"Watch yourself, Ranel, I haven't beat any ass since my first year in prison. Muthafuka's' didn't want to deal with me anymore after I broke a nigga's face against his cell and showed everybody the flavor in that bitch- so watch what you say to my friend you understand?"

Ranel eased his eyes off me a little. "So what you gonna' do about this little situation?" Casper wanted to know.

"Aint much I can do. Like I said, the money is tied up." Ranel dismissed the conversation and dipped a rag into his bucket and began to wash his Lexus.

"Well untie it," I lashed out.

"It's not that easy. That money is already tied up in the street -in the game. You know what I'm saying? It's workin' on the streets."

"All of it?" Casper asked.

"Every last penny," Ranel answered, then he bent down, picked up the hose so he could start rinsing off the suds on his car. That's when Casper kneeled down and picked up part of the hose and bent it with one hand, preventing the water from coming out when Ranel tried to spray the suds off his car.

"Fuck that, Ranel. You livin' too nice up in here? You got to give up something?"

Ranel looked at Casper. "Nigga', do you mind letting go of the fuckin' pressure, before the sun fades my shit?"

"Yeah, as soon as you give her some cash or I'm goin' to start wrappin' this motherfucka' around your little bony ass neck."

"Come on, man...you fuckin' up the paint," Ranel whined.

"It's going to be your ass in a minute. Now talk to her."

That same night, Ranel laid two-hundred thousand

of cold cash on the back seat of my car. We began negotiating as soon as the sun began to beam down and dry the soap on his car. I didn't think two-hundred thousand was that bad of a deal. Casper did most of the talking and don't you know he drove off in a1997 BMW 750iL that Ranel won in some card game and never drove. Shoot, after that, I gave Casper five grand and took my merry ass on my way. I put about five-thousand dollars in the house with me, then asked Teresa if I could put some of my money in one of her accounts. I wanted to make sure the fed's weren't watching me. Then I opened up a couple of small accounts for myself and my kid's college. I'd began job hunting and was going to let all the money sit in the bank forever and collect interest, because we were set and I was never ever, ever going to be broke again. I made up my mind that I was going to find myself a job and use the money from my job for expenses and leave the other money alone, as long as I could. It really was a good ending to some bull that tested my patience-like I never imagined.

The kids were about to start back to school and I wanted them to see their father, because they began asking a lot of questions that I couldn't answer about him. I hadn't talked to Keith, so he didn't know anything about the money and how funky Ranel was acting, nor the deal we made. The kids had been acting kind of quiet, so I thought I would cheer them up by taking the drive out to see Keith. When we arrived at the prison, the car seemed like it had gotten ultra quiet. The kids were frozen. My heart even began to pump a little harder, as it was being filled with joy to see Keith and sorrow that it was in the worst place anyone could ever be seen in.

We were sitting in the family visiting area when they brought Keith out. I don't know why they had him shackled by his ankles and hands, like he'd killed somebody or something.

The guards brought him over to us and watched him struggle to sit down. Keith just sat there, unable to move, unable to hug, just silent, letting his eyes run down each of us, one at a time.

Keith didn't look like my Keith. He looked tired, cold, his eyes were red and his hair had grown to a length that I had never seen before. My baby girl couldn't take it. The man she was looking at was not the daddy she knew. Her daddy had wide bright eye's, always smiled, always had something for her behind his back. She put her head in my lap and began to cry, as her brother stood, standing tall, looking at his daddy in total shock.

"Kye, why you bring them here?" Keith asked.

"To see you." I tried to smile. "Look how big they're getting Keith."

"You could've sent me some pictures or some shit, Kye," Keith mumbled as harsh as he could without startling his son, who was still staring at him.

"But they wanted to see you?" We both noticed Keith Jr. take one step closer to his father. Then he reached out and ran his finger down the length of his handcuffs.

"Get him, Kye. Get him away. I don't ever want him to have to touch this shit again," Keith explained looking down at his handcuffs. Keith Jr. backed away, then all of a sudden he fell into his fathers lap head first and began to cry.

I'm not going to say the little ones got used to seeing

their father the way he was. But when we left, they seemed a little more at ease, they at least had a chance to see Keith's face. But I knew they were hurting to see him that way. Keith surprised me-and I never saw him before turn on his negotiating charm. He went to another level, and quickly, to after he couldn't stop them from crying. He talked to both of his kids quickly and convincingly, as though his life depended on it. He wanted to let them know he was okay and that everything was going to be all right. I sat and wondered how he became that way. It was almost like that's what he spent his entire time inside doing. On the drive back home, the kids were in the back seat.

"Twenty, twenty-one, twenty-two." Pam stopped counting. "I'm going to be twenty-two when daddy come home."

"Uh...uh... you can't count, you'll be......Twenty-three, twenty-four, twenty-five, twenty-six, ...Twenty-Seven. 'Cause daddy ain't getting out until he do twenty years. Didn't you see how they had him chained up like a dog?" Keith Jr. said to his baby sister.

"Shut up, you don't know! He might be able to come home to see me graduate, or my prom! Ain't that right, mama?"

"Well, I don't care," Keith Jr. said.

I looked back at him and he was staring out the window, squinting his eyes. I didn't have enough nerve or guts to try to handle the situation. I just continued to drive and hoped they were through talking about it. It couldn't have been two minutes after we got home that the telephone rang. It was a collect call.

"Hello?"

"Hey, baby," Keith said into the phone. "You make it back okay?"

"Yes, yes we did."

"Thanks for coming. I was surprised."

"No problem, Keith."

"You know, you and the kids make me feel so much better. You're all that I have," he said. "Are they okay?" I looked around for them. Keith Jr. was getting a bowl of ice cream and Pam was watching TV. "Ummm...hmmm they're fine."

"Good. I want you to bring them back again. Maybe next month sometime, because something about today motivated me."

"Keith?"

"Yeah, what is it?"

"It's not going to be a next time," I decided.

"What? Kye, what are you talking about?"

"I'm getting a divorce."

"A divorce? Why? You can't do that? Why would you do that?" Keith asked frantically.

"Because it's for the best."

"But you said, you would always love me?"

"Oh, I do love you. But I'm doing this for the kids."

"The kids?" he asked.

"Yes, the kids."

"Kye, you know I wish I could do for you and my children?"

"Keith, I do, too. Now I have to be going. Take care."

Benefit of the Doubt

It had been raining the entire day in our fair city of N'awlins'. It was as if someone was standing above and having a good time, turning on the faucet that plummeted everyone down below, on and off all day long. My car was already in need of a wash before the rain, but after all the splashing of dirt and mud, the wash that could have waited another day or two had turned mandatory because 'Sexy Sharon' don't ride rain shower dirty for nobody. Once I was sure the brightening sun was out to stay, I was forced to drive into the first car wash I could find.

"Well, I'll be damn," I heard someone say from behind me, right after I began to watch my car creep through the automatic wash. I turned around slowly.

"It is you. Hey, girl, give me a hug!"

The man standing in front of me extended his arms out to me. I didn't know who he was, so naturally a sista' was very hesitant.

He pounded his chest."Girl, it's me. Nate. Nate from high school. Shoot, it's probably been fifteen, sixteen years, since I seen you! How have you been?"

I quickly zoomed back into my past. I tried to go back to my high school days and focus on this man who was standing in front of me at the same time. This Negro was blue black, plain ol' midnight, with about three inches of hair neatly cut in a small afro on his head. He stood about six feet, but through everything else about him, his dark skin is what tipped me off and brought back my recollection.

"Blue?" I called out.

He laughed. "Yeah, that's right! But don't nobody call me Blue no more, that was a high-school phase. It's Nate, and welcome to one of my four car wash establishments I got spread out all over. It's so good to see you Sharon. How are you?"

"I'm fine," I said back. "It has been a long time since we've seen each other hasn't it?" We stood standing looking at each other both reflecting on the past and how quickly the years had gone by. At least I was. I remembered Blue being really cool, back in our day. Matter of fact, we were kind of tight. Tight enough to put a book or two in each other's locker if our classes were nearby and cool enough to sit down and eat lunch at the same table everyday for lunch with the same clique. I was positive the last time we both saw each other was when we walked across the stage at our high school graduation. When people say, *those were the days*, that's exactly what they are. It's hard to explain and maybe, because we were all seniors in high school and we really didn't have much to worry about, that everyone enjoyed how things use to be. Most of us were just beginning to listen to rap music...I was really into B Angie B and Cheryl the Pearl, I just loved them. My song was, *"Funk You Right On Up"*.

"Sharon, you okay?" Blue asked. I mean Nate.

"Yes, I'm fine. Just drifting a bit about the old days, you know how it is when those years catch up to you."

"Yeah, those were some good times. I don't get to see much of the old crew anymore, except by chance, like I saw you here today. So what you up to these days?"

"Well, I have my own computer web design company now."

"Computers?"

"That's right. Nowadays, if you aren't on the world wide web, you're really not in business."

"You know, that's exactly what my wife was telling me. Why don't you come into my office and tell me what you do? Maybe, we can do business. I'll just go out and tell the fella's to detail your car while we talk. It's on the house-how's that?"

"Fine, that's fine, Blue. Sorry Nate."

Two hours later, Nate and I were signing contracts for me to design his web site to include all four of his locations. Right before I was about to leave, his wife walked into his office. She was wearing a pretty sun dress and her hair was combed to the back. She was taller than me but a little heavy for her height but still, she was pretty because she had gorgeous skin and breath taking facial features. When she walked completely in, she kind of gave me a wondering look. So, I smiled and said, "Hello."

39

Nate did the introduction. "Sheila, this is Sharon. She's an old schoolmate of mine and guess what Sweetheart?"

"What's that Nate," she said. I suspected she was a little leery of me being there because she sure sound like she was.

"She's going to put me on the world wide web! Advertise my establishments on the internet. I finally took your advice."

"Oh, really now?" Sheila asked then she finally smiled.

She seemed really interested, so I jumped into the conversation. "Yes, I was telling your husband how important it is to have a web site these days."

"Good, because I've been telling him the same thing for the last year or so."

"And that's why I took her up on her offer, baby. Why don't you oversee the whole thing, Sheila? You're more up to speed with computers than I am?"

"Sure, sure, Nate. No problem, it sounds like fun."

I was about a good month into the design of Nate's site. Sheila and I had met on more than one occasion to discuss the look and layout. The first time we met at a restaurant. The second time, at my place.

"So, what do you think of the site so far, Sheila?"

"I'm impressed. You really do good work," she said.

"Thank you."

"You're welcome. You know, Sharon, I was wondering if I could ask you a question?"

"Sure."

"Well, I don't hang out with a lot of girlfriends and very rarely discuss things going on in my life. I guess I'm truly the definition of a loner."

Her honesty made me smile. "Don't worry about it, I'm the same way," I revealed.

"Really?"

"I'm an only child and I've always had a hard time letting someone into my bubble. I feel more secure that way. You know what I mean?"

"Yes, I certainly do."

"So, what's the question?"

"Well, it's about Nate. I think he's seeing someone, but I can't prove it and I need to know what I should do about it?" Sheila confided.

"Wow, Sheila, I wasn't expecting that?"

"I know, I know—but I had to tell someone before I burst into little pieces. Just thinking about it drives me crazy."

"Oh, believe me, I understand. That's why I'm on hiatus from men at the moment."

"You are?"

"Girlfriend, I've been man free, going on six months."

"That's a long time."

"But it's been a good break. It truly has."

Sheila paused for a moment.

"If I find out for sure, Nate's cheating on me, I'm going to start my little hiatus, too," Sheila snapped.

"There must be a reason why you think he's cheating?"

Sheila huffed, "No doubt about it and her name is Brandy. I've never caught them doing anything, but the fact remains, she's always around him every time I look up."

"So what does Nate say about her?"

"Oh, he just dismisses her and assures me nothing is

going on. But I can't get past the way they look at each other."

I don't know how it happened, because when I broke up with my man I swore I didn't want to be involved in any more male, female problems, but Sheila and I started to hang out a little and I was like forced to listen to her. I guess, I was feeling sorry for the way she felt. I remembered feeling the same way, and definitely could relate to her situation and probably could've used someone to talk to, about my own situation when I was going through the same drama in my life. But Nate was now paying me a salary, a very good one at that, and I didn't want to get too deep into their business. After all- it was their business.

I arranged to meet with Nate, to pick up the new pictures he had a photographer take of all his car wash sites, to add to the website. He asked me to meet him at his car wash, which was twenty miles outside the city. I didn't have a problem with that, because the actual look of an establishment up close and personal allowed me to really develop a better site. When I pulled up into the car wash, I noticed Nate stick his head inside the window of a black Mercedes Benz. I couldn't see what he was doing or who the other person was he was talking to, because his body was blocking my sight. I waited for about ten minutes, not wanting to disturb him, then soon enough he pulled away from the window, laughing hysterically, and the car began to drive away. At the same time the power tinted windows began to roll up, but I could tell it was a woman driving because I saw her earring sparkle from the reflection of the sun. I got out of my car.

"Nate!" I called out.

He turned around, "Hey, Sharon! Hi you!"

"Fine, I'm here to pick up the pictures and take a look around the place, just like you asked."

Nate looked at his watch. "Is it time already? I'm tellin' you, I just can't seem to keep track of the time these days," he admitted.

Nate began to show me around the car wash. It was much larger than the others and he told me it was his favorite location. It was in a very high traffic area and to say the least very busy. I never imagined a car wash being so. After the tour, he took me back into his office to pick up the pictures for the site. I was surprised to see a bed inside.

"Don't mind the bed," Nate pointed out. "I need to fold it back up into my couch. Sometimes I have to catch some Z's when I'm out here, so I can stay fresh."

I've seen a lot of beds in my day that have just been used for other purposes than sleeping and the bed in his office was sure close to the ones I remembered. The pillows were scattered all over the bed, the sheets endlessly wrinkled and the cover was crumpled up into a ball and thrown into the center of the bed.

"Wild sleeper, huh?" I teased.

He turned and looked quickly at the bed. "Uh...yeah. I guess you can say so." Then Nate began to rush. He sat down behind his desk and began looking for the pictures. "I know they're around here somewhere. I was looking at them not too long ago," he acknowledged. He continued to look on his desk, then he stopped and looked up at me. "I notice you and Sheila have been hanging out a little, huh?"

"Yes, we've managed to go out for a drink or two."

"That's good, I really appreciate you spending time with her. I've been so busy around here, that I haven't been able to spend as much time with her as I would like. You know what I mean?"

"Um-hmm, I know, Nate. You're a very busy man."

He caught my sarcasm. Maybe it was the look on my face and my eyes going back and forth towards the seemingly fucked out bed. "What? What's wrong, Sharon?"

I didn't want to comment on what I was feeling I swear I didn't. But a possible cheating man is not high on my list of favorite people. So, I told him, "I don't know, Nate. I didn't really want to say anything to you and I wasn't going to until I walked in here and noticed the condition of your bed."

"The condition of my bed, what about it?"

"It just looks like it's been used," I told him.

"It has, I told you-I was sleeping in it." He noticed my expression again. I wasn't convinced. "I'm serious, Sharon. And who would I be in the bed with? There's definitely not anyone around here I'm interested in. If you haven't noticed, nothing but men work here." Nate opened the drawer of his desk still looking for his pictures.

"Who was the woman, Nate?"

He looked up at me. "What?"

"The lady you were talking to outside?"

"Oh, uh, she's someone I know." Nate looked at my unbelieving face and then over to his messy bed. "Ohhh, no, Sharon. Don't even try it."

"I haven't said anything."

"But you're thinking foul."

"Because things—look—foul, Nate. You know Sheila

thinks you're fooling around, don't you?"

"Yeah, I know. She's never been quite secure with herself. That's how she is."

"My goodness, do you blame her?"

"Yes, because I'm not doing anything to make her feel that way." Nate let out a sigh of relief, "Here they are!" He pulled out the pictures from under a stack of papers. "Care to take a look at them?"

"Sure, Nate. Why not?" He handed me the pictures and I started to go through them. "Sharon, there's no way I would cheat on Sheila. No matter how things look, I wouldn't do it," he tried to explain. But it sounded like he was pleading to me.

I called Sheila and asked her to meet me for a drink. I was in deeper than I wanted to be. I'd seen too much and I've always believed sisters needed each other, when things were not quite right. I was just hoping I could let her know what I saw, without calling the situation absolute. When she arrived, Sheila noticed me looking at a couple who were embraced in a deep kiss, in a booth across from our table.

"You think they might want to go someplace where they can stretch out?" She chuckled.

"They really should?" I commented. "I already ordered our drinks," I mentioned.

Sheila took off her jacket, "LongIsland iced teas?"

"Yep, you know it."

"So, what did you want to talk about?"

I was blunt, "Nate."

"Oh?"

45

"I went to pick up the photographs of the car wash out on the west highway and there were a couple of things I noticed that weren't quite right."

"Like?"

"Well for one, when I pulled up, I saw him with his head inside of a car, talking to a woman."

"A Mercedes?" Sheila asked.

"Yeah, how'd you know?"

"It's Brandy's."

I didn't want to say anymore. I was even thinking how to change the subject.

"What else did you see?" she asked.

"Well, when I went into Nate's office, his couch bed looked like it had just been used for more than sleeping, but I can't say for sure."

Our drinks couldn't have come at a better time. We sat and sipped on them, without commenting any further on what I told Shelia, until they were almost completely gone.

Sheila finally spoke. "Now you see what I mean, don't you?"

"About him fooling around?" I clarified.

"Yes. That's exactly what I mean."

"But I didn't actually see anything, Sheila. I just wanted to tell you an odd detail or two."

"And I appreciate it, Sharon. All of these odd details are the things making me think he's cheating anyway, because I've never seen anything myself that would make me say he is for sure. Don't you know I got a call earlier today from a man."

"What man?"

"He didn't leave his name. He asked me if Nate was my husband and I told him yes."

"Well, who was he?"

"Didn't say, but he did say that his wife was messing around. He sounded like he was crying or something. He told me to watch out. Then he hung up the phone."

"That's it?"

"That was it," Sheila acknowledged.

"I don't know if I could sit back and wonder like you do, Sheilia. I don't have the patience," I told her.

"I've been wondering for years, Sharon, but since I haven't found out anything for sure, all I continue to do is give him the benefit of the doubt."

"Well, do me a favor, okay?"

"Sure."

"Do you know much about his business dealings?"

"No, not really, I basically let him handle everything."

"Don't do that, Sheila. Get involved. Learn everything you can. Everything from the type of soap he uses to the water temperature. You never know what you might need to know later on down the road. You understand?"

"Why do you say that?"

"Because I've seen it time and time again, when men try to keep total control of establishments their wives help them build, and I don't want you to get burnt, that's all."

"Yeah, I better huh? Don't want to give him the benefit of the doubt that he'll always take care of me.

"There you go. It's only for the best." I lifted my glass to her, "Cheers."

Love So Deep

Twenty–two powerful years of marriage. Time had tiptoed upon Cuffee and I and placed its tightening grip on our shoulders, stern, like a crazed thief in the night. Its unwavering element of surprise was strong, ferocious, more than enough to make me stand in astonishment of what had been, and what hadn't become of our lives. Yes,.....our black lives. Our simple, but very complicated, black lives.

Twenty-four years ago, Cuffee had asked of me a single question, more of a request. Her tone of voice that night had been similar to the tone the Black Panthers, which we were a part of, adopted when dealing with folks we didn't fully trust, those who claimed to be interested in our mission and our goals.

We were engaged in serious business. The business of liberating our people from the strong grip of a government that wouldn't...couldn't...dared not release its stranglehold on the black people of America. We didn't trust a soul, including some of our own people. Those black-Tom's, who did manage to infiltrate, didn't fully comprehend our objective. There was no way they could. Most of the black infiltrates, sent to spy on us, didn't fully understand what they were sent to do. Those uniformed rats. Those faint hearted souls. But we understood. Their families were hurting too.

In the late 60's and early 70's, nothing about being black was fair. A job, any job. Yeah…any job, no matter if it meant bringing down your own people in the process, was a good job. A job kept families from sloshing around in squalor. A job, any job, kept families fed. And clothed. And warm. And clean. It was the same thing with slavery, when our own people sold us for profit.

The same shaking intonation we used to rattle new faces, so we could determine spies from the CIA and other counter intelligence rats, is what was present in Cuffee's tone to me. Cuffee wasn't harsh, she just wanted to know. Curious. Wondering. Needing to know. I've never forgotten the question she asked me, as I stood before her, a young, twenty-three year old man, with nothing but bold optimism and passion about our future, as long as she was by my side.

It was 1975. We were standing in the parking lot of an A&W Root Beer joint in Pittsburgh. It was one of the very last A&W's to still service outside and the atmosphere was heavy…yes, heavy. All the cars in the parking lot were tuned into the same radio station, listening to the *Isley Brothers*. Slick hand shakes, high fives and head nods were exchanged by the brothers who pulled up every twenty seconds or so in their Chevys and Buick Sedans, searching for a place to park. Their dates sat as close as they could on their arms, in a daze from the lyrics the *Isley Brothers* sang into their ears. And, yes, you could smell the pot. The pot, the marijuana, the bud. Even without its presence though, the night would have felt *mild…..light…..mellow.* It was as though everyone had put our struggle behind us for a couple of hours. No minds were focused on the police brutality, rampant riots, discussions of why Malcolm and Martin had been killed, blatant discrimination, and why bodies of our black men, women and children were being found dead on a nightly basis down in the south. It was simply peaceful. The struggle we were fighting as a tightly formed brethren, with the larger agenda being the entire nation, was not our fight that night. The *Isley's* weren't singing *Fight The Power.* For once, we tried to do nothing but tune our battle out. Our minds were clear, relaxed, enjoying the uncommon scenery of wide and genuine smiles on faces that were ever so close to becoming frozen in anger by the exhausting job of liberating our people. Black souls who, at any other time, any other moment, would be ready to make our presence known by any means necessary by ways that would have been labeled beyond radical, creating blood and tears if need be. But that's not where minds were that night. What can I say? It was just a damn good night…a <u>damn</u> good night. So good, there was nothing else left for me to do. The presence within me was still, the eyes before me astonishing, like diamonds in a stream. So I let it be. Let what was on my mind be….Yeah…that's what I did, just let it be.

The gesture of shaking my head and licking my lips made my strong, deliberated question come from my mouth as if it was a grunt.

"Cuffee, will you marry me?" I asked, as I stood still,

standing cool with my hand wrapped around her waist. Yeah I was cool, among the other brothers and sisters who were standing around cool as well. I remember seeing "Fight the Power" T-shirts, along with, red, black and green necklaces draped around necks, picks in Afros with fist molded on the handles, brightly colored dashikis draped on strong backs. We stood for something in our day. Our dress, our appearance, reflected the power we had within, a power we shared with one another.

Today's "hip-hop" fashions are a pale shadow of our time, driven and controlled by big name corporations. Today's trends are being set by marketing types, who've never talked with us about our culture, our goals, the image we wish to establish. To me, hip-hop is vague, a blurred and diluted version of all we created, a sad ghost of all we fought to attain. And I say this because the question remains, with the jury having been out for years. Concerning their *fight*. "*Are these young hip-hop types fighting the good fight*?" — It's the main question coming from those still deep into our liberation as a people, still this day. When I'm confronted with the question as we sip coffee, my answer is yes. I would have to say, yes. But they are not Figh......Tinggg! The young generations fight, as I see it now, is more about acceptance of being. They even encourage their parents to join. And they do, because they're just as shallow as what they've brought into the world.

"We want our music to play loud, without you telling us to turn it down. Let the large percentage of our tasteless, meaningless, violent lyrics drown out the sounds of your community and what you have created and what you're trying to capture as a community," they cry. *"Aren't these my ears?*

And I'll deal with my attitude and future when the time comes. But for now, I'll just be!" they scream and shout and advertise. That's why I question the fight in their bones. I cringe every single time I hear their corporate, public relation written rhetoric and sound bites, because it *s*eems to be the basis of their *fight.* Their shouts of, *"Don't look at me, 'cause I wear an earring, or plait up my hair.* Their reasoning of, *"It's an extension of my being, it's my essence,"* is very insulting to me.

What on earth could the younger generation know about an extension of being? Did they not come into this world with a path, a path that had been made for them to follow? A path associated with a rich history at each turn, which was built with the blood, sweat, tears and determination of those who knew what they would need in order to survive. The builders of the path, prayed that those to follow behind them would not only walk through the path of righteousness, but run through it quickly, fighting, figh-ting, figh—ting, figh--ting to continue to build on what had been laid out before their very precious eyes. Those who prepared the path, know about extension of being. They know. We know.

My afro in my day, my earring in my day, my strut in my day, were a display of power. Of ancestry, of roots, a proud lineage that was unmistakably being taken for granted by the power structure of our country. That's why we displayed our heritage with pride. But the afro today, the earring today, the plaits today, the strut today—these are displays of fashion. It negatively replaces and wipes away everything we did to allow young black asses to walk into stores and buy the clothes they now wear on their backs, without having to slide in the back entrance or only being able to touch what had been brought back, worn before, perhaps even torn before they could purchase-even touch. The younger generation has diluted anything brothers stood in front of. Anything brothers died for. Anything we were locked up for. Anything we were bitten by killer dogs for and beaten over the head for. *For the sake of fashion. For the sake of fashion. For the sake of fashion.* It has turned out to become what they mimic on a daily basis. None of the Panthers would ever stand up to make someone except how we looked. We just wore our attire and continued to move on. We all understood the underlying content of our objective. Liberation. Liberation. Liberation. We never gave a shit. The battle during our time wasn't with the cutting glancing eyes who wanted to do us harm. It was with the system. The system that had the entire black community in chains, but swore up and down my people were free and a part of society. This was our fight, a battle which we were on the verge of changing, forever more, and in the midst of that struggle, I found a woman as committed as I was, a woman I wanted by my side for all time.

"Ashanti, did I hear you right? My brother, did you ask me to marry you?" Cuffee whispered.

I studied the parking lot, then looked at Cuffee. I stood proud and strong, as I imagine the first of our male ancestor slaves must have appeared. Heads unbowed, even though shackled from head to toe, as they stood on unfamiliar soil while full of pride, unknowing that several hundreds, thousands, millions of stinging, whelping, forever scaring lashes were awaiting them— to beat them into submission, to beget their undivided attention for the constructing of this country. And the lashes from the whip were not just intended for them. They were meant for *their* sons, *their* sons offspring and *their* sons and still *their* sons. The intentions of slavery were forever. It was planned. But still-he was proud as he stood.

"Yes, yes I did, Cuffee. You're a precious commodity, sister, and I love you with all my heart," I told her.

Cuffee looked at me. She adored what I said. I had always respected her. It was the only way I knew to treat a woman. I'd never known my father. He was killed before I was born. By the police. My consciousness and dislike towards them still burns inside my soul. My mother told me my father was always respectful. Didn't matter what was going on in their lives, he was always respectful. I thought I should be the same, emulate what he did, make sire proud, while he sat next to the heavenly father. With my premise of respect always alive inside of me, I've never understood why the word "*bitch*" has become so popular. Men calling ladies bitches, women calling each other bitches, even women calling themselves bitches. Cuffee was no bitch to me. She was my beloved, my truth, my wisdom, my future, my past, my soul. I wanted her to always be my mate. She was amazed by my question as we stood in the parking lot. A light went off in her head. I saw it flicker through her wide brown eyes.

"Married, Ashanti?"

"Yes, married," I repeated for her.

She smiled, her eyes were beginning to moisten. "Promise something?" she said.

"Sure, anything."

"Promise me you'll take me from all this. I want to go far, far away from this. Will you promise me that, Ashanti?"

I did. I promised. We were married. Now, years later, my beloved and I are still enclosed in the craziness and unpredictable turn of black events. We're still living in the same neighborhood, bloody but unbowed from what I've failed to deliver, as I understood her request to be, so many years ago.

The time to disseminate into shallower waters never has evolved in our lives and even though our relationship is still as strong as ever. I've never been able to get enough courage to ask her what she has thought about me, not moving forward after all these years to take her away. Away from this decaying neighborhood, away from the screeching sirens, away from the young girls--babies themselves-- who push babies all day long, up and down the neighborhood streets, with nowhere to go. Away from the drugs, away from things that have drastically changed right before our eyes, in so little time. Sometimes, I wonder if, after all these years, she remembers my pledge, my promise that night.

She's been so busy in the struggle herself, as a tenured professor of African American Studies at the University Of Pittsburgh. She's spreading the word to all who'll listen about our past and future as a people. That's what kept us together so long. Our belief in education and dissemination of current information, events, past happenings and future movement by our oppressors that hasn't eased one inch. That's the reason it has never been the right time for us to leave. Every time I've thought about taking her away, moving to a place of solitude, finding a place where the two of us could enjoy, something in the community, something in the nation, something has held me back from doing so. When the thought first dashed into my mind in the early eighties, about leaving the community, Ronald Reagan became president and, along with him, came the recession. I was working for CETA. I loved the work I did there, preparing our children and helping black families who needed assistance in housing and employment. Then the program began to take hits. *Reaganomics* struck our program by halting funding. The community began to experience a rise in crime. My job was discontinued and the entire eight years of Mr. Reagan became a living hell.

The gates of hell opened wider, as Mr. Bush closed his eye's as his military leaders infested our streets with crack cocaine and I fell into the burning flames of drug rehabilitation. I began fighting on a daily basis, to rid our people from the destruction that was awaiting our community. A battle, a fight that not only took its toll on the community and many families, but on me, on me, Lord on me, as well. The deaths, the cons by souls living high from cocaine, the disenchantment that I witnessed, put me in a horrible mental state and charged me to push, to fight. I went to war against the cocaine in our streets and tried to help everyone, every family, every crying mother, every worried father, who was losing their child from the tight grip of crack. Just every-damn-body seemed to be touched.

Things are still bad, the war is still underway. Ohh…it's never over…never over. But I never wanted my wife to doubt my love and promises made in love. I wanted her to know I never forgot about my promise to her, despite my busy days, trying to control what had happened to our people.

Soon, the total essence of our love, my promise, my pledge, began to work at my mindset. The death of my people had set itself into my marriage. This death…this death…this type of death.....this death was not what I meant, when I said to my Cuffee years ago, "Until death do us part."

I set out to find out if Cuffee was happy with her life. I needed to know if she was disappointed in me. Me, the caretaker, because I'd never taken her away from our surroundings. There wasn't an inkling of evidence that her love for me had faltered, but something was pushing me to find out. I sat back and wondered, what was driving my feelings?

It didn't take long before I came to somewhat of a conclusion. The realization of what our men have gone through, and what we are going through this very moment, as an internal society was a part of what was eating away at me. I understood that in order for me to believe something was wrong in my own relationship, I had to be buying into something. Something either so real, it was going to eventually destroy Cuffee and I all together, or so superficial, it was being carried by the devil and I had let it sneak into my thought process. With all the wisdom and knowledge I had attained just by living and reading, reading the facts of black love, black heritage, black achievements, black history, black pain, I still was not prone, prone from destruction myself. My proactive voice in the community was not some type of oil based solution, rubbed into my pores, that would stop me from being like any other black man connected to life's truly confusing vine of love.

While sitting before a cup of tea, swirling my cinnamon stick around and around and around in the depths of the brew, I listened to the strong sounds of Zimbabwe drummers magnify through my speakers of my stereo. As the congo's continued to blare, they became louder each time they were struck. I was taken away, to a state-of-being, of thinking. One that I loved to be in. One that many of my brothers and sisters, who were on the same living high as I, experienced many times before together. But this time, this mellowness, this lightness, this high, were all mine as I drifted into my own thought of meaning, of why my mind had me were it did.

I drifted into the zone of our hell. The black man's hell, here in America. Hell in the greatest country in the world. My passion for trying to explain and educate on a daily basis took me on this ride. Many folks seem to dismiss the affects of slavery and what it's done to the black male and female relationship. Those who do know, look at it and look at it often. They constantly dissect, cut, and analyze the fallout and the end result of what chains and whips did to us as a people, as a family unit, as individuals. I was there. There was something I needed to realize with my mind, with my inner thoughts, to assure my sanity in my own life, because I knew where the roots began.

My journey was difficult. The music in the background had long stopped playing, as I sat still and let everything I knew, the concrete information and facts about our past, run through my brain and enlighten me. I quickly realized that all these years, after dealing with other people's problems, it had become even more problematic for me to deal with my own.

But I fought through it, then stopped in a specific part of our history, which my thought process had always been unable to digest. I stopped at the chapter in our history, in this country, where our men were forced to sit back, with the noses of rifles and guns pointed in their faces, their tired and dazed eyes focused on long, thick, leather whips, dangling in the dust before them. Forced at the same time, dared to assert their natural will as men of any color, to protect, while inhumane indecencies and dehumanizing things went on right before their very eyes—to keep them in line— to the women who were their wives. These times in our past have always been embedded deep within my emotional fervor. But what? What about these times would make me believe my beloved was disappointed in our journey? Most black men do not. But I did a self check. Self checks today by black men, any man, are almost inconceivable on a large scale. There was a time when most black men blamed their mistakes, problems and sloppy situations on everyone but themselves. But those days are long over. Yes, the excuse was good and the success rate extremely high when used on others, when we weren't educated and didn't know the truth. But we have studied the truth, truths have been revealed and I wasn't going there. I wanted to look deep into myself, our history, my past, to find out why...why, I was feeling this way.

Early in the morning. That's when it came to me...early in the morning. Way before dawn. Deep into the morning night. One should never disclaim a revelation a spiritual awakening, when it happens early in the morning it usually begets a beautiful testimony. I realized, early in the morning, in the still, in the dark, what had been eating at my soul. It was celebration! Celebration! Celebration! I realized it was celebration. The path of our past brought out the truth, the understanding for me, the reasons why I didn't feel my wife, my angel, was content with what I had provided for her. It was not so much our past as a people, which pushed out the realization for me, as it was the current state of our people and what we all are going through. The now, the presence of all of us, wading in the water without much understanding of anything that matters to us. I'd been trying to hard to convince unhearing souls, locked minds and *we're okay* attitudes that we as a people were in a very bad situation in America. All the mind blowing statistics of not only black men but black women confined to prisons seem to go unheard. My continued challenge to better our primary schools in our neighborhoods haven't been enough to unlock parents minds for their childrens future. All our future. The everlasting gun fire and black on black crime to this day burns at my soul. All of these situational aspects of the communtiy had bared down on my being. The game that I'd been fighting for decades had turned its evil, wicked deceit on me internally and attacked my confidence in my relationship with my wife. My cries to my beloved people had not been heard and we've remained stagnet as well and it's power shifted to what I hadn't accomplished for the person who meant the most to me and it's a shame because through it all I did not celebrate my union with Cuffee.

Not celebrating, not shouting, not showing, not giving words of love and telling Cuffee constantly how much I loved and cared for her was the culprit. There was no celebration of my commitment to her. Everything that I'd been doing had been done out of habit and respect. Respect for her being my wife, without any emotional celebration to let her know that I loved her and was happy she was my wife. I realized that, without celebration of our union, without celebration of our love, my failure to keep the eager promise I'd made, would haunt me daily, because it made me feel as though I had failed. Without celebration of our love, that failed pledge threatened the strong walls of our marriage. Celebration. Celebration is deep.

I was sure my theory was correct, but I had to know for sure. I had to talk it over with Cuffee. So many evenings at home, she'd caught me staring at her, working through the questions in my mind of how I would present my question to her. She never commented, concerning my looks. Never questioned me, but she had to be curious, wondering what I was thinking, what was on my mind. But I never asked and let days go by but still I wanted to find out if my premise was correct and ask Cuffee how she felt about things.

Cuffee was in class when I arrived in the auditorium. She was standing before at least two-hundred of her students. I'd forgotten it was the week when she lectured on everything that she had discussed up to the midpoint of the semester to all eight of her classes. It was really good to see her smiling as she did her thing. It reminded me of home, when we would discuss political and social events. Cuffee was on one standard keel all the time. There was no "at work" Cuffee and "at home" Cuffee. She was one. The one I loved.

I tried to be as quiet as possible, as I made my entrance into the auditorium. There was an empty section in the center of the hall. I wondered if the students wondered who this old man was? I even stepped on a young sister's book bag, then her foot, as I made my way through. I could tell Cuffee spotted me, because she hesitated in mid-sentence, right before I sat down. After I became comfortable in my seat, I tried to get some type of eye contact, but she had already made her way to the far side of the stage, as her voice echoed throughout the auditorium hall.

I'd always enjoyed listening to Cuffee's powerful voice blaze into her speaking audience. As usual, she had everyone's complete attention. Her demeanor demanded it. Her stunning, proud look, along with her movements as she made her points, always pausing as if going to ask a question of one of her students, kept them alive. Her students loved her for it. It kept them on their toes and interested in what she had to say. They also loved her because she wasn't afraid to be different. Different from the other tight-lipped professors, who very rarely gave it to the students straight. Cuffee didn't bow down to University politics, didn't care what the University opinions on certain topics were and damn sure lectured on any damn topic she chose. She connected with the students and they loved Cuffee for being herself. They loved her style, too, the fro' she sported, picked out wide and free, like the essence of a bird. The wide, long shirts. She was distinguished in every way and I quickly became engulfed and tuned in to what she was saying, as she stood strong in her dangling gold earrings that sparkled against her golden brown skin.

"So students, future leaders of our families, communities and country. This is what I mean by evolution, in terms of the media. The NAACP has issued statements and statistics, regarding the three major networks in our country, concerning the lack of people who look like you and I on the television screen. And now they're getting major networks to sign agreements that say the networks pledge to 'do better'. But I want to discuss how this situation has evolved, find out what's led us to the programming we see today.

"First, why did the network powers think they could get away with showing no faces that represent you and me? They managed it for a long time and, if you ask me, we have never had a comfortable proportion of us on the screen. But— do you think because we don't support and challenge what we already have. What has always, from its inception, been called black and reached out to the black community the networks believed they could shut us out on their shows all together? You all know who I'm talking about. I'm talking about our station, the one we don't support. Our cable station that plays the videos, all day long. It shows the re-runs of shows that were not only money makers for the networks that are closing us out, but for the most part showed us always in a laughing and joking matter. I'm talking about an entity that considers itself black. I just want to get you students in my class to think, without being too critical of what is ours. I do believe they have some outstanding programs. Particularly the late night talk show that enlightens us, keeps us informed, and promotes advocacy -because we all know that we won't get it from the networks. They also have a few shows on Sunday that air, when everyone's at church. But my question is- after all these years-- has our station evolved?"

Cuffee paused for a moment and noticed the shaking heads of her young students. "Why is it that at least one sitcom on *our* station's roster cannot be written, produced and directed by employees of our station? Don't we have outstanding black writers, authors, directors and beautiful actors and actresses? What I'm saying is, what we already have in place can set the standard and show the country that everything about us is not only about laughing and dancing. Maybe that's why the majority of everything in the past about us, is of that nature, because that's what the network executives see when they turn the channel to see what we're being fed by our own people. Think about this...If a person watches someone give a cat a bowl of milk and the cat drinks the milk, happy and content, is this person going to give a cat a bowl of grape soda, when it's their turn to feed it- if he wants the cat to be happy? Absolutely not. They're going to give the cat what it appears the cat likes."

Cuffee stopped pacing the stage and leaned towards her students. "Work with me here, because I want you all to understand. When a show that's supposed to represent us does appear on a major network, its something *we* don't want to see Ninety-nine percent of the time it doesn't represent us. Because *we* are not hired to produce or create the program. And what I'm trying to say is, it's our own fault. We haven't screamed enough at our own people, who are feeding us what we've seen for generations, over and over again. It's a shame that what some of your parents saw when they were coming up, you all see on the screen every night every single-night...over and over again. And that image that we see is feeding the American public, therefore we don't look like we've changed, and the sterotypes continue, which is not accurate. That's what I mean by evolution. Ours. What we have, what we can really establish as ours, hasn't yet evolved.

The NAACP is right, in that the laws ensure we're seen on television as often as is required by the demographics of this country. But that's as far as it goes. Now, the NAACP hasn't come knocking on my door, to see what I think about all this. I doubt they ever will. But, I'll give you my opinion on their efforts anyway. Their fight is worthy—a little late, but worthy. However, I think they should begin focusing on advertisers who are willing to put their dollars into what we've already established—meaning our station—our black cable station. Then they can gather up the black writers, producers, directors, actors and actresses. Show by example. Even raise some money for our station. That's what will show our importance in the overall scheme of things. And once our importance is realized, we'll never again have to beg for inclusion. And it doesn't have to take forever to get a program in place." Cuffee appeared eager to say more, but she glanced at the clock and stopped. "Have a nice day," she concluded, with a smile.

I sat still, listening to the applause Cuffee was given from some of her students who'd been charged up from her lecture. The auditorium quickly cleared and Cuffee spoke with a couple of students, who wanted to give her their opinions on the subject. After the last question was asked, Cuffee made her way up to me, exhausted, but smiling.

"Why didn't you tell me you'd signed up for my class?" she said.

"Thought I'd surprise you," I told her.

She sat down next to me. "How are you, brother?"

"Fine. I enjoyed your lecture. Really strong."

"Yeah? You think they knew who I was referring to?"

"Yes, they knew. How could they not? I really dug, that you didn't call them out."

"I came close. But I have to tell it like it is, Ashanti. You know these kids have been lied to enough times already. And when they watch that stuff on that channel, eighty percent of the programming is a lie. And we can help it to do better-by getting the right people involved because the initial premise of the station was brillant."

"Indeed, sister. Indeed."

We sat quiet for a moment, as a student came running back into the auditorium to pick up the book that she'd forgotten.

"Make sure you do your reading. I'm going to call on you next time!" Cuffee shouted out to her.

The student looked back and smiled.

"So what brings you out?" Cuffee asked.

"Wanted to ask you a question, something that's been laying heavily on my mind."

"Sure."

Here goes, I thought. "Lately, I've been thinking about something I promised you, the night I proposed to you."

She smiled, "My...you've gone back some years, haven't you, my brother?"

"Tell me about it," I agreed. "But the journey back into what we dreamed and what we've accomplished has brought me to a question that I need you to answer for me."

"Sure, anything."

"Well, the night I proposed to you. Do you remember that night, Beloved?"

"Yes, I'll always remember it. It was beautiful, Ashanti."

"Well, I remember you asking me, if I would take you away?"

Cuffee was surprised, "Yes, I remember."

"I've never done that for you, Cuffee. We haven't moved much economically. We've stayed pretty much in one place— I wanted to know if you had any problems, any regrets, for marrying me, because of it?"

Cuffee grabbed my hand. "Brother, are you all right?"

"Yes, I'm fine. I just need to know if you feel like I've cheated you, by not fulfilling the promise I made to you, by not taking you away?"

Cuffee looked away from me for a second. She looked as though she was going back to the moment I asked her to marry me. She turned back towards me, looked into my eyes and, once again, went back to the parking lot, went back to the days of our young ambitious love. Yeah, she was going back.

"Cuffee? Cuffee? Are you okay?" I asked.

"Just trying to remember, that's all. Just trying to remember all this."

"Well, do you remember asking me to take you away?"

Cuffee was still in sort of a daze. "Yeah, yes I do, Ashanti. But...as I remember..." she smiled. "I wasn't talking about leaving, Ashanti. I never wanted to leave the community."

"What? But you said—" She put her finger on my lips to silence me.

"Brother, I remember asking you to take me away. But I remember asking you to take me away from having to meet as a people, in a bunch, in a gathering, in the section of the city, to feel like we were somebody. I was tired of trying to feel like somebody in this country and the basis of my lecture today has made me see nothing for us has really changed, because we're still at it. Still trying to be accepted. That's all I meant. Ashanti, I was referring to our struggle, Sweetheart. Nothing but the struggle."

"The struggle?"

"Yes, the struggle. That's all. What's gotten into you, love?"

I was relieved. "I don't know, I really don't," I said. "After all these years, I thought you wanted to move away and I hadn't done enough to grant you what I promised."

Cuffee exhaled, "Ashanti? Our love is much deeper, much deeper than that black man. Our love transcends beyond death. And I really do mean that. It transcends beyond death and everyone will know about it, when we're in heaven together holding hands."

I soaked up her words. "Well, it sounds like we need to go celebrate this love," I said to her.

Cuffee smiled and her eye's widened, "Now, that's a place I wouldn't mind going for sure."

A smile covered my face then Cuffee stuck out her hand.

"Give me five...." She sang.

I began to place my hand in hers.

"On the black hand side," she coyly instructed. I did and the back of our strong black hands met. Then our loving, heartfelt embrace confirmed her words to me, as well as our strong black love. It was just the beginning of our *celebration, celebration, celebration.*

Miles Away

The day I stood at the altar, surrounded by family and friends and professed for all to hear, *"Until Death Do Us Part,"* I meant it like nothing I've ever said before. The words I so passionately uttered to Darla were honest and sincere. I even felt a vibrant quiver run through her body, as I held her hand. Her widened eyes were like puddles of water, about to release down her beautiful brown cheeks. My eyes were just as honeyed. Then Darla repeated the same words to me, *"Until Death Do Us Part"* with complete confidence. Her emotional expression touched my heart. I felt a tear drift down the side of my face. At the same time, a tear journeyed down hers. I was ecstatic. She was enraptured. We were full of energy and ready to fulfill our commitment to one another. Forever.

Then it happened. Four months into our marriage, I was offered a job at the University of Seattle, as the head coach of the men's and women's track teams. That's right, opportunity was knocking in Seattle, Washington, where it rains eighty percent of the time and the suicide rate is sky high. Darla and I lived in Philadelphia and we both loved living there. But Seattle was a wonderful opportunity. I had run track at Temple, then moved on to coaching, after barely missing qualifying for the 1988 Olympics in the two hundred meters.

I had forgotten I'd even applied for the Seattle position. My name had found itself on so many applications that I really couldn't keep track of them all. When Mr. Davis, the Athletic Director, called with the offer, I started thinking about my future and how it could be the start of something special for Darla and me. The head coach I was working under at Temple wasn't leaving anytime soon and I felt I was better than just an assistant. I'd made it through all the obstacles that usually kill first time coachs, who begin coaching at the school where they were once athletes. I was able to deal with the youngsters on the team, who knew me personally as a teammate. It wasn't easy gaining their respect, but I set out to do it my first day at the helm. No more would I answer to simply Hennet. It was Coach Hennet. I careened my way through the heads of my ex-teammates. No more partying with them, which had been my norm. I pushed study and training habits, at the same time motivating everyone to perform at their highest peak every single time on the track. Three years later, the guys from my era were gone. The eyes that had witnessed my bad training habits were no longer around to tell incoming freshman about my crazy past and how I still made it to the national finals, making my runners feel they could do the same. If they only knew what my partying, inconsistent diet and lack of sleep had done to me. Maybe one less party or one less dance, somewhere in my career, would have given me that tenth of a second, that last extra push I'd needed, as I leaned towards the tape in the photo finish. It took the officials thirty minutes to decide who would represent our country in the biggest games of them all. To this day, I've never forgotten how hard my heart pumped, waiting on their decision. When I finally found out, I collapsed where I stood, in complete exhaustion, after realizing I didn't make the cut. Whenever any of my runners asked about my history from the trickling down of rumors from year to year, I quickly dismissed the stories, because I wanted them all to give their best each time out on the track.

Finally, I looked around and realized I'd accomplished my desire to be respected as Coach Hennet. All of a sudden, I was the coach the runners came to before anyone else, including the head coach, if they had a problem. My big break came when our leading sprinter appeared on national TV and gave thanks to me. He gave me an endorsement for helping him break the one hundred meter world record. The very next day, U of S called and offered me a contract, with a salary four times as much as I was already making. Consideration and thoughtful deliberation, regarding the opportunity, was definitely called for. I was pushing thirty-five. Five years away from THE BIG FOUR O, and I needed to start putting heavy chunks of money away for the future. I planned on retiring at the youthful, exuberant age of fifty.

I'm from Philadelphia and Darla grew up in Pittsburgh. The east coast is the only thing we've ever known and we both loved the lifestyle. I couldn't imagine life without cheese steaks, for example. Or life without the Sixers. Hell, we had season tickets even when the team couldn't find the basket. Now, they were finally coming into their own, proving they could play and play well. But not only that. The good times Darla and I had on our dates going to the games were really special. It was our night out. Our moment to scream, hold hands and smile together.

Our relationship had been that way since we met. My five foot-four golden brown, bright eyed Boo' was only sixteen when she stepped on the Temple campus. Right away I was intrigued with her accomplishment, once I found out about her academic achievement. I'd seen Darla on campus a few times before I stepped to her and, believe me, nothing about Darla was sixteen. In fact, the first couple of times I saw her, I thought maybe she was a transfer student in her senior year or something. Darla was smart as a whip and very fragile at the same time. Her friendly smile and constant conversation quickly began to give ideas to some of the brothers on campus, who took her outgoing personality as weakness and they'd planned to do her wrong. I used my notoriety, played detective and found out when everything was going to go down, then asked Darla to the movies that same evening. From that night on, we saw each other constantly. That's how I found out about her family background. She grew up with both of her parents in the home, and it was apparent she cared about family as much as I did. I knew right away I was going to make her my wife. I didn't have a lot of standards, like most of the brothers I knew. Hollywood smiles, large chest with long perky nipples, the nice round ass and show stopping qualities that all of them searched for, didn't place high on my list. I just wanted my wife to know and understand what a family unit was all about. It didn't hurt that Darla had assets, too. Her father was Puerto Rican, her mother Black and they created a very very hot pepper.

When we were married, she wanted to keep her heritage and her maiden name, Santiago. She always smiled wide as can be when someone called out her name after we said our vow's. Darla Santiago-Hennet. It took some time for me to get used to and, of course, the credit card companies always trip and the mail is never right, but she was happy and that made me happy. We lived in a nice four bedroom home, comfortably furnished, with a small yard. In a lot of ways, we had it all. But I didn't have a future in Philly, at least not a bright one, not one that included the title "Head Coach." Still, I suspected Darla's immediate reaction would be less than enthusiastic. I was right.

"Seattle?" she asked. "On the other side of the country? Where it rains all the time? Why in the world would you consider Seattle?" She frowned. The look spoiled her smooth, bronze face. "Seattle?" she repeated. "We don't know anybody there. Mikhail, we don't know anybody who lives west of Cincinnati!"

We talked about the opportunity. We talked about the future. Darla's willingness to leave decreased the longer she thought about it, although she never actually said "No" to the idea.

While she wavered in her non-committal attitude, I was getting really hyped about the idea. Not for Seattle, particularly, but for the opportunity, the challenges. I could sense the resentment of the head coach, as runners continued to come to me with problems and questions. Quietly, subtly, he was reducing my responsibilities and attempting to slow

73

the interaction I had with the team members. Then, during an intense team meeting, Coach and me had words right in front of the entire team. Something had to give. When the call came from Seattle, demanding a decision, I accepted. I was excited and desperate. But I knew I should've talked with Darla about my decision so I took her to dinner to break the news. After ordering dinner and being served a glass of wine and hearing about her goings on at her job, I reached across the small table and took her hand.

"Baby, I've got something to tell you." I hesitated. "It's not quite...It— wasn't supposed to happen like," I stumbled.

"You took the job in Seattle, didn't you?" Her voice was quiet, flat. She withdrew her hand from mine.

I nodded. "It's just too good an opportunity for me to pass up, Darla. It means our future. It means we can afford to have children, which we damn well can't do on an assistant coach's salary, not if we want them to have the advantages of college and all. This means you can stay home with our kids, if you want to, at least for a while. Or we can afford a nanny, if you prefer. This job means we have options now."

"You're doing this for our children?"

"I'm doing this for our family," I corrected.

Darla's eyes gazed. I suspect she was thinking of our families. We were among the fortunate few who'd been raised by both our parents, who'd not endured the averages of divorce or separation, the pain of a one-parent home and family. Our parents had never been separated for more than a day or two our entire lives, growing up.

"Mikhail, you know how hard I've worked on my

project? You know how important it is to me. I can't just leave in the middle of it. I may be good at what I do, but this project will prove it. Walking out in the middle, at the critical point, could mean the end of my career."

"Baby girl, listen. I don't expect you to walk out on your project. I want you to finish it. I want you to complete anything and everything you start. Hell, I suspect you can write your own ticket, anywhere you want, once your Y2K experience is on your resume and part of your credentials." I paused and took a healthy sip of wine. With a sigh, I continued but what I was preparing to say, wasn't going to be easy. "Look, I'll go out to Seattle. You finish up here, then join me. It's June now so it will only be for six months."

Darla stared down at her glass. When she looked up at me, there were tears in her eyes. "I love you so much, Mikhail. I've never considered you being away from me. Never thought about not laying next to you at night. I...." She used her napkin to wipe the tears from her cheeks and forced a sad smile.

I stopped her before she said anything else. "I won't go. The last thing I want to do is make you cry."

"No...no. It's all right. It's only a few months right? All I need to do is finish up here and I'll be out there with you when my project is complete. We can do this," Darla sided.

"Are you sure?" She nodded and smiled. "Thank you, baby." I said.

"No need. I thought you heard me when I said *until death do us part?*"

Seattle

It's May now. And the new millennium began five months ago. Of course, it's raining outside as usual and I'm sitting in my high rise condo, looking out my window, by myself, thinking about Darla, who's still in Philly. What can I say? Darla is the type of person who finishes what she starts. Although she was successful in her initial job of making sure all flights remained safe during the Y2K scare, there were some unexpected bugs that popped up and she decided to stay on her watch and see them through.

Initially, I was upset, but I thought about it and realized her relentless attitude was one of the things I loved about her most. Even back in college, when she took on her double major in computer science and math. Everyone including myself thought it was a bit much, but she stayed the course and graduated with honors, which led to her job. But being away from Darla hasn't been an easy thing for me to do. I couldn't explain how many times I've sat in this very recliner, with it fully extended, and thought about our situation. The way I felt when I first said good-bye to my wife has haunted me and caused pain ever since. Hands down, it was the hardest thing I've ever had to do in my life. But what I've done to our relationship since leaving Philly feels almost like death itself and now things are much more complicated.

First of all, Darla and I began to pull apart by the decision I made for the betterment of my career, our lives and the future. I called myself going on a recruiting trip across the country and found myself in Philly with my wife for five straight days. Darla was happy to see me, but it wasn't enough and

76

she didn't have to tell me so. Yes, the sex was great. We were non-stop but, mentally, we both had drifted a bit. The distance between us pulled us a part, I know it did to me. I didn't think separation would be so cruel. And all of our troubles didn't start to affect me until I came back to Seattle and sat down in this chair to think about what I've done to our relationship. At first, it was romantic, talking to the one I loved, looking out at the ocean, and contemplating our future-knowing that she would soon be with me. The whole concept of waiting for Darla to join me was doable. But not even love can prevent loneliness from entering your heart. If I could only explain how many tears of mine have trickled down the windowpane, right along side the many raindrops that have touched my window. Not to mention how I have struggled, trying to stop Darla from crying every night, before we hung up the phone. Most of the time I just had to wait, until Darla finished saying whatever was on her mind. I'd never been able to stop her from crying for any reason, since I've known her.

"Darla...come on, baby. It's going to be all right," I promised her.

"But this is not how it's supposed to be, Mikhail. We're supposed to be together. You and me together-no other way." She would sob uncontrollably into the phone, while I sat still, mouth opened wide, without words to comfort her.

After a while, I began to become hardened to Darla's cries. I think I felt cheated she didn't come to be with me, even though I understood her reason why. When July rolled around, I even lied to her and told her that over the Fourth of July weekend I couldn't make it home, as promised, because of a recruiting visit to Compton. I don't know why I did it. I

77

just did. Seeing Darla, then having to leave her, was becoming too painful for me. I didn't know if I could handle it again and I knew there was no way I could handle her pain. Not up close and personal. We were at a crossroad in our relationship and I knew it. Especially after she told me her latest news, a few days after she decided again to come out west to be with me.

"Mikhail I'm going to be promoted."

Then it became a game of who was going to break first. We both wanted our marriage to work, but we both wanted our careers to progress and I wanted her to move to Seattle as we'd planned. At the same time, Darla began to toss around the idea of me moving back to Philly. Her suggestions were becoming strong, so I had no other choice on the holiday weekend than to stay away, because I wanted Darla with me in Seattle and that's when things became difficult in our marriage.

I'd planned to sit in my apartment, go over my next year's roster then surf the internet high school websites for the top rated runners in each state. Afterwards I was going to read the latest happenings on Blackplanet.com. But the sun, coming through the window, drew me outside and I ended up laying on a blanket, under a tree on the practice track, all by my lonesome, close to falling asleep. My eyes were beginning to close, when I noticed Deshelle, a runner on my ladies team trotting onto the track.

Deshelle was cool, a coach's dream. She was all about business and was a great example to the freshman. She walked down lane three, unaware that I was lounging under the flock of tall trees. Deshelle had on shorts, a T-shirt, white cross trainers and she was carrying her spikes and towel in her hand. She walked onto the football practice field, placed her towel on the fifty yard line, then sat down to switch from her cross trainers to spikes. Deshelle had never been a very big talker, at least not around me. It was the only problem I had with her. She set a very good example, being business like through the course of the season. But I thought she could be more vocal, because most of the athletes on the squad looked up to her. Deshelle had made all conference every year and placed either second or third in the conference in the one hundred and two hundred meters in her first three years. She was a graduating senior and, for the first time in her career, she won the one hundred meters in the conference championships and was invited to the national championships to qualify for the 2000 Olympics. I offered to continue coaching her through the trials, but Deshelle wanted to go at it alone.

I didn't have a problem with her decision. She was very focused and she knew what she needed to do. Plus, she was finally peaking as a runner and I could see her motivation. Deshelle was a hometown favorite. I didn't recruit her. She was already a fixture on the team when I arrived She was born just up the road, in Tacoma, and everyone treated her as well as Ken Griffey, Jr. She could have easily gone to any of the top flight track programs in the country, but she enjoyed it so much in her home town, she decided to stay close to family and friends.

Deshelle made her way back on the track and pranced down to the 100 meter start, turned around and delicately pranced about 25 meters then pranced back. She looked a little tight from lifting weights or maybe from an early morning swim. I watched her strut about. She continually stretched her neck from side to side and tried to work out the kinks in her thighs. She bent her back and began rotating her arms, one at a time. I'd thought about walking over and saying hello but decided against it. To be truthful, I was enjoying looking at Deshelle because she reminded me of Darla. Even though I didn't want to be with my wife, because of our situation, I didn't mind seeing someone who remotely reminded me of my love. Physically, she was a little bit leaner and longer, but their mannerisms and movements were damn near identical. The first time I saw Deshelle, it was like my life stopped for a brief second. It was after a night that Darla and I sat on the phone for most of the evening, talking about our plans for the future. I had called an upper classmen meeting the next morning, to meet and greet everyone and to explain what I expected from them in terms of leadership. Deshelle came strutting into the meeting, looking like my baby. I think she even noticed my stunned face and brief stare.

Deshelle must have felt good and loose by now, because she'd began sprinting down the track. She'd do about fifty meter's or so, then turn around and trot back, only to do it again. Deshelle was a lanky five-feet eight and had been wearing her hair in braids since the track season started. She was built just like a sprinter, wide shoulders, small chest, and you would never catch her not walking on her toes. After a while, she began doing knee lifts about thirty meters down the track. All of a sudden she stopped.

"Hey! Come here!" she shouted. I looked in the

direction she was shouting. A small, floppy-eared Beagle had made its way onto the field and was carrying one of her cross trainers across the field like it didn't have a care in the world.

"Hey! Come here…Come here!" Deshelle shouted out. The Beagle paid no attention to her and kept moving steadily across the field. That's when she kicked off her spikes and took off after the Beagle, who began to play a game of 'keep-away' with her. I sat up. The humor of the situation eased my thoughts of Darla for awhile. Deshelle was now getting the workout she'd come to the track for. Every single time she got close to the white and brown patched Beagle, it would dart in the opposite direction.

"Give me my damn shoe, you silly ass dog!" Deshelle screamed. The dog felt her frustration. It stopped and sat down, about eight paces away from her, and they stared at one another.

"Look," she said, out of breath and bending down with her hands on her knees. "I don't know why you think I want to play with your little dusty butt. But I don't. You hear me, I don't so drop the shoe." Deshelle took one good deep breath, as the Beagle looked up at her, then she lunged forward towards the dog. It darted out of her reach.

"Give me my shoe, damn it!" she screamed, then she was off chasing the playful dog again. I was almost in tears, laughing at Deshelle's efforts and the dogs antics. All of a sudden, the dog began to back-up and make its way in my direction, as Deshelle approached it. I stood up and walked gently toward the situation. Deshelle was surprised to see me and threw her arms up in the air. I placed my finger over my lips, instructing her to be quiet, because the Beagle hadn't noticed me. As I inched my way behind the little dude, I could tell the dog was full of play. He was looking up at Deshelle, wagging his tail, as he faced her. He was panting hard now and I was just about upon him. When I finally reached down to grab the shoe out of his mouth from behind, he looked up with his bright eyes and darted away. I began to give chase and there we were. Coach and top notch athlete on the practice field, chasing a silly dog with a shoe in its mouth for nearly twenty minutes. Finally we gave up hope, too tired to continue.

"You might as well forget about your shoe," I told Deshelle, as I sat down beside her towel, around the fifty yard line.

"Damn dog," she snapped. The Beagle was about twenty yards behind us, laying down, panting like crazy. "If I had a pistol, I'd shoot him! She chuckled.

"Would you do that?" I joked.

"For those cross trainers? Maybe so." Deshelle took her towel and wiped her face.

"So, what are you doing out here today?"

"Relaxing, I thought," I said to her. "I came out to look over some prospects on paper and to sit back under the trees. I've been here since you got here." I pointed towards the trees where my things were still laying on my blanket in the shade.

"Coach? You mean to tell me you've been here the entire time?"

"Yup'."

"Why didn't you help me earlier?"

"Didn't want to disturb your workout."

Deshelle picked up her lone sneaker and looked like

she wanted to toss it at me. "Fool ass dog took my right shoe to my favorite pair of trainers in the world. This is the first time I've ever worn them, when I'm not competing in a meet. I took a chance today and now look. In the mouth of that crazy ass little dog." Deshelle caught me staring at her, in a daze. "Coach, you all right?" Her voice kind of squealed when she asked me.

"Yea…yea..I'm fine."

"I thought you, of all people, would be in Philly over the holiday. What's the deal?"

I'd never discussed anything going on in my life with anyone since I'd moved to Seattle. I hadn't become close enough with anyone to even talk about the weather. I don't know, I thought people out West were kind of stand-offish and aloof, so I just contemplated my situation by myself all the time. Still, I answered Deshelle's question as politely as possible. "No, not this time. Maybe Labor Day."

"You going to the park tonight, to see the fire works?" She apparently sensed my loneliness at the same time I saw her peek over at the dog.

"I'll probably watch them from the window at my place."

"That'll be nice," she said.

I looked back and saw the Beagle inch closer to us, like he couldn't hear our conversation well enough. "So, how's the confidence for the trials? You ready?" I asked.

"Think so, I've been working hard. Still doing the same thing that's gotten me to this point. You wouldn't believe how happy I am, now that graduation, school work and everything is over with. This is the first time I can honestly say I've ever

83

been able to just concentrate on track."

"Take it from me. When it's time to run, take it one race at a time. Go through the prelims with complete concentration and have your mind set on qualifying for the next round. Make sure that's the only thing you're concentrating on. Then, when you reach the finals, anything can happen."

Deshelle blushed, as though it was her life long dream. "Believe me, if I make it to the finals, I'm going for broke," she assured me.

I smiled at her enthusiasm. "There's a chance you might have to go for broke a time or two in the prelims, so keep your guard up. I remember I did, in the quarterfinals. If I remember correctly, the quarterfinals were deeper in talent than the finals were." We were quiet for a brief second.

She smiled at my going back into the day. "So, you like it here?" Deshelle asked me unexpectedly.

"It's doable. Why do you ask?"

"Just don't get too many people who move out this way, that's all." Deshelle confirmed.

I had to stop myself from explaining to Deshelle the major plan Darla and I had together. I tell my runners all the time. 'Talk about it, get it off your chest,' but again, I didn't go into my situation. We talked for another hour or so.

After a while, we moved from the hot sun to my blanket between the trees. The dog watched our every move. He was close by now, in the shade himself, rested and looking as if he would be ready for the second quarter at any minute. Our conversation had become very one sided, mainly because I kept the student-athlete, coach relationship intact. Deshelle was trying to get out of that mode. I did the same thing when I first graduated from college. I didn't lose any respect for anyone, but when I graduated I began to try different things and communicate with people on a different level, to let them know that I had arrived and my college education was well worth the time. I have to admit Deshelle was doing a damn good job.

"You know? I was thinking about getting into coaching one day," she said.

"That would be great," I told her.

"Right here in Seattle. I thought about starting off with my own track club, with a bunch of third and fourth graders, and moving along right with them, as they progress in school. Then I'd recruit them all for U of S and have the top track and field program in the country."

"Oh really, now?"

"Hmmm...hmmm. That's if–you aren't still here. I wouldn't want to take your job, you know what I'm sayin'," she teased.

I glanced at the Beagle and whispered to Deshelle, "Look...his eyes are shut."

Deshelles eyes brightened. "Here's our chance." She began to get up. I touched her hand and she looked at me and I looked at her for a brief moment.

"No...no. We have to be quiet, if you want that damn shoe back." I couldn't help but grin.

"You think this is funny, don't you?" Deshelle asked, looking down at her feet, which were covered with only one shoe.

I nodded yes. Deshelle smiled and we contemplated

85

how we were going to get the shoe back. The dog was about ten yards away from us.

"Okay...okay. You ever play twister?" I wanted to know.

"Huh?"

"Twister? You ever play?"

"I think...yeah. When I was younger." Deshelle looked at me strangely.

"Okay...we're going to have to make our way over to him like wheel barrels, on our arms and legs. If he doesn't hear us...lunge and get your shoe back." Deshelle shook her head and couldn't believe how her day had turned out.

"Okay, you with me?"

"Ready," she whispered.

I started off first and moved about three yards closer to the dog. When I sat on my rump, I motioned for Deshelle to do the same thing. When she reached the point where I was, we both started to laugh. The dog hadn't moved and its eyes were closed, with the shoe still in its mouth. I moved again and stopped. When I was close enough to lunge at him, I could see Deshelle motion towards me to take a chance. I shook my head no and told her to join me. When she made it over to me, she was on the right of the dog and I was on its left. I held up three fingers and mouthed to Deshelle silently, "On three." She nooded her head okay, and I held my fingers up. "One......" I dug my feet into the ground to get a good lunge at the mutt. "Two." I noticed Deshelle do the same, one shoe and all. "Three." As soon as we both lunged at the dog, it looked up and darted forward and ran about twenty yards away from us. Deshelle and I lay flat on our stomachs, in the grass, looking directly at one another and couldn't help but laugh. The dog pranced away from us, wagging its tail, letting us know it played us like suckers and he was champion.

Philly- July 4th

I'm not going to lie. Mikhail's last minute cancellation hurt. It hurt so bad, I went over to the concourse after my shift and came five minutes from boarding the plane to go see him. But I didn't, because he would've had me and won this bout. His victory would have given him confidence to pour on his charm and persistence to get me to move to Seattle with, him while we were in bed. I did want to be with my man, don't get me wrong. But I didn't like the game Mikhail was playing. To me, our situation was cut and dry. I was the Deputy Director of Air Controllers, which means I was now making the money that I'd thought we both prayed for me to make. It also meant that Mikhail didn't have to worry about money and if he had to get a job at a high school, as a teacher, and coach track it shouldn't have mattered, because we would've been together.

My weekend wasn't a total loss though. My father was visiting the states from South America and wanted to spend at least one night with me, while he visited some of our family members and long time friends. So I invited him over to spend the night with me, before he made all of his rounds.

I served Papa a heaping dish of red beans and rice, having used Mama's recipe for his favorite dish. He savored his first bite, licked his lips in satisfaction and smiled up at me.

"Baby girl, it's so good to be here. I thought maybe you didn't want to see your Papa no more."

"Papa? Why would you think that?" Papa had moved back to South America to be with his brothers and sisters after mama died. Being around him instantly brought out my heritage as I spoke.

"It just crossed your Papa's mind. It's been so long since we've been together, ya' know?"

"I know, Papa. But I missed you, too. So how do you like the red beans and rice? Like Mama's, no?"

Papa put down his fork. "Could stand a little more spice, but it tastes just like your Mama's when she first started cooking for your Papi," he admitted.

It was good seeing Papa. After Mama passed away, Papa acted as though he wanted to die, so he could be with her. I could understand where he was coming from, knowing how I felt being separated from Mikhail. I sat and thought about it, while Papa masterfully placed his beans and rice on his fork. I felt like my situation was just as bad as Papa missing Mama because my mate was still living and I couldn't be with him as well. Death was final and the separation, plain and simple, had to be dealt with. But Mikhail and mine's was truly hard to deal with. I knew that I could be with him. If one of us would just make the decision to leave what we were doing, so we could be together.

"So, how do you like this new job, baby girl?" Papa asked.

"I love it!"

"Tell me more about it. I know you've told me what you do over and over again on the phone. But phones are impersonal. Come on, nice and slow, tell Papa everything."

I smiled. Papa hadn't changed a bit. He always wanted

to be up close and personal. "Well, I'm Deputy Director of the Air Traffic Controller Division. I make sure all the flights coming and going out of Philly reach their destination safely. I'm responsible for every aircraft that flies into or out of our airport."

Papa thought for a minute. "That's a lot of stress on my baby girl, no?"

"Ummm..hmmm. Sure is. But I love my job, Papa. In a couple of years, who knows? Maybe I'll be promoted to Director!"

"Your Mama always said that you were special," Papa told me.

"She told you that?"

"All the time. I can still remember her rocking you to sleep and telling you how important you were going to become one day. She was right."

"Thank you, Papa." I can't explain how much those simple words from Papa meant to me. Mama was my life. I was so depressed she couldn't be at the wedding, when Mikhail and I committed to one another. I'd watched her and Papa for years, sharing their lives together, and I wanted to show her their actions taught me well. But she probably wouldn't have been so proud of me and Mikhail's situation but I know she would have given me some excellent advice.

Papa wasn't an alcoholic, but he loved himself a margarita with his meal and I made some for him.

"Ummm....this is good," he said. "So, baby girl. How's Mikhail? He couldn't make it home for the holiday?"

"He's fine, Papa. He just thought he better catch up on some work." I poured myself a margarita.

"Is everything okay with you two?"

I didn't answer right away. "Sure, Papa." I tried to smile.

"No...no...no...no. Don't try and give your Papa that fake smile. I brought you up and that's the same smile you give to me when you fall off your bike and I asked you if you were okay..and your butt hurt you soo bad. Come on...tell Papa what's going on with you two?"

I didn't want to talk about it, but the look on Papa's face was stern. When I saw how concerned he was, something told me to talk to him about it, even though I knew he was protective. When Mama was alive, I never told Papa anything. I would tell Mama and left it up to her to tell him anything important, if that's what she felt like doing. That's how things worked, when I was growing up. I learned early on in my life not to tell Papa something directly. He was way too protective of me, he wanted only the best for me, and he'd go right to the source when things weren't going well. But I could feel Mama telling me that it was all right to tell him. I didn't look in his eyes when I spoke, because I was sort of embarrassed about my situation. "Well, Papa. Me and Mikhail are both being stubborn, that's all."

"Stubborn? What's this all about?" Papa took more of his drink this time, almost finishing what was in his glass.

"He wants me to move to Seattle with him. To live."

Papa looked like he was trying to recall something. His eyes shifted left then right and he licked his lips and said, "Isn't that what you told me you were planning to do, baby girl?"

I stared at my glass, kind of shocked he remembered.

"Yes, Papa."

"Well?"

"Well, I didn't know I was going to be promoted on my job the day before I was going to resign, Papa."

"But you two are married. Married people should be together."

"I know. But is that all that matters? We're still together, even though we're apart." I didn't even believe what came out of my mouth.

"Basaura," Papa said, matter of factly.

Oh my, I'd made Papa go into his native tongue. Papa was seventy-six and if he'd said the word in English, it would have meant rubbish. He calmed himself, before he continued.

"Why are you thinking like that? You're not together, if you're apart." Papa's words were strict. He knew, I knew better and, with the look on his face, he didn't have to say anymore to me. I knew how he felt, but I had to tell him how I felt.

"But, Papa, haven't you always told me to be the best I can be?" Papa's face eased a little and I could tell he was searching for something to say. Before he came up with a response, I continued. "And that's exactly what I've tried to do. Papa, it's not easy doing what I do. The position I have may never come along in Seattle. I've always wanted to get the best out of myself, for others in our heritage to see, to show things are obtainable. It's what you've always taught me, right?"

Papa's stern face eased a little more. I'd grown to love the wrinkles that lined his cheek bones. Papa wasn't a tall man, but he was still strong and handsome. I even relaxed, when he smiled a bit.

"You know you're right, baby girl. I did teach you that our people, especially in this country, need all the positive images we can get. There could never be enough. We're almost the number one minority in the states and are the least recognized." Papa took a sip of his margarita. "But what about your marriage? Marriage is so sacred, Sweetheart."

"Papa, Mikhail and I are still married," I told him. "We're just apart and have to decide. We need to decide on our circumstances, that's all."

"I bet you two are into a pissing game, huh?"

"What, Papa?"

"You two are trying to figure out who will break first."

I smiled, "You're right."

"Both of you *are* stubborn."

Yes, Papa was right on target and I began to fill his glass again and while he watched me pour, he told me.

"Well, one thing you should know about men, baby girl," Papa said. "And this is the truth from the streets to where I grew up in Spanish Harlem all the way to our mother country."

"What's that, Papa?"

"It's hard enough for a man to keep the words of commitment on an everyday basis, when his wife is accessible to him because there's a lot of distractions everyday. So I believe it's safe to say, it's almost impossible for a man to do when his wife isn't anywhere around." Papa raised his glass, "Salute." Then he drank his margarita, never taking his eyes off me, or saying anything else about the subject. He wanted me to understand.

Seattle

I don't know what got into me. Yes, I do. Being so close to Deshelle, on the ground, after making a swipe for the dog, got the best of me. Just for a brief second, I looked at her resemblance to Darla, her golden brown skin and rapturous smile. The invitation came out in a mad rush.

"You want to join me for the fireworks tonight, at my place?" Deshelle didn't seemed to be surprised.

"What floor do you live on?"

"Twenty-fifth, number seven."

She consented with a head shake, as we continued to laugh at the dog, who was obviously waiting for us to chase him. But it never happened. The shoe was his.

Later that afternoon, returning to the condo, I had a funny feeling someone was following me. I stopped and turned abruptly. That crazy dog, had followed me the entire way home, still holding Deshelles shoe in his mouth. This time though, when I approached him, he didn't run. I walked directly over to the Beagle and it dropped the shoe. When I bent down to pick it up, the dog licked me on the back of my hand.

"Aren't you a good dog," I said and I bent down and began to pet it. I inspected him and he was a boy. He whined and wiggled, then sat down and enjoyed my hands, rubbing him all over the top of his little round head. He couldn't have been over four or five months old and looked like he was in excellent condition. As soon as I started rubbing on those floppy ears, he had me and I had him. I didn't even give it a second thought. He wasn't wearing a collar and my building allowed pets. I stood up. "Come on," I said, looking down at him. We walked into the building together, stepped into the elevator and rode up to our place.

It had been a long time since I entertained someone besides Darla. Confusion best describes my thoughts regarding why and the heck I'd even asked Deshelle over. Maybe the closeness of laying next to her on the ground excited me and made me horny and my invitation slipped out. While I was shaving, I wondered if the loneliness of being all by myself for so long had finally gotten to a point where I couldn't take it anymore. I didn't really know what I'd gotten myself into and how I was going to react, once the moment of truth came knocking on the door.

I went to check on my dog. He hadn't moved since he saw the view from the window. I don't know if he was amazed or scared. All I know is he was frozen still. I sat some water in front of him and he just looked at it, then looked back outside. I left him alone and began to think about the night.

A million thoughts ran through my mind. At first, I started to make some margaritas, the exact same way Darla had taught me. When I remembered that Deshelle was in training, I broke out all of the fruit juice I had. Cranapple, orange and apple. One thing I did realize, while getting things together for Deshelle. I had been out of the game for way too long. What was I going to talk to this young girl about, other than track? I knew about most of the rappers and groups she probably listened to. But rap didn't really do it for me anymore--not enough to hold a lengthy conversation about. All that lick 'na..na', get paid bullshit had gotten boring to me. I could barely stand to listen to it. Yeah, I would tap my foot or move my head to the beat of the music, when one of my runners would be listening to it while lifting weights or warming up in the locker room before a heat. But I wasn't into rap like that anymore. I was more into jazz, which made me reflect on life and where I was headed. I put on Paul Jackson in the CD player and let it roll.

Next, I had to decide what to wear. Not that I was one of those guys who let his wife dress him, because it wasn't like that. When Darla and I hung out, it was nothing for me to put on a pair of Dockers and a T-shirt or something and look good. But I didn't want to seem like an old, outdated thirty-five year old who had forgotten everything about fashion. I wasn't even going to let myself go out like that. I saw the kids and how they dressed everyday. Plus, my generation created what the college students were wearing. I stopped worrying about it and put on a pair of my jeans and my T-Shirt and a touch of Polo Sport Cologne.

I checked myself out in the mirror, and joked, *"Damn, thirty-five, brown-skin, bedroom eyes, still with a body,* they can't stop me," I pumped myself up, then walked into the living room to check on the dog again. He still hadn't moved. As I watched the dog, I began to question what Deshelle was thinking about us getting together. Was she suspicious of my intentions for the evening? One thing I do know. Young women can be either naive or sophisticated to the point of frightening a man. As a coach, I'd had plenty of opportunity to catch the swiftness with some of the girls and overhear even more from my male runners about how fast things move with the younger generation. I questioned even having her over again. I was really walking a tight rope, but it was too late. Nine o'clock rolled around and there was knocking at my door.

I opened the door and there was Deshelle, looking at me, then past me, into the condo, wondering if I was going to let her in. *"What the hell am I going to do if Darla calls?"* was the first thought that entered my mind, as I stood looking at my company.

Deshelle didn't give me much time to think about my question to myself. She smiled and said, "Hey coach!" She was cheerful, she wasn't bothered with the situation one bit.

"Hey, you," I said back as calmly as I could, but nervous still. "Come on in."

Deshelle walked in and hesitated, she was struck by the amazing view from my condo of the ocean. Then her eyes caught my dog. The sound of her voice made my roommate turn his head for the first time all night. He stared up at her.

"Why, you little bastard...come here!" Deshelle screamed. My dog yelped and took off and scurried under my couch. You could hear his paws scraping my hardwood floor, trying to get as far away from Deshelle as possible.

"Hey..hey...leave my dog alone!" I joked.

Darla looked back at me as I stood there smiling, "Your dog? What do you mean, your dog?"

"He followed me home and doesn't have a collar, so I'm going to keep him," I told her. Then I walked over to the closet and pulled out her shoe.

"You mean to tell me, he followed you home with my shoe in his mouth?"

The fireworks didn't start until around eleven thirty. Deshelle and I sat near the window and waited. We must have talked about everything under the sun, including her love life. She brought it up, I didn't.

"Coach? You remember the guy who always used to come and watch me practice? He would always sit in the first row of the bleachers and holler out to me that I wasn't working hard enough?"

"Oh…yeah. I remember him and you can call me Mikhail," I let her know.

"I don't know if I can. But I'll try," Deshelle said back to me. "But anyway, he was my boyfriend."

"Was?"

"Umm..hmm. But he started to get way too possessive and I couldn't handle it."

"Possessive?"

"He wanted to know where I was all the time. What I was going to do and who I was going to be with. You know the routine."

"You sure he wasn't in love?"

"Well, yeah, he said he loved me," Deshelle admitted.

"That's not such a bad thing. He just didn't know how to handle his love for you, that's all."

"I guess," she frowned. "But I had to get rid of him. I couldn't deal with him any longer."

I nodded my head and really for the first time all night looked Deshelle up and down. She looked more like a tennis player than a track star. She had on shorts, but the shorts had a connecting flap that made them look like a skirt. At the bottom of the flap they were colored with three stripes, blue white and blue again. Her shirt was a white, tight T-shirt that was exposing her nipples. She noticed me checking her out.

"So...how's your wife?" Deshelle asked, without any hesitation. Her frankness set me back a second or two. I got up from my chair and looked under the couch for the dog, to give myself a couple of seconds to think about my answer.

"She's fine," I replied.

"Does she know I'm here?"

That question made me take a deep breath. "No, she doesn't," I admitted. "Is that going to be a problem for you?"

"Not if you don't make it one," Deshelle shot back. Right then and there, I felt a little bit more easy with Deshelle. She knew I was married, I confirmed I was and she didn't seem to mind.

"So, me being married doesn't bother you, being here?"

Deshelle squinted her eyes. "No, I know lots of married men."

"Like who?" I wanted to know, as I chuckled at her surprising answer.

"Like my father. Who never seemed to be happy with my mother," Deshelle said bluntly, as she stared at me with her poker playing face.

My eyes didn't move from her and I guess I got a little understanding from her right away. She'd seen love at its worst and understood how situations occurred, when a union wasn't as beautiful as it should've been.

"So what's the deal with you and your wife?" She turned her head away from me, trying to catch all the massive bright bronze flares that were beginning to dance in the sky.

When the first round disappeared, she prodded. "So?"

"Me and my wife?"

"Yeah…your wife?"

I could've lied to Deshelle and brushed her question off, but she was more forward than I ever imagined. Her questions were more of what I'd expect from a woman my age in the same situation. She just wanted to know. "Well, see, it's like this."

Deshelle stood up from her seat, before I could begin to explain, and took one step over to me and sat in my lap. "I'm listening," she let me know.

It wasn't but a few seconds before my partner woke up and began to rise as though he'd been in deep winter hibernation. My boy sensed his pleasure nearby. Deshelle noticed I was surprised at her sudden move. She seemed to enjoy the surprised expression that covered my face then she started to gently trace my eyebrows that she kept telling me were so nice, earlier in our conversation.

"Deshelle it's like this. My wife and I are at a crossroads in our relationship at the moment."

Then she bent over and blew in my ear, like she knew it was my favorite thing in the world. "Ummm…hmmm," she purred.

"But it's gotten to a point where we both think we're in the best place for our careers and we don't want to give that up."

Deshelle started gnawing at my ear. "Do you still love her?"

I pulled away and Deshelle bent down to look into my eyes, waiting on my answer in a sassy manner.

"Yes. Yes I do," I told her. Deshelle paused for a second, like something laid heavily on her mind. She watched two more flashing displays trace the skyline, then she went back to my ear, blowing and nibbling. Another bright flash of sparkling combustion brought me from under her young and surprisingly aggressive control.

"I do love her Deshelle," I repeated. As I spoke, I heard my dog's nails rasp the floor again, trying to get further under the couch.

It's no secret. Probably no surprise. Deshelle spent the night at my place. While she laid next to me, completely naked and showing off her fine tuned body, I began to think about what the hell I'd gotten myself into. I don't know why people wait until something has been done wrong before we worry about it, but that was the case with me. It was like things went lightening fast. First the ears, then down the neck. When my hands went up under her shirt and felt the longest, sexiest nipples I've ever touched in my life--it was on. It was like it was her boiling point and the key to unlocking her young desire. She arose from the chair, took me by the hand and led me into my own bedroom. I was surprised to find the same take charge attitude I wanted her to display to her younger teammates being used on me.

Deshelle was in control of the night and I wondered how and the hell she got that way. I had my day with a few women while I was coming up, but when I was Deshelle's age the ladies I bedded were under my control. Signs of the times I guess. Deshelle's aggressiveness didn't stop once we reached the bedroom. She took off my shirt. She took off my pants. When I was completely naked, she sat me down on the bed so

I could watch her undress. Placing one of those sexy nipples against my lips, she jiggled slowly out of her shorts and there was no stopping us. Deshelle must have needed the night, as well. When I finally had the chance to touch the spot that I couldn't wait to get into, she let out the most seductive scream I've ever heard. I heard her mumble through the darkness. "It's been so long, so long...." Over and over again.

We continued our encounter until the early hours of the morning. She was on top of me, grinding, grunting, panting as though she was trying to prove a point, make me scream out loud. She tried, she tried, she tried some more. She almost succeeded. Finally, she fell off of me and into a deep sleep. I think my dog's pacing, back and forth in the hallway, brought me out of my fulfilled state of mind right before I fell off to sleep. Honestly, when I thought about what I'd done, the commitment I'd broken, I wanted Deshelle to leave. And I must confess, the thought of waking her up and telling her to leave brought back memories of Mike Tyson being locked up for the same thing. Hell, I really didn't know Deshelle. She'd already surprised me with her aggressiveness behind closed doors. I didn't know what she'd think if I told her to leave so early in the morning. Who would she turn into? What would her attitude be? So, I laid there, sweaty and confused but sexually satisfied. Then she opened her eyes and noticed me staring at the ceiling around seven thirty in the morning.

"Hey...you're up." I nodded. She stretched as best she could as she looked at the clock on the side of my bed. "Hmmmm...dang, I wanted to leave afterwards." She frowned at me. "You know I have to do a double workout today, since your crazy dog interrupted me yesterday." I guess she noticed the blank expression on my face. "What's wrong?" She sat up and began slowly stretching out her back. "I know? I know what's wrong with you." She caught my eyes for the first time since we'd had sex. "You're thinking about your wife aren't you?"

I huffed.

"See, I knew it." She began looking around in the bed. "Where are my panties?"

"How did you know?" I asked her.

"I just do. Mikhail, you're a very nice man. Don't think for one minute I didn't feel you staring through the night, when I was sleeping."

"So you understand?"

"Sure. You're not the first, believe me."

"First what?" I wanted to know.

"Married man I've slept with." Deshelle's comment surprised me. "But you're the best." She kissed me on the cheek, then bent over towards the floor and grabbed her panties. "Go'head and ask me," she pushed.

"What?"

"Ask me how many married men I've slept with. Ya'll always want to know."

I did want to know and she could tell.

"You are my fourth," she said bluntly, as she began putting on her shorts and shirt. Before I could respond the telephone rang. We both looked at it. It rang again, then a third time.

"Aren't you going to answer it? It's your wife. Don't worry about me." I looked at her and arched my eyebrow. "Go ahead," she encouraged, nodding towards the phone. It was the worst situation I'd ever been in. The phone rang a fourth time and Deshelle huffed then picked up the phone and handed it to me.

"Hello?"

"Good morning, Mikhail," Darla said.

"Hey..hey, baby," I said in a groggy voice. Deshelle stood in front of my mirror, straightening out her hair and looking at the cologne and other personal items I had on my dresser. Her movements distracted me for a second.

"What's wrong?" Darla asked.

"Oh...nothing. Just waking up, that's all."

"Papa's here and he told me to tell you hello."

"Oh, that's right. How did yesterday go?"

"We had fun. We sat around and talked. You know how he is."

"I sure do."

"What did you do yesterday?"

"Who, me?"

"Yes, you."

"Uhh..what did I do yesterday. Well....." Deshelle noticed me stumbling and moved her lips and pointed out into the living room.

"The dog," she whispered.

"I got me a dog, baby! That's what I did." I placed my fingers to my lips, instructing Deshelle to be extra quiet.

"You got a dog?"

"I sure did. I was out at the practice track and this cute little Beagle followed me home. When I went to pet him, he got me hooked right away. So, I'm going to keep him."

"And it's a Beagle?"

"With white and brown spots. Wait until you see him."
Darla became quiet. I waited, uncomfortable. I looked at
Deshelle before I spoke, letting her know I needed some
privacy. Thankfully she opened the door and walked out.
"What's wrong, Darla?"

"I just want to know when we're going to see each
other again. This is the first time that we've missed each other
after we've made plans, Mikhail."

"I know....I know."

"I'll come to see you. How's that?"

"No...no. You don't have to do that," I explained. I
almost panicked. It wasn't like she could have made it to Seattle
in five or ten minutes, but having Deshelle all up in my space
made me kind of jittery.

"Why not?" Darla demanded.

"Well...right now, Darla, I'm right in the middle of
recruiting and I need to get at least one top notch runner in
here, so my time is pretty much taken."

"You don't have enough time for your wife, Mikhail?"

"That's not it. It's just that now isn't a good time."

"Well, when?"

I pulled the phone away from my ear because I heard
the dog's bark. It was the first time he'd made any kind of
noise since I brought him home.

"Sweetheart, let me call you back in a couple of hours.
The dog's barking and maybe he's trying to tell me he wants
to go out or something. I don't want him pissin' all over my
floors."

"Okay," Darla agreed with a slight giggle.

I went into the living room and Deshelle was trying to

get at my dog. "Come here, you. Come here," Deshelle said. "He doesn't like me."

"Now why would you say that?"

"'Cause, Mikhail, when I walked out here he was sitting by the window and when he noticed me, he barked and ran under the couch. That's why."

"He likes you. He probably thinks you want to hurt him for taking your shoe."

I bent down looked under the couch. "Come here Paco."

"Paco?" Deshelle inquired, "Where did you get that from?"

"That's what he looks like to me...he looks like his name should be Paco," I told her, while I laid on the floor snapping my fingers, hoping he would come to me. He finally budged forward. In no time at all, I had him in my arms. Dehselle came over to me. Paco barked at her. "She's not going to hurt you," I let him know.

"So," Deshelle said. "What did your wife say?"

"About what?"

She shook her head, giving up on her question. I was not going to let her aggressiveness into my marriage. Then she changed the subject. "You know you're going to have to take him to the vet, don't you?"

"Yeah...I guess I should."

"I know one, not far from here."

"Good, I'll go get him checked out, then run to the store and pick him up some food and stuff."

Deshelle wrote down the vet's name and address.

"Well, I better be going." She started walking towards

the door, then turned, "Will I see you later?"

I thought about it for a second. "Let's see, okay? Lets see."

Philly-Same Day

Mikhail called me back, like he said he would, but there was something really strange about him. All of a sudden, he was more depressed about our situation. He kept saying he never realized things were going to end up like this between us and he was thinking about coming back home and forgetting about his job at the University. He hinted that he could take a job here at a high school, if he had to, like I suggested time and time again. I told him he didn't have to do it for me, but Mikhail didn't want to hear it. He said it was probably best for our marriage and kept telling me he was so, so sorry for putting me through our separation.

Mikhial's constant repentance and amends went on for weeks, then I figured it out. Mikhail had cheated on me. Face it—a loving man, one who really, truly loves his wife, can't cheat and continue as if everything is normal. His phone calls came more often, but they weren't as long. Even the time of day of his calls changed. We used to take turns waking each other up in the mornings. Now, Mikhail began calling every morning, and not just once, while I was trying to get to work. Three....four, sometimes five times, telling me how much he loved me. That's how I knew. I wondered if I could get him to admit it. So I probed. "Baby, can I ask you a question?" If he answered my question quickly, he was lying. If he laughed, he was telling the truth. I knew my man, having loved him and studied him for so many years. "Are you cheating on me?"

"What? No, baby," he shot out with lightening speed.

I knew it. I sat silent for a while. He knew all about my silent treatment. If he got it, it meant I didn't believe him and I was upset. We must have been silent twenty to twenty-five minutes and his silence explained even more to me. "Who is she, Mikhail?" I asked in my strongest accent.

"Darla, what are you talking about? I thought what we have is strong."

"So did I. Now who is she? You've changed and a woman is the reason why."

"Look, I have to go," Mikhail said.

"Where? To see her? Why are you making this more difficult than it is? Mikhail, I know you'd never do this to me if we were together. Papa warned me of this weeks ago."

"Papa told you what?"

"Papa told me that it's hard enough for a man to be committed on an everyday basis with his wife and damn near impossible, if they aren't together." We endured another twenty minutes of silence.

"Darla, I'm sorry," Mikhail whispered. I hung up the phone, wondering if I would ever be so forgiving as to break our new silence.

Seattle-At the practice track

"Hey...aren't you going to tell me what my time was?" Deshelle huffed, as she tried to catch her breath while she walked towards me. I could sense she was frustrated with me. I held Paco in my arms and she must have figured out I wasn't watching any of the things we were working on. "When I asked you to make sure my mechanical looked good, I was serious, Mikhail," Deshelle barked.

I looked down at my stopwatch. "Yeah..yeah your time was...." She was right. I didn't time her. "Let's do it again," I hollered out. Deshelle rolled her eyes at me but what could I say.

Nothing was on my mind but Darla. We hadn't spoken in weeks and although I was dead wrong for sleeping with Deshelle, I thought at least she should return my calls. Darla didn't realize it, but she was making matters worse. I didn't know where we stood. I really thought it was unfair she didn't return any of my calls. I was man enough to admit I was having an affair. And at that time, I was prepared to tell Darla it was only a mistake, I'd never let happen again. But Darla hung up on me and refused to talk to me. And that, to me, is like something is final--finished and I wasn't going to let Deshelle fly out the window without knowing where we stood. I was use to having someone around in my life, no matter how selfish it seems. Being away from Darla all those months showed me I needed company, because I hated every single day of being alone, by myself. And I'm not saying I was ready to make Deshelle my wife or a permanent fixture, because I wasn't. I missed the mental stimulation that Darla gave to me and Deshelle sensed it. At one point, while we were laying in bed, Deshelle even encouraged me to see what the deal was with Darla. I wanted to but Darla, I think, was salivating she had me where she wanted me and really didn't want to hear an apology, unless I decided to come home. But I wasn't going home, if I didn't think things could be forgotten and we both could move on with our future together and chalk this whole separation thing up as a very bad decision and experience.

"So, what was it?" Deshelle asked.

"What was what?"

"My time. My time?"

Damn it. I'd forgot to time her again. "Do it again. Let's see how you make out."

Deshelle walked over to me, took her towel off my shoulder and wiped her face.

"You know, you need to get yourself together."

"What are you talking about?"

"You're slippin', that's what I'm talking about."

"What?"

"Put it like this. Just like your wife knew, I know. You're worrying yourself crazy about your marriage." Deshelle put her towel back on my shoulder and began to walk back to where she started her three-thirty yard sprints. She was doing them to build up her endurance.

I kept my eyes on her spandex runners. Her hands grabbed her hips, as she walked away.

"Wait a minute," I called out. "Don't you think my situation is important?"

She turned around, "I guess?"

"You guess?" She nodded.

"Well it is, Deshelle. I've been with Darla for too long to just throw our relationship away."

"I thought that's what you did when you moved out here, then slept with me?"

"You thought I moved here to get away from my wife?"

"Yeah. Marriage is a crazy philosophy. I don't know

why people even try to attain the standard the whole silly concept calls for."

"I told you I loved her, before we slept together Deshelle. There's no denying that."

"But your actions have told me different."

Deshelle was now walking back towards me, hands still on her hips. I could tell she was going to try to get up all in my face with her flirtatious suggestions and those roving eyes that always moved themselves down to my partner. She stopped in front of me and began to slowly pet Paco on the top of his head while he rested in my arms. "Look, Mikhail, why don't you just enjoy me for now? If you love your wife, like you say you do, you'll get back together. Then all you'll have of me is memories. Wild, sexy memories." Deshelle turned around and began to walk away again. My eyes were focused on her strut. She turned around to see if I was looking at her, while she teased me with her backside. When she saw that I was, we both knew where we would end up after the workout.

That's how things continued for weeks and weeks. Deshelle and I took our frustrations out on one another every time we got a chance. My frustrations centered on the total lack of communication with my wife, Deshelle's on making the Olympic team. Still, through all the frustration and sex that we were definitely having, Deshelle and I became somewhat closer together. There were three times I recall Deshelle staying over at my place for three straight nights in a row. As many times as we had made love-- No, had sex,-- we were beginning to get used to each other's rhythm in bed. I didn't know if it was me, because I'd been without so long, or that Deshelle's loving was just that good. One night I turned to her and asked the question I'd wanted to ask after she told me about her past. "Is there a reason you've slept with so many married men?"

She pulled back a little, but she answered me. "At first there was. The first time, my girlfriend during my freshman year talked me into it."

"Your girlfriend?"

"Ummm...hmmm. He was the owner of a club in Tacoma. She knew him better than I did. Later, she told me she'd slept with him, too. But I guess she noticed the way he always looked at me, when we'd go to his club, and she introduced us."

"And that's all it took, was an introduction?"

"Noooo. I got to know him and I started listening to her tell me how much money he had."

"You didn't need any money. You were going to school free on scholarship," I pointed out.

"It wasn't really about the money. But a little spending money never hurt anyone," Deshelle chuckled.

"Well, what happened between you two?"

"Nothing. Basically the same thing we do, but I didn't spend as much time as I do with you. Plus, I didn't like having sex with him. So things just faded."

"Did he go back to his wife?" I wanted to know.

"He never left her."

I thought about her answer.

"The other two men were simply for my pleasure. That's all."

"Your pleasure?"

"Yep. Being able to see them while I was in school, without any ties, was the best thing for me. I wanted them for one thing and they wanted me for one thing. It was an even trade."

I felt Deshelle's hand touch my boy under the covers, then I grabbed her hand.

"So, what do you want me for?" I asked her.

Her hand moved again. This time she was too quick to catch.

Philly

Where was Mikhail? That was the question on my mind. After I busted him, I figured he'd be on the next flight home, anxious to explain, to show me how sorry he was, to talk about rebuilding our marriage. I left the recorder on the phone and refused to answer or return his calls. I stacked his letters on the counter, refusing to even open them. I wanted him home. I wanted him here, in our house, in our bed. Once he got here, I was planning to show him what good loving was, if thats what he needed. I'd show him he didn't need another woman.

But my strategy wasn't working. He didn't come home. And as the silence strengthened, my anger grew. I wouldn't crawl after him though. I wouldn't beg like a desperate fool. He had to come to me. Fortunately, my situation at work offered me the perfect outlet for my energy and an escape from my personal problems. My boss Douglas surprised everyone and announced he would be retiring in the next six months. Oh…how much I wanted his job, as director of the agency. His six months was mainly a bunch of comp time that he wanted to take and I knew, while he was away, it was my shot to show everyone I could run the place without him. The night he made his announcement, I sat at the kitchen table, thinking, planning. *'Six months. I've got six months to show the Board I can handle his job. I'm next in line. There has never been an assistant passed over in the agency after a director has left.'* More important, Douglas had told me he wanted me to have the job when he left. He offered to provide his endorsement to the Board, if I wanted it. It wasn't long until I discovered the price of that endorsement.

"Darla." Douglas hesitated, as if thinking what next to say. We were at one of the tables in the break room. As always, it was loud because the planes were coming, and going past the control tower. Douglas had come to where I was eating lunch. "I think this is a good time as any to tell you what I'm thinking, to give you enough time to make a decision," he said. I'd known Douglas for years. In fact, he was the person who interviewed me for the agency, when I applied for the job out of college. Douglas was about fifty-eight and looked like he'd been a jock in his younger days. I think he played football in college or something. I knew he was stone crazy about the Eagles. He never missed a game and was always the one responsible for the football pools during the season. He'd come into the office after every game, acting like he himself had made a saving tackle of a sure touchdown or something.

"You know I want you to have my job, Darla," he said

in his deep, husky voice.

I could see a plane out the break room window about thirty or forty seconds away from landing. I smiled at Douglas the best I could, while I tried to get the bread from my sandwich from the roof of my mouth. "I want you to have it and I think you'd be excellent for the position."

I finally succeeded with the bread and said, "Why thank you, Douglas."

"However, I need something from you." He had to speak a little louder because the plane approaching was almost right overhead of us.

I nodded my head. Then the plane was directly over us and he said something back to me, but I couldn't make it out. "What did you say?"

"He smiled then looked around to insure we were still alone. "I want to have you, in exchange for my endorsement."

Without a word, I stood up and walked away from the table, hearing Douglas chuckle, as I headed straight for the restroom. I couldn't believe what I'd heard. I couldn't believe Douglas had propositioned me. I rinsed my face with cool water. Maybe this was one of his crazy office pranks, I thought. Maybe this was his idea of a joke. He did those kind of things all the time. I returned to my office. When I saw him staring at me through my window that separated our two work areas, I knew he was serious.

What's a girl to do? This sort of thing isn't supposed to happen. This is the new millennium. I thought about going to personnel. I thought about contacting the Board. I even considered the NAACP. But I wanted his job and I didn't want to hear any accusations that I concocted the story in order to be placed in his vacant position.

It appeared Mikhail wasn't coming home and had no interest in our marriage. Apparently the little honey out in Seattle was taking care of his needs and he had no use for the sacred vows we'd shared. So, I started thinking. There's nothing like a highly employed sista' to bring out the highly employed brothers and if I could get this job, that's exactly what I would be. If there wasn't going to be any Mikhail, that's what I wanted to have in my life. Plenty of opportunities for a *good* man who lived in *Philly*. I thought about the offer from by boss. Some days it pissed me off, others it made sense.

One night I watched a rerun of *Boomerang* where Eddie Murphy's character had to sleep with Eartha Kitt. I was sort of in the same situation. Maybe it was the margaritas I was drinking, who knows? I started thinking about trying to stomach Douglas in bed. He wasn't a bad looking guy. Half Hawaiian and Asian with a sprinkle or two of Negro in him. He had a square head and a hairline that was almost too close to perfect. He was big, like one of those Sumo wrestlers. My mind drifted to going to bed with the man, wondering what it would be like, thinking it might not be so bad. Being horny probably didn't help the clarity of my thinking. I'd missed my action from Mikhail when he played me to stay in Seattle on the Fourth of July. It was the end of October and I was past due. The more I drank, the more I became mad that Mikhail slept around on me. So I thought about Douglas finally giving me some pleasure. Then I thought about reporting him again. But if I did, everyone in the office would know and think I got the job only on those merits and I would've never been respected.

It was time to have a little chat with Douglas. We were in his office during a shift change, so my visit to his office looked as sound as could be.

"Were you serious about your offer, Douglas? The exchange you mentioned, regarding your position?" When he nodded, I continued. "I've given it some thought."

His eyes lit up and he leaned across his desk. "I think it would be for the best Darla. We both win. And just to let you know, I think I should let you in on a little secret. Some of my golfing partners who are on the Board were talking about maybe looking at someone else from the outside to come in to fill the position. You know that's never been done here. It's been a family for years, so I think my recommendation would really seal it for you because they really wanted to know how I felt about you taking over. "

'Those son's of bitches. ' I thought. I had to do it now. "There's just one question," I pointed out to Douglas.

"What's that?"

"How do I know you'll go through with your end of the deal? What guarantee do I have of your endorsement?"

Douglas relaxed. "We'll set a date and time. I'll commit and make the recommendation. You'll know you have the endorsement, before we meet."

"Okay. But this will only happen one time, Douglas? If I decide to do this, once is enough."

"One time," he agreed, his eyes lighting in anticipation.

Seattle

I was by myself again. Deshelle had already run in the Olympics and was now on a world tour with the team. She'd trained like a woman possessed and proved her abilities. She'd placed second in the Olympic finals and also ran a leg on the 400 meter relay team, which won a gold medal. She called the night she was presented with the gold. But our conversation had been more between a coach and runner, than between two lovers or even two friends. She was too excited to tell me she missed me. Maybe she didn't. I hadn't talked to her since that night and sometimes I wondered if she was all right, making her rounds around the world. Paco was doing his best to keep me company, but he had his limitations. He was a damn dog. I dug through my address book and decided it was time to call Triggs. I hadn't talked to him in way too long. Triggs was my boy in junior high, high school and college. He was the brother who would always support me in all of my pursuits, good and bad. He was even the best man at my wedding. I needed to talk to him for sure.

"What's up Mac Daddy!" I demanded, soon as Triggs answered the phone.

"What? Who's this?" He knew.

"Your daddy. That's who it is."

"What's happening, Slim!" It was good to hear his voice and my nickname at the same time.

"Same'ol, same'ol. You know how I do it! What's going on with you?"

"Maannnn' I just found out that Rhonda is pregnant again."

117

"Again?"

"That's right...number six in the oven, baby!" Triggs boasted.

"Ya'll some children-making folk."

"That's what you do, when you get married, my brother....you make them babies. So tell me what's going on with you?"

"Aww, man. Just coaching, trying my best to get my team to win the conference this year."

"Hey, I saw one of your girls made the Olympic squad! I know you feel like a proud daddy!"

"Yeah, she worked hard for it brother. She's a real nice girl."

Something in my voice must have clued Triggs. He'd known me for too long. "What you talking about a *real* nice girl, Slim?" Triggs tone of voice was cooler by several degrees.

"Just what I said. She's a nice girl."

"Come on now. Talk to me, brutha'. We too old to be playin' word games."

I took a deep breath to collect my thoughts. "Where's your wife?"

"Sleepin,' man. I told you she's pregnant. Now tell me what's going on?"

We stayed on the phone for three hours. Triggs was surprised and somewhat angered to hear about all the drama that had happened in my life, especially since he stood beside me when I promised to forsake temptation. I felt like I'd let him down. But as I began to get into specifics about my situation, it was like Triggs was treating me as if I'd done something he wished he could or had the balls enough to do.

"Slim, I saw her on the tube brutha'. Tell me, is she as good as she looks?"

I chuckled at his question. "Better. You hear me? Out of this world."

"So you and her were carrying on for like months, you say?"

"That's right."

"So that means you two did it more than a couple of times then?"

"I stopped counting after the first night."

"Slim, you in your mid-thirties man. How you keep up with that young girl?"

"Wha'? I'm still in shape man, believe that. And she's so sensual, so sexual, it's not like you even putting in work. She just takes it-- like I give it."

Triggs laughed into the phone. "Oh, my goodness, oh my goodness," he repeated. "And she was so good you let Darla find out, huh?"

His question silenced me. "By the way, has Darla been by there?" I wanted to know.

"Naww'... I think Rhonda called her once or twice and if I remember she said Darla·was talking about being up· for another position or something."

"Another position?"

"That's what Rhonda told me. So what you two going to do, Slim? This long distance thang' is the least of what I expected out of you two and that's for real."

I didn't have an answer. I still loved Darla, but I didn't know what to do or I would've tried it. She still wouldn't answer my calls. The letters I sent certified to her job were never returned. Triggs interrupted my thoughts.

"Well, like I say, Slim. There's nothing like having a wife and a house full of kids. I don't care what anybody says, I wouldn't trade it for the world."

Philly

A couple of weeks passed and Douglas had already taken one whole week off and, just like he said, gave me his recommendation to replace him as director. Right away my co-workers who felt qualified for my position, began lobbying for the slot almost immediately. Then it seemed as though everyone else who heard I was recommended for the position were instantly trying to be my best friend. Everyone. People who'd ignored me before or didn't say much to me out of the ordinary, except for work related issues, were suddenly telling me about their entire lives and how happy they were for me. I began to understand how the men in these positions had the balls to make propositions, like the one Douglas had offered me, because everyone kissed their ass.

I called Papa and told him about the recommendation. It was so nice to hear how proud he was of me. It helped soothe the still nagging feeling that it was not how things should have worked to get it. I guess I was naive, in believing society was past the point where a woman had to sleep with the boss, in order to climb the corporate ladder. It made me wonder how many other women were still battling the same dilemma in the workplace. Things hadn't really changed all that much after all.

After Douglas' recommendation for the position, it

really didn't matter much to me what happened next. My self-worth had taken a nose dive, when I realized Mikhail had cheated on me, had broken the vows of our marriage. What difference did it make if I slept with Douglas? I wasn't sleeping with my husband. Or anybody else, for that matter. I knew my decision wasn't living in the spirit and knew some of my sister girlfriends would be appalled at what I was going to do, but I had little trouble justifying my actions. Sleeping with Douglas would get me a job that would give me the power men have always had over women. Even though what I was doing was wrong, I was doing the wrong thing for the right reasons. I'd never do it again, but my position would allow me to hire and place women in jobs they couldn't otherwise attain. And not one of them would have to lay on their back to advance. I was working for the good of the cause and I knew I wasn't the first woman who'd had to lay down to get what she wanted, whether literally or figuratively.

I pulled into the parking lot of a nice sea food restaurant on the outskirts of Philly. It was where Douglas and I were going to meet, before I paid my dues. I was to meet Douglas at eight o'clock. I parked near the door and waited until I saw his Jaguar pull in and watched him walk briskly to the entrance. Taking a deep breath, I got out of the car and followed him inside. His smile was possessive, almost predatory, as he greeted me, like he didn't believe this was going to happen. He didn't say a word until we were seated at our table.

"You really look nice," he said.

"Isn't that why I'm truly here in the first place?" I asked him. I had on a black slip on dress. My hair was pulled back into a long pony tail and I had worked on my make-up to get the most seductive look possible. I don't know, maybe I was even trying to look like an entirely different person. Douglas really made me kind of nervous, because his big ol'sumo wrestling self barely said anything over dinner. I got real tired, real quick, looking at his dark blue suit jacket along with his shirt and tie that looked like they were to small for his massive shoulders and neck. He ordered an oyster platter and the way he worked on them I instantly wondered if he was going to eat me the same way. If he was going to get it. Believe me, he was going to eat it first. I never did say that Douglas was physically a dog. Mentally, yes, but physically, he was decent. Nowhere near Mikhail, but I could use him the same way he was using me.

Mikhail had the audacity to have his little fling and I knew just this one night would make Mikhail realize never to mess with me. Yes, I intended on telling him. Telling him every single detail of the night with Douglas. Every kiss, every hump, every pump, every lick and every stick that we shared. I knew that one night probably couldn't even compare to whoever and the hell Mikhail was stroking. But when a woman does the same wrong to a man, that has been done to her. A man can never, ever get over it, because every man thinks what he's ever laid inside to always be his and only his territory. I don't care if you were a fast ass sophomore in high school and saw the man who took your virginity twenty-five years later. I'll bet one thing. He's going to want it again, after all those years, because in his corrupt mind, he's still claiming it. That's how they think. And Mikhail was no different.

"Douglas, why are you so quiet?" I asked, as I fiddled

over my chef's salad.

"Oh...uh. I don't know. Just trying to have a nice time, that's all."

"So, are you having a nice time?" He nodded yes. "Do you plan on being this quiet later?" He looked up from his plate and, for the first time, really, really looked at me and smiled.

"I'm kind of worried about what you think of me, Darla?"

Out of all the nerve in the world, I thought. *At a time like this, he has the nerve to act like he has some scruples about himself.* "You're worried about how I feel about you?"

Douglas slurped down his last oyster and I thought his suit jacket was going to rip. He wiped the corners of his mouth with his napkin and smiled."Darla, I know you couldn't have been too terribly surprised at my offer?"

"Douglas, to tell you the truth, yes I was," I assured him.

"You mean to tell me you've never noticed my stares." I shook my head no. "Okay, granted I knew you were married and I was trying to be discreet about my interest but, after all this time, I seriously thought you noticed."

"Sorry," I said.

"Well, it doesn't matter. We're here now. But I have to tell you. If I hadn't overheard Janet and Sylvia talking about how your marriage failed, I would've never confronted you like I did."

"Janet and Sylvia?"

Douglas grinned, "Yes, during my last surprise inspection on the red eye shift. There wasn't to much happening in the control booth that night. Those two had brought in some cookies and ice cream and were sitting around in the break room chatting. I just happened to walk in and overhear them discussing your marriage and how you and your husband had separated. That's why they were suspended for two days without pay, because they weren't at their post." Douglas grinned again.

"Sorry to bust your bubble, Douglas, but Janet and Sylvia don't know anything about my relationship with my husband."

He snickered, "That's exactly what they said. But you know Janet is the one who listens to the recordings on our phone lines and she said you never returned any of your husbands calls. They were just speculating, I guess." We exchanged wondering smiles, "So everything is okay between you two?" he asked.

"As a matter of fact, no," Shoot, I was tired of my situation. I didn't tell Papa anymore about it because I didn't want him to worry and I hadn't talked to Mikhail about our situation period. I'd kept everything inside of me and it was time for my feelings to come out, even though I cared nothing for the person sitting at the other end of the table. Then I thought to myself, *"That makes it much better."* I looked at Douglas and told him to order me a margarita. I quickly drank my first margarita, then the second. By the time I started on the third, Douglas and I were sharing our opinions on marriage.

"I know exactly what you're saying," Douglas admitted, while he sipped on his third gin and tonic. "I've been married four times. And one out of the four, nobody ever knew had taken place. After my first three, and my fourth wife's second, we decided if no one knew that we were married, we wouldn't be distracted by others."

"So what happened?" I asked.

"We got bored with each other and decided to call it quits anyway."

There was no doubt I was buzzing from my drink, because I asked the man who wanted to sleep with me, for the exchange of a job, about *God*. "So, do you think God is really upset with us?"

He must have thought I was buzzing too, 'cause he laughed at my question, "God?"

"Yes, God," I repeated, "I'm just asking because the vows you take when you're married are the most sacred words you ever say in your life. I mean, much more sacred than any other words that ever come out of your mouth. When I said my vows, I really did mean them. What about you, Douglas?"

"Each time I said them?"

"Yes, that's what I want to know. Each time you said them. Was it ever different? Did you mean it any less any of the times you were married?"

"I don't think so. To be truthful, each time I married I thought it would be for the last time."

"See, that's what I want to know about God. Do you think he's going to hold those who don't keep their vows in marriage responsible?"

"If he does, I know I'm in trouble," Douglas laughed.

"I'm serious."

"All marriages aren't reconcilable, though," he said.

"It just seems like the hardest words you stand before

God and say, *til death do us part,* are the most difficult in life to achieve," I explained.

"I'm a living example. But I'm sure, all things considered God knows the circumstances," Douglas said.

"You think he understands the circumstances you presented to me?" I asked flat out.

Douglas looked at me with squinted eyes, then finished his drink, "Only I will ever know."

During the fifteen minute drive, I did a lot of thinking. Douglas was still kind of nervous. It was obvious during dinner so I decided to take control. It seemed the closer he got to his goal, the more he seemed to freeze up. By the time we left the restaurant, I wondered if we'd ever make it into bed and, if so, whether it would be worth the effort. Sleeping with Douglas had become more than a route to the director's office. It had become my pay back to Mikhail and with the help of the margaritas, I was ready to go through with it. I thought of all the things Mikhail and I had shared, thought of him now sharing them with his lover, and I was infuriated. I wanted Mikhail to feel the same pain. I parked in the drive and Douglas pulled in behind me. As I got out of the car, he came to my side. His smile was hesitant, almost shy. His eyes were a hazy brown and the margaritas made him have a nice smile, even if he did have fat cheeks to go along with his fat head.

"Ready?" I asked. At his hesitant nod, I took his hand and we followed the curved walk to the porch. We were at my house, so I felt comfortable. On the porch at the front door, I turned and smiled up at Douglas, forcing some resemblance of sincerity. Reaching up, I placed my hand against the back of his neck. He lowered his head to meet my lips. I noticed a silhouette appear near one of the street lamps, right before I closed my eyes to kiss him. Douglas sensed my hesitation, heard my sharp intake of breath, and turned to follow my gaze. We both watched Mikhail's shadow fade into the night.

Philly-Same Night

The sight of Darla, lifting her face to receive another man's kiss, was more than I could bear. Shocked, I stumbled down the street towards my car, my mind replaying the scene I'd just witnessed, my hands trembling, my stomach rolling. Numb, acting mostly on instinct, I checked into a hotel and called Triggs, asking him to meet me at the bar. By the time he arrived, I was well into a bottle of cognac. The numbness had vanished, replaced with the heat from the cognac that I was drinking non-stop.

"So, what's the deal?" Triggs said, coming up behind me while I sat at the bar.

I turned around to greet him.

"Damn, look at you, Slim. What's going on, you're wasted?"

"It's Darla."

"Darla? Is she all right?"

I shook my head no.

"What happened?"

"Nothing."

"She's all right then?"

"No."

"No?"

"Uh…uh. I saw her tonight, with another man."

Triggs took a deep breath. He sat down next to me. "Man, damn. Is that all?"

"Is that all?"

"Yes, is that all?"

"That's enough," I shot back, "Come on, have a drink with me." I pointed towards the bartender, who came over with a glass for Triggs and poured me another.

"Tell me what happened," Triggs said.

"Well, I came home to see Darla. You know, talk to her face to face, because she hasn't returned any of my calls or answered my letters. As soon as I got here, I went to the house and she wasn't there. I drove around for a couple of hours and, when I returned to my place, I see her standing on the porch, about to kiss this guy."

"Kiss him?"

"Kiss him," I confirmed.

"Man...that doesn't even sound like Darla." Triggs questioned.

"Saw it with my own two eyes."

"Did she see you?"

"Not sure, I didn't wait around to find out."

Triggs took a sip of his drink, "You're my boy, Slim, but I can't say that I blame her."

"What?"

"I'm just sayin', you did it to her. It's like, what goes around, comes around."

"Fuck that. I never believed in that childish bull shit." I tipped up my glass.

"Well, it just happened to you."

I didn't want to hear what Triggs was talking about. I

looked over in the opposite direction of the bar. He was my boy. He was supposed to be there to support me.

"It's always funny to me."

I looked back at Triggs. "What's that?"

"How brutha's always get upset when the tables are turned."

"Who's upset?"

"Your drunk ass, that's who."

"So what." I sharlpy conceded.

"So, you need to just deal with it. Darla dealt with what you did to her."

"It's not the same."

"It's exactly the same."

"Look, Triggs, I didn't mean for you to come down here and lecture me. I asked you to come down here to drink with me."

"You've had enough, Slim, and I have to work in the morning. You need to get yourself together and handle this shit like a man. When was the last time you drank like this, anyway?"

"When we were in college," I slurred, "You remember how we used to do, don't you?"

"Yeah..yeah, I remember. But we're men now, husbands. Got to do right." Triggs finished his drink and slid his glass away.

"No...no..no. You're a husband. I ain't nobody's husband."

"You and Darla can work through this, Slim."

"Naww.., we can't, there's no way now."

"How do you know? You need to sit down and talk

first."

"There's nothing to talk about."

"You two have a lot to talk about. For one, all of the time and effort you've put into your relationship. There's a lot of years between you two, you know what I'm sayin'?"

"Man, you sound like Oprah Montell, or some damn body."

"And you sound like you're hurting."

I was. I'd never in my life thought I would see Darla puckering her lips and getting ready to lay one on anybody except me. Way too many things were running through my mind, as I sat at the bar. Triggs must have understood I was reminiscing, because he sat quiet. I took a quick glance at him and, for the first time, I was in awe of another man. Triggs had a wife. Kids. The complete package. He looked to be doing well, too. His head was still full of hair and it looked like he was able to sneak in a workout often enough to stay in shape. He still dressed snazzy, wearing a blue jean baggy outfit. Brother looked like he was in his twenties, like he was motivated and had places to be.

All of a sudden, I began to wonder if I should sit down and talk with Darla, like he suggested. Hell, Triggs must know something about the marriage business. He'd been married since we were freshman in college. I never will forget all the drama he and his wife had while we were in school but, according to him, they were still going strong.

"So you think I need to talk to her, huh?" I asked.

"That's right, I do."

"And start where, Triggs?"

He smiled, "Start off with an apology. It works every time."

"That's it?" I asked.

"Oh, hell no," Triggs chuckled, "You might as well prepare yourself for the stand."

"The stand?"

"You heard me right. Being drilled. Question after question about your lady friend."

"Shit, man. I don't want to get into that."

"And she's going to know that, too. You think she wants to hear it?"

"Well, why is she going to ask about it?"

"To see how you react when you tell her."

"What?"

"Yeah.... She wants to see your facial reactions and see if you're truly remorseful. I told you, bru', you goin' to be on the stand like a murder case or some shit."

"So what should I do?"

"Tell the truth."

"That's it?"

"That's it. But if you truly aren't sorry for what you done, Slim, I'm telling you, don't let her know it."

"But what about her. I saw her tonight. She owes me, too."

"Nope."

"Nope?"

"Uh..uh, she can say it's the first time they were ever together. Even if it wasn't. See, women aren't going to tell if they mess around. They'll keep that shit to themselves until they die. That just shows how stupid we are, 'cause we can't stand the pressure and we tell on ourselves in a heart beat."

"Triggs, I told you, she figured it out."

"She didn't figure it out. She had a feeling and your ass got nervous and told on yourself. Isn't that what happened?"

I knew Triggs was right, but I wasn't going to admit it.

"Right?" he asked again.

"So, what?"

"So, don't go in that direction with her or she'll twist the whole situation around and you two will have even more drama. What you want to do, is talk about it one time and move on."

"One time?" Now I was listening to him, but that seemed to be asking too much. I knew Darla and I knew her Spanish heritage was going to be in rare form. It always was when we had a disagreement. Darla loved to talk, until she was sure she had her point across.

"So, you goin' to give it a try?" Triggs wanted to know.

I thought for a moment, then looked at Triggs, "How do you know so much about this particular topic?" I was curious. Triggs pointed to the bartender for another drink. He watched his shot glass as it was filled to the rim. Triggs picked up his drink and drank it straight down then turned to me.

"'Cause I do." He waited until his drink went all the way down then slid off his bar stool and patted me on my back, "Call me, okay?"

"Yeah, I will," I promised, as I finally understood.

Day's Later

It took three days to work up my courage. Three very long days of making plans and discarding them. I considered going out to the house and making myself comfortable. I had a key, my name was on the mortgage, I helped make the house payments. My favorite box spring and mattress were in the master bedroom and it would have felt good to lay my tired behind on it. I gave up on that idea and remained at the hotel. For two days I followed Darla to work and back home, trying to figure out what to say, trying to find the nerve to approach her. Finally, the third day, I drove over to the house and waited. As Darla got out of her car, I approached the driveway, Paco in my arms.

"Darla? Darla, could I, uuuh..., talk to you for a second?"

She looked at me and Paco, then glanced at the sky, "It's going to rain any minute."

"Well, we can go inside, can't we?"

She frowned again at the dog, then at me. With a slight shrug of her shoulders, she turned toward the house, "I guess,"she decided.

For the first time, I was uncomfortable walking into my own home. This had always been a haven for me, a place to relax and enjoy the fruits of our labors. But it felt different. Even my trophies, lining the fireplace mantel, offered no warm feeling of home or belonging. Silent, Darla walked through the living room and into the kitchen, dropping her briefcase on the counter. Without a word, she began sorting the stack of mail collected nearby.

She neatly placed her mail in one pile, then added the remaining envelopes to a huge stack at the end of the counter. "You might want to take this with you, when you leave," she commented.

I'd dropped into one of the chairs at the table and Paco laid at my feet.

"That's all my mail?"

"Umhmmm," She turned to face me, "Did you come to pick up the rest of your things?"

"No, as a matter of fact, I didn't."

I was still unsure how to open a discussion about my lover that put us in our situation and I needed something to help me relax. I walked over to the refrigerator. I looked at the bins on the inside of the door. I checked the shelves. I stooped and looked to the back of the refrigerator.

"What happened to the bottle of wine I was saving?"

Darla snapped, "I poured it out."

I turned towards her, "Why? That was..."

"Look, Mikhail, say what you came to say. It's been a long day."

I sat back down at the table and rubbed Paco on his head. "Well, I just wanted to tell you I'm sorry for what I've done and I'm hoping you're willing to accept my apology."

Darla laughed at me, then pulled a chair out from the table and sat down. "What are you sorry for?"

"You know, sleeping around on you in Seattle."

"Is that all?"

"Yeah," I was a bit confused.

"What about all of my sleepless nights," Darla popped at me. "The tears I've cried and constant heartache and headaches I've been having since I found out about you, Mikhail?"

I looked down at Paco. I'd told Triggs this shit wasn't going to work. Darla had already thrown out four other topics, besides the one I apologized for. I didn't know where to begin and I guess my face told Darla so.

"I don't even know why you're here, Mikhail. You have no idea what you've put me through. I think you should go back to Seattle and be with you friend. Forever."

"Darla, what are you talking about? We're married."

"You don't need to be telling me that. You need to understand it yourself." Darla stood up from the kitchen table, opened the refridge' and retrieved a bottled water.

She was in the mood to argue, I could see it all over her face. Her eyes weren't bright and shiny. They were narrow, coming close to becoming red and watery. Her voice shook. I knew, any minute, she was going to throw a tantrum. I felt myself becoming upset. The thing Triggs told me would happen if I wasn't careful, was happening right in front of my eyes and I didn't think it was right. And I knew I wasn't going to be able to handle it.

"Look, you're not going to turn the table here and try to make it look like I'm all at fault," I told her.

"It is all your fault, Mikhail. No one else's but yours."

"Wait a minute. I seem to remember seeing you on a romantic excursion, too?"

"It's different. You would never understand and I don't care to explain it to you, Mikhail."

"Well I want an explanation. I'm still your husband."

"You're not going to get one. Husbands don't leave their wives and go miles away, then sleep with other women."

"I told you I was sorry, Darla. Besides you agreed with my decision to leave, in the first place."

"Well, sorry is not going to do it." Our voices were starting to echo through the kitchen. I felt Paco try to get my attention, by bumping his nose against my leg. I eased a little and tried to laugh off our circumstance, while Darla moved the cold bottle of water up to her lips.

"Look, Darla. I think our first mistake was moving apart from each other in the first place."

"That was your decision," she shot back her voice was lower this time.

"Which you supported," I calmly told her, "But I don't think we were ready for it."

"I tried to tell you that."

"I admit you did. But what I honestly want to know is if you still truly love me? If you don't, I'll leave and we'll have lawyers straighten all this out."

Darla looked at me. Her eyes penetrated every part of me as I waited for her answer.

"Yes, yes I do," she answered.

"Then we can work this out, because I'm still in love with you, Darla."

"No. No, Mikhail, it's not that easy. I do love you. But I didn't say I trust you."

"Well, move back to Seattle with me. We can live there liked we planned, right?"

"No...I can't. This opportunity here, Mikhail, is more

promising. I can't leave now. If you love me so much, move back here?"

"And do what?" I asked, "Work where?"

"I don't know. Take some time, think about your future."

"I already know what I want to do with my future," I told her.

Back in Seattle

Three weeks later, Darla called me. She told me her boss helped her get the job she'd always wanted. It was funny though? She didn't seem as happy as I thought she might be, seeing that she's the first woman of color to hold the Director position in her agency. But it's what she wanted and we both knew our marriage was over. I didn't question her about our situation again. Matter of fact, I had to rush off the phone, there was knocking at my door. It was Deshelle. I guess death isn't really what do us part.

Laying on Silk

Sharon was very hesitant about making the call to the popular late night radio show, *Better Sex and Love*. Three times already, after getting a dial tone on her phone in order to call in, she was made to hang up the phone again after the annoying constant 'hang up and try again' sound woke her out of her deliberation of putting her business on the airwaves. She was undecided. The thought of someone recognizing her voice was enough to make her chug along and suffer with her scarred sex life with her husband, Tommy, as she had for the last two years. But Sharon was frustrated, she was not easy, she didn't like the feeling of not being satisfied sexually and the last segment of the show was so "hot and nasty" it had made matters worse, as she'd seemed to wonder if she was the only grown-up in Chicago not having good sex.

Sharon and Tommy had been married for five years, but they'd been together for a total of ten. For the first five years they were non-stop. Going at it every chance they could get and having a variety of favorite positions and trying them out any place that would give them enough time to pleasure one another. But the good sex had quickly faded after they were married and now, Sharon was tired of her situation with Tommy and wanted more.

Apprehensive, Sharon reached across the pillow where Tommy laid his head. Tommy wasn't home. He'd gone out. And last night, too, as well as the night before that. He'd become upset a while back, when he and Sharon were 'doing the do,' and he noticed things weren't quite right himself, but never once asked Sharon what the problem was. They'd begun having sex in their same normal way, which, Tommy blamed on the wicked hours he worked on his job. Tommy, noticing Sharon was awake and turning to face her, giving her a few kisses on her breast, then neck, then plopping on top of her and wetting his fingers with his own saliva and moistening her, then inserting her all in one minutes time. Goodness. It's not what Sharon wanted, so she just laid on her back with her eyes open, watching Jay Leno. She wanted to feel the fire, the desire, burning between her legs and all over her body as it had felt years before they were married.

Most of the time, she understood the circumstances. They'd both come home dead tired from work. During working hours, both would think about coming home and having wild sex together, but the burden of their jobs and headaches of getting to and from work had put their sex lives on hold. So, when Tommy noticed her disposition and lack of grind and hump, while he was on top handling his business, he thought about rolling off of her. But finished what he had to do, and hadn't tried it since.

Sharon looked at the clock. *Better Sex and Love* had only thirty minutes left. It was one-thirty in the morning. The hosts, Hot Mona and Pumpin'Mike, had already begun bragging about how the city of Chicago was going to be bumping and grinding after the tips they'd shared, when their show was over. Sharon didn't want to miss out, so she picked up the cordless and dialed.

"No way I'll get through," she thought. She listened to the phone ring one time, two times then a third. She listened to the radio. They were in commercial. Then a fourth ring.

"Hello? *Better Sex and Love* and this is Pumpin' Mike," she heard. Mike's electrifying deep voice startled her. She was unable to speak. "Hello, this is Pumpin' Mike.. goin' once... goin' twice," he prodded.

"Uh…hello?" Sharon whispered.

"Yes?"

"I have a question?"

"Okay, give me twenty seconds and we'll be on the air. Hold on, okay?"

Sharon began to disconnected the line. But Pumpin' Mikes voice startled her.

"Will you hold?"

"Yeah, sure," Sharon pushed out.

In the twenty seconds, Sharon tried to collect herself. She didn't know if twenty seconds was enough time to get her thoughts together and calm the nerves she felt beginning to rattle her. But she wanted to know what she could do to spice up her sex life. It was an emergency. A very bad emergency that could possibly save her relationship. All of a sudden, it was time.

"Hot Mona?"

"Yes, Pumpin'?" Mona asked over the air, as they sat together in the studio, addressing their listener's.

"We have on the line.....Uh...caller, tell us your name?" There was silence.

"Caller, are you there?" Pumpin' asked.

Sharon forced herself. "Yes, I'm here."

"Tell us your name, Sweetheart," Mona hissed.

"My name is Sharon." Sharon hit herself on the leg. She didn't want to do that. She had made up her mind, in the twenty seconds that she was on hold, to use Tina. Now it was too late.

"Sharon, thanks for calling. What's your question on *Better Sex and Love* with the marvelous Hot Mona and me...Pumpin' Mike?"

"Oh I like how you say that," Hot Mona purred.

"Thank you, baby. Okay, Sharon, the floor is yours."

Sharon looked around the dark room, rubbed her hand over the silk sheets on Tommy's pillow and forced herself to speak. "Well, I have a question?"

"That's why we're here, baby," Mike said.

"Well, my husband and I......well, our sex lives are nil and void."

"Oh...wow....you mean you and your husband don't have sex?" Mona inquired.

"No, no. We have sex. Not as much as I would like but, when we do, it's not any good and I don't know what to do," Sharon explained.

"Okay, okay. We've had this type of call before, so what I think you need is some tips from Pumpin' Mike and

Hot Mona. What do you think, Sharon?"

"I guess so."

"Well, I'm not married, but I think you two should be having knock out sex. Tell us a little about you two first, before I give you something that will put the spice back into the bedroom, girlfriend?" Mona instructed.

"Let's see...We've been married for five years, and I was seeing him about five years before that. Uhhh, lets see, when we weren't married, it seemed like he would go out of his way to satisfy me, you know what I'm saying?"

"What would he do?" Pumpin'Mike asked.

"Well, he would do whatever I needed him to do, to satisfy me."

Pumpin' didn't stop there. "Yeah, yeah, like?"

"I don't know if I can say it over the air?"

"We all grown," Mona squeaked.

Sharon chuckled a bit from embarrassment, "Okay, say for instance, whenever I wanted him to, or after we had sex and I didn't reach orgasm, he would go down on me. Can I say that?"

"You just did. Hey......" Mona sang. "Now we getting somewhere."

"So, so, Sharon. Are you sayin' he doesn't do that anymore?" Pumpin wanted to know. "And you're in need of a downtown shopper perhaps?"

"That's exactly what I'm sayin," Sharon confessed. "All he wants to do is get on top of me at night, before we go to sleep, and if I happen to get satisfied, then that's icing on the cake. Most of the time if I do get that feeling it's the result of me pushing myself to that point and nothing he's doing to get me there."

"Oh...my goodness. Now this is the call I've been waiting on all night. Let's do this. Let's take a break and come back with Ms. Sharon and give her the Pumpin' Mike and Hot Mona freaky tips and suggestions that have never been heard before, so we can help Sharon and her husband get back their groove. Is that all right with you, Mona?"

"Fine with me, you know how I freak."

"Sharon, you cool with that?"

Sharon giggled, "Yes."

Pumpin' became really excited, "Alright Chitown'! We'll, be back in two! You are listening to *Better Sex and Love* with Hot Mona and me, Pumpin' Mike. 'Bout to get freaky up in here! Stay tuned."

Sharon was flushed now. But her nervousness and hesitation had disappeared. Sharon didn't tell the D.J.'s, but her situation was more serious than what she'd let on. She was seriously thinking about packing her bags and leaving. Every married couple has items high on their priority list. And sex and trust were the main two on Sharons. She had always enjoyed sex. As a young girl, she highly anticipated giving up her virginity and, when she turned eighteen, she went away with a twenty-seven year old man and was taught the ways of the world on a three day weekend that was both satisfying and delightful, which she has never regretted. Now she was eager to find out what kind of suggestions they were going to give her. Already, she'd decided she was going to wait up for Tommy, if any of their suggestions interested her and tell him exactly what she wanted or it was over.

"We're back with *Better Sex and Love*, with me

Pumpin' Mike."

"And me, Hot Mona."

"With our caller, Sharon, who's discussing with us, how she and her husband's sex lives have completely stalled. Am I right, Sharon?"

"Yes, that's right, Pumpin'," Sharon answered into the phone.

"Well, we were discussing your problem over the break. And what we've come up with is......maybe you need to try new things, that are more exciting, to get your sex life back on track and sparkling and bublin' like a class of MOET. Now answer me this? Have you and your husband ever, taken the time to leave the bedroom and get away somewhere, a place where there are no distractions to be together?"

"Sure, we'd do it all the time during our first year. But just to let you know, we went to Indianapolis for the Black Expo last month and stayed in a pretty hotel and everything and still, the same result."

"You mean--you didn't do it?" Hot Mona inquired.

"No, no...we did it. But it just wasn't hot. Just wasn't what I needed. Put it like this. I could've stayed at home for what I got and done it a lot better myself."

"Ohhh, my," Mona belly ached, "That's terrible gurrl'."

Mike chimmed in, "Depends on who you ask?"

"You're soo bad Pumpin'," Mona told him.

" I know, what can I say? Well, stop me if I'm wrong now but, Sharon, to me, you sound like you got a lot of freak in ya'? Is that true?" Pumpin' Mike chuckled.

"Yes, Mike. I can't lie to you. I love having sex."

"Well, I know exactly what you need then!"

"Oh, you do?" Mona interrupted over Sharon's embarrassed laugh.

"We need to break out the sex kit, for Sharon ya'll!" Mike shouted. Instantly in the background, sound effects began to blare and it sounded like someone ripping open packages. There were moans as well.

"Let's see what, we have for Sharon. We're here on *Better Sex and Love* and we're trying to give her ideas to spruce up her sex life. Let see, here?"

Sharon began to laugh, "I don't believe this…" she said.

"Ahhh, believe it, sister girl, because we're going to get things poppin' in your bedroom! Pumpin' Mike, tell her what we have for her," Mona directed.

"Well it looks like…..hold up…what is this? What's up with all these straps? Hot Mona, help me with this? I'm quite sure you have one of these at home?"

"Let me see," Mona joked.

"Oh my, and you're right, I do have one of these. To be truthful, me and my man have two! Girlfriend…Girlfriend?"

"Yes?"

"Let me ask you? Do you like oral very much?"

"Ummm, love it! Got's to have it!"

"Well, what we have for you is a harness, girlfriend! Now if this don't get it! I'm telling you, Sweetheart, you get your man to hook this up to the ceiling and lift you up in it and have him stand before you and take care of you like never before. Woooo, this one is nice!" Mona declared.

Pumpin'Mike was surprised at Sharon's silence. "Sharon, are you all right? What, is it too much for you?"

"No Pumpin', but I've already been there and done that.."

"Well now, looks like we have our work cut out for us," Mike tells his audience.

"So, do you have any of the vibrating toys?" Mona asked.

"Yes," Sharon replied.

"Which ones?" Pumpin' jumped in to say.

"I've probably tried all of them. Even the one that looks like a tongue and moves up and down."

"Girlfriend, you have that one?" Mona sparked out.

"Yes."

"Don't you know I've been looking for one of those?"

"Well, it makes too much noise for me," Sharon explained.

"Wow, Mona, you are hot," Pumpin' said.

"What about sexy underwear?" asked Mona. "Now I can always entice my man with a thong. Do you have sexy garments, Sharon?"

"Oodles."

"Well, I just don't get it. If you have all these things, why aren't you and your man having the times of your lives? I know me and my wife don't have this harness do-dad. I mean we do now, since you already have one. But me and wifey keep it going damn near every night, it just don't stop."

"How long have you been married?" Sharon asked Mike.

"We've been together two years, two hot years!" Mike bragged.

"See, that's where I think the problem is for us. I think

we've been together for too long and now we're bored with each other. I've been with this man a little over ten years and I'm only forty."

"You mean that really happens? Getting tired of your partner?" Pumpin' asks.

"I've heard it does," Mona replied.

"Believe me, it's true. And there's nothing you can do about it," Sharon sulked.

"I'm sure there is," Pumpin' assured.

"What, go out and cheat?" Sharon wanted to know.

"No....no, you can't do that. You've taken your oath."

"That's right, *til'death do you part*, sister gurl'."

"Come on, Pumpin' it must be something we can do for her? Think, baby think. Everyone needs to be satisfied," Mona declared.

Sharon slowly let out her frustration with a sigh, then crossed her fingers, hoping they could help her in the worse way because she really wanted things to work out for her and her husband.

Forever Love

The crisp air blowing early in the fall season, high in the mountains of Georgia, was moving steadily across the roof top of Harry and Melinda Hayes. The couple had awakened early in the morning, as they'd done together for the last thirty-five years and were in the kitchen, preparing to start their day. Harry was seventy-two and Melinda sixty-seven.

"Harry?" Melinda called out.

Harry had just unfolded the morning paper. He was relieved. His newspaper boy heeded to his cries of how important it was for his paper to be at the doorstep at 5:00 AM, instead of 6:30. For years, Harry would eat breakfast and go on his morning walk with his wife. "Yes, dear?" He answered.

"For once in your life, can you not eat, scrambled eggs, two slices of bacon, toast and drink two cups of coffee? Let me cook you something else?"

"Something else?"

"Yes, something else, Harry. Maybe, some pancakes and sausage, perhaps?"

"I don't want anything else. I want what I always have. It's not only what I like, but it's what I'm used to eating."

"I think it would be good for you to try something else," Melinda offered.

"No thank you. Is what I want to eat, ready yet?"

"No, I thought we'd walk first, then come home to eat, Harry."

Harry looked over the top of his morning paper and stared at Melinda. "I want to eat, then walk, Melinda. What's with all the changes today?"

"Because I'm tired of the same old grind. I think we should change our schedules from time to time."

Harry dismissed his wife's request. He loved the way his schedule was set up. His eyes moved from his paper and onto Melinda's dim gray sweat shirt. "Do you have to wear that sweat shirt again today?"

Melinda stopped counting the scoops of coffee and looked down at her sweat shirt. "My sweat shirt? What's wrong with my sweat shirt?"

Harry's eyes were now back to his paper. "You wear it everyday, is it the only one you have?"

"No, but it's my favorite, you know that, Harry."

"It would be really nice to see you in something else, Melinda. That's all I'm saying." Harry licked his thumb and turned a page of the newspaper.

"Well, let's say this, it won't happen today because I'm wearing this one, you got that?"

Harry and Melinda sat in the kitchen for another hour,

Harry eating his breakfast, Melinda drinking orange juice, a half cup of black coffee and nibbling on fruit. All of a sudden their conversation--what little they had to say to one another that morning-- had turned into a dispute about what the other has done for years. Every so often this would happen between the two.

Finally, it was time for the two to journey on their early morning walk. Harry locked the side door of the house and put his key in his pocket. While they walked down their long driveway, Harry noticed he needed to call the tree cutters to cut back the branches hanging over the drive. At the same time, Melinda focused on the mail box, where the wild flowers she'd planted were still doing fine. Once they reached the edge of the drive, Harry and Melinda stopped. It was time to decide *together* which route to take. Harry pushed his gloves tighter on his hands with his index finger and thumb. Melinda wrapped her scarf around her neck, nice and snug. They didn't speak when they were finished adjusting their gear. Both remembered their chat in the kitchen and were still uptight. They both took steps at the same time out of the drive. Harry turned right. Melinda left. Instantly, they realized they'd be walking alone, but continued walking anyway, quietly, making their point to one another. It was what they wanted to do, without compromise, but at the same time knowing they'd get over this disagreement, too. As they'd done for years.

Sippin', Thinkin' and Singin'

It's not important to know what happened with me and my girl. Just know it's over and I managed to cover all the bases of wrong doing. I was the one at fault. Put it like this...I couldn't complain one bit if I heard on the street that I was the blame for my girl disappearing before my eyes. Anyway, this half-empty bottle of GRAND MARNIER and my spinning head have me thinking and when I sip, I usually think of song and when I sip and think enough, I usually end up singing, emulating somebody who makes money, singing, like I wish I could. But I don't know how far tonight will take me. Or who the singer will be. I'll just have to wait and see where my buzz takes me.

It took an hour. But I chose the voices of all voices, as I sipped. I placed Luther Vandross on the turntable and went straight for _A House Is Not a Home_ and as soon as I heard his one of a kind, trembling voice, I started to think about how Luther could sing this damn song so passionately, like it meant everything in the world to him? It's like he knew one day I--along with many others--would be in this very predicament of instantly being without a partner and realizing that your house, isn't a home when your sitting all by yourself.

After the fourth time I listened to the song, and realized I was going to play it over and over again, I pulled a chair up next to my turntable and sat down right in front of it, so I didn't have to keep that back and forth shit of walking over and starting the song over. I wanted to hear Luther tell it like it is...all night long. More importantly, I didn't want to stumble and fall on my face, going back and forth through the dark room even though my girl had taken most of the furnature when she left while I was at work. I just sat my drunk ass down and began to listen and interpret the lyrics from the maestro. No doubt about it, I'm sure I'm not the first to sit in a dark room listening to words, explaining through song, and pondering why I even attempted to accomplish what has always seemed to be so virtually impossible to conquer for everybody-anyway.

Commitment is a bitch, married or not. The way I look at it, the way everybody be trippin' nowaday's, if you claimin' somebody is yours and they claim you back? Shit, you married. If you livin' with somebody? You married. You got kids wit' somebody? You married. You givin him or her money and payin' they bills? You married. You driving his or her car? You married. So, that's how I feel about committment, 'cause that's what married people do. They claim, live together, have kids, help out with the bills and drive each others car's. Oh yeah-I almost forgot. If you sleepin' with somebody-- guess what? You married. 'Cause don't nobody want no dirty ass sex partner.

These days, that's death. So these crazy people, need to stop looking for the rings and going through whoever you claimin' purses and wallets and all that nonsense. 'Cause more than likely, everybody doing something with somebody and whoever they doin' it wit' more than likely, damn near feel like--they married.

Anyway, anyhow, I'm sure I won't be the last to sit with my eyes wide open and only see total darkness, without a clue as to why things couldn't work out in my situation. I never dreamed that *two* months of union, on the highway of love, would end up in a long screeching skid, then crash and burn right before my eyes. It's not what I expected to happen after all this time. We said things to each other that I thought was real. That's why I'm sitting here, drunk, numb and amazed that this entire situation feels like death. It's the end of what me and my girl had, something we'll never have again 'cause it's over.

I already admitted I was drunk. But Luther has brought all this out of me tonight, in the darkness. I don't care how old this song is. I first heard it around 1981 and if you ask me it would've been a hit in 1921 and will be a hit 2021, too. Luther's simply pointing out *A House Is Not a Home* is so, so deep that it demands you take notice and I suggest to anyone, if they ever get to a point in their life, where I am. I suggest you listen, sip and think, just like me. 'Cause when I read the note my girl left, on the only chair she left me in the living room, that said, "Calvin, I'm gone," I couldn't do nothin'--nothin', you hear me. But start listening to this damn song and pray to God she at least left me a blanket to cover my ass--'cause it gets cold in here at night.

Franklin White

Shh, shh. Listen, listen to this song. Listen, listen –
this humming shit, this scatting thing he's doing with his voice?
It's like he's trying to push the words out of his soul with
tones and shit. Masterful, that's what it is. He's humming and
my drunk ass is sitting here babbling in a similar sort of way.
But what's actually had me all messed up since the first time I
played this song tonight is his analogy of those damn chairs
and what they continue to be, even though they're not in use.
And this damn house--the house--the house--the house analogy
is enough to make you want to go and beg for another chance
or burn this bitch down to the ground, because being here
alone is a hell of thing to have to get used to. But I'm not
going there, 'cause she's never coming back to me. This song
is **Poetry! Damn it!** That's what it is, and to tell you the
truth--if I only knew, what I know now. Hold up, I like that?
If I only knew, what I know now.......uh oooo, I feel one
coming on--and I have to sing it over the violins and harps
and strong bass stringing in my mind as strong as Luther does
it. Here goes.

> I just can't figure this out—
> And I've long........ had my doubts—
> But, 'cause it was something so strong as love—
> I thought- it was truly possible—
> To stay with you—
> Without giving my all to you—
>
> I admit.... my eyes were unwilling to see—
> and my mind....... unwilling to believe—
> all the things..... already set in-stone

now I'm sitting.....all alone

Chrous
But if I always knew-
what I know now-
If I only knew
What I know now-
But if I always knew
What I know now-

There would have always been conversation—
There would have always been anticipation—
You'd never known what I was planning next
A simple song-- even shoppin' at the mall—
A bite to eat or a simple glass of wine-
I would love to hold you right now knowing you
were all mine
Maybe......... if I'd taken a long look at things—
Our life wouldn't have become twisted and framed-
Like a blank picture hanging on the wall.
If I only gave you my all

Chorus
But if I always knew-
What I know now-
If I only knew
What I know....now
If I always knew
What I know now
If I only knew

Simple as it may seem...love is but a dream—
Creative and wonderful....but I failed to bring it
to you and give you my all.....Keep you near
Closer to me...It's always what I felt you needed
my dear

But one thing is for certain
the game of love is full of pain—
I admit in dealing this hand to you—.
So I don't blame you, for doing what you had to do
If I only knew
No way I would have left you alone all night
If I only knew
I would have realized it wasn't right
Theres no way I would've tried to slip in bed while
you were sleepin'-It's so sad now -cause I lost you
and got back my twenty-twenty vision

But If I only knew...
What I know now...
If I only knew...
What I know now...
But-If I only knew...
What I do now...
I'ma say it again
If I only knew...
What I know now...

Yeah, that's it. That is it! Where's my drink?

Change of Heart

Continuation of Bestselling Novel
Fed Up with the Fanny

Kelly sat down next to me in my Range Rover, flopped her hands in her lap and sighed. It was obvious. Kelly was defeated, embarrassed, ashamed and tired. There was no removing the embarrassing plastered mud, which was becoming harder by the second from her face. When she turned and looked at me, it was evident everything she was going through and had done was heavy and at the moment, I must admit, so were our lives.

"So, Deric what do we do now?" Kelly asked.

I was surprised she even asked me, my opinion. It hadn't been her *Stello'* since I knew her. Anyone who knew our history, I'm sure could understand my shock and astonishment of her question. The first thing that came to my mind was to do what I always wanted to do with Kelly. And that was just to get away, something I asked her time and time again to do with me. Even if it was only going to be for a few days, so we could regroup and straighten things out, way before things had gotten out of hand.

"We need to get out of here. Go someplace else. Just you and me," I told her. My words didn't register to Kelly and I waited for her response. It never came. The only thing I got from her was a brief stare. "Want to move east?" I asked.

She broke out of her trance. "East?" Kelly finally acknowledged, "You mean, further out on the eastside, away from everybody?" Kelly began to shake her head. She was feeling the move.

"Yeah, how 'bout Jersey? Is that far enough away for you?"

"Jersey, when?"

"Yeah, New Jersey. As soon as possible."

Kelly shrugged her shoulders, then wiped the last teardrop away from her face and looked back up at the house she and Cece had been the best of friends in together. Kelly couldn't believe their friendship had stalled. "Might as well, nothing else to do around here," she decided.

I remember putting things in perspective and thinking twice about my offer. I had heard Kelly's words of reassurance before. "If you're serious about us starting over, I'll do this? Picking up and leaving isn't going to be easy. But I really want to, because it will do us some good. But you're going to have to want it, too, Kelly." I reached out for her hand, "We have to become as tight as ever. No more games." She must have noticed me glance down at her stomach. I couldn't forget about the addition to our world. It definitely wasn't going to be easy. "Deal?" I asked.

Kelly took one more look at the house and said, "Deal. I'm just happy you even want to be with me after all this."

I put the transmission in gear and slowly began down

the street, "Like I've always told you, Kelly, I love you." Days later, we were on our way, without saying good-bye to a soul.

The first year was definitely a learning experience, but the love and commitment I always wanted to share with Kelly in Detroit met us in Jersey. If someone would have run across Kelly in Jersey that knew her from Detroit, they would swear she wasn't the same person they'd known in the Motor City. She had become literally another person and, for me, I was impressed because she'd become the person I always knew she could be.

Completely gone were the days of opportunistic money schemes and fast talking her way into situations that were not any of her business. Kelly had changed for the better and we were in love. And yes, I was sure, because we were flat broke and Kelly had always been about money and materialistic items. But she definitely stepped up to the plate and stuck it out with me, when times were hard. When we first started out I was looking for a good paying job, while at the same time working two jobs just to pay rent and keep food on the table, and Kelly hung in there with me just the same. She was full of encouragement and faith, even when I was feeling really low about dragging us out to Jersey, just to get away. Especially the nights I had to buff the floors at the local Pathmark grocery store. I was just trying to weather the storm and, at the same time, help Kelly with her pregnancy as best as I could.

We went downtown to get married. Forget a wedding- we barely had enough to pay the application fee to be married. But all of our troubles turned out to be well worth it. Our relationship couldn't have been better. We were finally one and on the same accord. All I wanted to do was hold on and continue to work and put in applications at every opportunity that I could get. At the same time, I was praying for a healthy economy, because I knew there was a job out there for me.

We were renting in Montclair, New Jersey, north of East Orange and Newark. Not very much different than Detroit, if you ask me. Still, the change of venue was a good decision for us. Finally, I had Kelly to myself. When the baby was born, we became even closer. Kelly named the baby, Kahlil, after CeCe's husband. I was surprised about the name, until she explained she wanted her son to have the same qualities Kahlil possessed, when it came to doing for people and being honest. I had no problem with the name or the man. I would've felt differently if lil'Kahlil was mine, but he wasn't. He was Scooter's son. She'd been sleeping with Scooter behind my back, behind Cece's back, and when she got pregnant, Scooter wanted no part of her or the child. So I wanted to become his father and still give him all the love he would always need, no matter what his name was or who his father was.

But all of that drama was behind us. 'Lil Kahlil was sprouting up like a weed in water and was way too smart for his age. He'd already shown signs of inheriting his mother's high quality taste. I remember holding him on my lap, after coming in from the grocery store and he pointed at my ear and said.

"Guymonds?....Guymonds?" in his little squeaky voice.

I glanced over at Kelly, "What is he talking about?"

Kelly snickered, "Diamonds, Deric. He's trying to say diamonds. Every time I go past the jewelry store on Bloomfield, we stop and look at the diamonds in the window. He noticed mine in my ear and, every since Kahlil thinks everyone is supposed to have diamond earrings in their ears. He's been going *guymond* crazy up in here today. He just hasn't mastered how to say it yet."

"Diamonds? Already?" I asked.

Kelly nodded and Kahlil pointed at my ear again. "Guymonds? Guymonds?"

As if on cue, Allah came into my life and presented me with a good paying job, a few weeks afterwards. I was grateful to the most high and Kelly as well, as she never once questioned my ability to get a better position to provide for my family. Of course, I took her out shopping--not the shopping she was accustomed to--we went to a family shopping store. But it was still shopping. I decided early that we would save every penny we got our hands on, so we could move to Brooklyn, near Prospect Park. The amount of money I was making was going to allow us to do that, with careful planning.

I was hired as a rover for the electric company in New York City. I know it wasn't the most fantastic job, compared to everything NYC has to offer, but it was damn sure a good paying job. I started off making twenty-three dollars an hour, way more than the minimum wage I was getting at my other two jobs. I wanted to take advantage of the blessing and make sure I moved my family out of the one bedroom apartment we were staying in. The main thing for me was to get through my probationary period at the job, save every dime, then move to a bigger and better place.

Two years had passed, since moving away from

Detroit, and I'd been working in Manhattan for about eight months. I have to admit, it turned out to be much more than I ever imagined. New York City was nice. The tall inviting structures, major news media, major sports, the aura of something always happening, the top notch, straight to the point business deals being initiated every minute of the day, even by the Yahoo' standing behind the counter at the corner deli, were exciting to me. Making a deal, for a dollar off some bomb-chicken soup, with a buttered bagel, and getting it every once in awhile, for me, made Manhattan the best place in the world to work. It reminded me of my car selling, wheeling and dealing days, but on a constant basis in Detroit. New York City is the only place I know where everyone is out to make a buck and everyone else knows it and embraces the ambiance just the same. The job kept me busy, though. I had to leave early in the morning, close to five o'clock, to beat the early morning traffic. My shift didn't start until seven, so I made it a point to take my sweats along with me and run three miles everyday, along with my friend and coworker, Trent.

Trent was a senior mechanic in the plant. He was responsible for working on all the elaborate controls that always seemed to get out of whack. I was a rover. I walked around the plant, checked systems and made sure they were operating correctly. Every morning, we would arrive in the parking lot about the same time. Already dressed to run, we would put our work clothes in the locker room, stand outside the plant and stretch, then take off on our run.

It's something, running through the city, early in the morning. Especially when the traffic is minimal and the city is just waking up. It's downright beautiful, getting a chance to see those big buildings, as the sun is rising from the east. That's when you get the total picture and realize what the city is really about. Trent always made sure I was aware of the surroundings.

"You got to love this, Deric," he said to me on one of our very first runs. "This is where I lived my whole life."

"Manhattan?"

"Damn right and wouldn't want to have come up anyplace else. This is where it all happens, baby. From the good, to the bad. And that's all the time."

"One thing's for sure," I said back.

"What's that?"

"It's a hell of a lot better than where I've been all my life."

"Yeah? Where's that?"

"Detroit."

"The Motor City?"

"Yep."

"I thought Detroit has its moments?" Trent asked.

"I've never seen them."

"Didn't like it, huh?"

"To much drama, for me," I admitted.

"Drama?" Trent chuckled, "You...associated with drama? Now, that's hard to believe."

"Wait a minute now, don't I seem like I could get caught up in a little somethin'-somethin'?"

"Nada. To me you're a choir boy, Deric."

"Please, to the contrary, that's what people thought and that's exactly why it was full of drama, in the Motor."

"Detroit was spinning like that?"

"More than you know. More than you know," I confirmed, as we continued to chug along through Central Park.

Trent and I started to become pretty good friends. I realized, friendship was what I was missing, when I lived in Detroit. There wasn't a single soul I could talk to about Kelly, except Kelly. I remembered trying to talk to CeCe about our relationship, when things began to get really bad between us. CeCe wanted us to work things out. I'd bared my soul to her one day and she turned around and ran straight back to Kelly with everything I'd said. It had only made matters worse between us. Moving out east had been a little scary, because I realized early on I didn't have anyone, besides Kelly, to call on if something happened or I needed help in a emergency. Kelly brought it to my attention a time or two. I think she became a little frightened herself sometimes, when she was out with lil'Kahlil. Kelly hadn't became close with anyone herself but I really wanted her to find another girlfriend who could possibly become as close to her as Cece had been. My friendship with Trent was turning out to be just what I needed, both from a practical and emotional standpoint.

"So, what-up' 'B?" Trent called out one night, when I was making my rounds through the plant. I could tell he was hard at work and motivated to get his work done, because when he was, his east coast slang came pouring out.

"Same shit, different day." I told him. "Ain't nothing changed and that's for sure."

"Well, that's good. Because this fucking steam leak is giving me fits." Trent pointed to the stream of hot steam pouring from a pipe.

"Spewing, ain't it?"

"Hell yeah, and this ain't the only one. I'm going to be chasing these bitches all night. What are you still doing here?"

"Working that overtime," I let him know.

"Damn, you love some overtime, don't you?"

"I have to, my son has style man. He has a thing for diamonds already and I know right off the bat, I got to save me some money for the years to come."

"Diamonds?" Trent yelled, over the steam, "He better get himself a job!"

"He's only two," I reminded him. "But he's expensive, I swear he is."

"That's right. My fault, I thought maybe you had another out there somewhere I didn't know about?"

"Nah', man, only got one. And the truth of the matter is, I didn't make him."

Trent looked up at me, his expression was though he was reading a book and realized the plot. "Oh, so you a soldier, huh? Taking care of other people's bidness'?"

"Yeah, man, that's what I do."

"That's cool. Be proud of that shit, 'B. I got two living with me that my wife didn't have."

"Two of your four?"

"That's right, a nigga' slipped up not once, but twice, with the same damn woman. And boy...my Boo still took me back and brought my girls in with us, when their mama started buggin' the hell out." Trent's smile was a combination of disbelief and thankfulness, rolled into a tight compact ball. "Damn." Trent went into thought.

"What?"

"Don't know too many nigga's, who stay around with their girl after she's creeped on them?"

"Don't know what to tell you about that one partner. But I guess you know one now. I love my son, man."

"You really must. What about her?"

Before I could answer the question, more steam burst out of the pipe and damn near knocked Trent backwards. I ran into the the control room, to tell the watch supervisor to back off on the line, until Trent finished up patching. Trent's question did make me think though.

I watched my son look through my photo album, and he made me wonder if anyone back in Detroit remembered me. I helped his little hands turn the pages and thought about everything that had happened, *Yeah, no doubt, they do. How could they forget, Ms. Kelly.* That part of my life would always be part of my legacy in Detroit, and couldn't be erased. Still, this was the first time I'd looked at the pictures, since leaving Detroit. I wouldn't had been looking at them at all, if 'lil Kahlil hadn't found them in the box at the back of the closet. There was a picture of CeCe and Kahlil. I tried to explain to my son, the tall man in the picture was the man I'd named him after. He listened, but I doubt that he understood what I was saying. When he gets older, he'll definitely know why he bears the name. Then there was the picture of me, Lee and Scooter, all standing together at one of Lee's crazy ass parties. I'd forgotten I even had the photo. My first instinct was to take the picture and throw it away. I looked down at lil'Kahlil and saw how much his eyes looked like Scooter's and decided I better keep the picture. It was the only one I had of him and one day I was going to have to tell him the truth about his father. I was determined my son would never go through what Kahlil's nephew had gone through. That was a terrible mess and I believe he had the right to know who his real father was and it was a shame how he found out. That's why I'm going to tell lil'Kahlil, when he's old enough to understand, who his real father is and leave it up to him, if he wants to reach out.

I gathered up the photo album and placed it back in the closet. I had enough of going back down memory lane. I never dreamed motherhood would change me the way that it had. Kahlil was my life. And Deric made things easier than I expected them to go, after we moved out here. Deric didn't say a word about me staying home, taking care of Kahlil for the first year and a half after he was born. I'd gone back to work, because I was getting frustrated with the sameness of my days and thought it was time for Kahlil to be around other small children.

The boy had grown up so fast and he isn't an ordinary two-year old. He's serious. Oh, he enjoys his playtime, there's no doubt about that, but sometimes, when I sit down and watch some of the things he does, it makes me wonder how he gained the insight he seems to have. He knows when his mama is having a bad day. He knows just when to give me a hug. He's never given me any problems, nor any reason to think having him wasn't the right choice, even after I found out Scooter wasn't about anything and had lots and lots of kids spread out all over the country. That's why I give Kahlil my all, whenever he needs anything. That's one of the reasons I named him Kahlil, because that's what I learned from Kahlil in Detroit. He gave Cece, his all and I learned to appreciate his honesty to Cece after the dust settled about the situation I put them through. I still can't believe I lied on him like that.

More times than I care to count, when I call out my son's name, it makes me wonder about the pain I caused Cece and Kahlil and our friendship. I don't necessarily think about the two of them and what they're doing. I know they're all right. The love they have is serious and impenetrable. Ain't nothing strong enough to take Cece away from Kahlil but death. He proved that, even when me and Cece's friendship put him to the test. I was just glad the whole mess in Detroit was behind me. I'd learned marriage could actually work, even with the warped feelings I'd had about the word "commitment" all those years. I had a wonderful son and I loved my job. I guess it's safe to say I'd changed in more ways than one. Marriage and a baby make a big difference in life. A good difference. At least, that's how I felt the first two years.

I was at work. I'd been working at an exclusive boutique in midtown Manhattan. This particular day is when the tide started to turn for me. Mrs. Price came in, having been referred to me by a mutual acquaintance. She was in her forties and sharp as can be.

"Now, Kelly, I've heard so much about you, hun'," she said to me. "And I'd really like to get a few items to upgrade my wardrobe. You know what I mean, Darling?"

"Sure, Mrs. Price. I'll have you feeling like a million dollars in no time," I assured her and I went to work showing her pieces I thought would work for her. By the time she decided she'd upgraded enough, girlfriend had purchased eight outfits with shoes and scarves to match.

"Thanks for shopping with me, Mrs. Price."

"It was my pleasure, Kelly. And I'll definitely be coming back, you can count on it."

I rang up her total and smiled as I mentally calculated my commission. Three hundred dollars. *"Yes, yes, please hurry back Mrs. Price,"* I thought to myself.

As Mrs. Price walked out the door, two classy divas waltzed in, dressed from head to toe. The first one was a little taller than me. She had a creamy, peanut butter complexion and her hair was pulled back under a FENDI scarf. She took off her FENDI sunglasses and smiled at me. After years of loving fashion and now working in the industry, I automatically catalogued her outfit. Under her ranch mink cape by Ben Kahn, she had on a sleeveless, black mock shirt and mini skirt. I would've bet money they were by Calvin Klein. No doubt about it, her shoes were by Valentino and she was carrying a FENDI handbag.

I smiled, "Hi, I'm Kelly. If there's anything I can help you with, just let me know, okay?"

She smiled back at me, "Hi, I'm Bridgette,"she said, then glanced toward the door, where her friend was waiting with her head sticking out the door, looking out towards the street. "Charla? Gurl', what are you doing?" Bridgette asked.

"Waiting on our sponsor, that's what I'm doin'. He's parking the Benz." Charla looked right and left, then shrugged. "Oh well, he knows where we are."

When she turned from the door, I realized how much she reminded me of Cece. She was shorter than me, had dark skin and slanted cat eyes. Her hair was cut short too. Charla was wearing a funky white stone polyuerthane coat with fur lining. Her platinum colored tank top sat on her perfectly, but her black leather classic bike pants set everything off. She glanced around.

"Hello," I said to her.

She placed her hand onto her chest. She was so prissy. "Hi, I'm Charla."

I could tell she was nice, right off the bat. Her wide smile and down to earth disposition put me at ease immediately. She looked over at Bridgette.

"So, this is Marco's, huh'?"

Bridgette answered, "Yup. I hear, this is where they've got what we need."

I chimed in, "And you heard right ladies!"

"This is nice," Charla said, as she carefully began to survey the store.

The boutique wasn't large, but it was classy and gave off an aura of good taste and top quality. Marco, the owner, was Italian. I'd only seen him twice. He sent his guys out to collect money at the end of the day and to deliver our checks every week. Everyone wondered if he was in the mob or something, because he was so distant. But one of the girls said that she knew his family and our store was just one of many that he owned.

The inside of the store was contemporary and fit nicely in Midtown. The dummy models stood on platforms connected to the walls and were dressed to a tee. We changed the outfits at least once a week. Most of our inventory was in the upstairs loft, visible from the main floor. In the center of the store was a leather couch and two chairs, which were set around a table covered with magazines. In the center of the table was an ice bucket and a bottle of chilled champagne.

Bridgette was drawn to the couch. She removed her cape and leaned forward, "Oh my goodness. Champagne! Yes, I don't mind if I do."

"Let me," I said, walking over to join her. I reached underneath the table and removed three stemmed glasses, anticipating their friend would join them.

"Girl, let me tell you, there's nothing like going shopping and spending somebody else's money. You understand what I'm saying?"

I nodded and smiled at Bridgette. I knew more than she could imagine. But I tried my best to dismiss the game, I knew all to well. Charla joined us, sitting in one of the chairs that flanked the couch.

"And getting a buzz, while you do it, is the icing on the cake!" Charla admitted.

As the two girls giggled and began joking around, the door to the boutique opened. In walked an exhuasted looking light brown skinned guy, with a light mustache and wavy black hair, who wreaked of big-big money. He stood still and glanced around in his leather jacket and jeans. Then he began pulling off his driving gloves and let out a sigh of relief.

"Come on down, Phillip," Bridgette said. "We're about to have some champagne." Then she turned to me, "So Kelly, you think you can hook us up with some nice stuff?"

I glanced around the group, who were all now relaxed and comfortable. "No question, I'm sure I have something for you that suits your tastes," I boasted.

Bridgette and Charla shopped for over three hours. I hate to admit it, but the old Kelly was running all through them. I could see it in their attitudes and actions. They were buying with a vengeance, trying on outfit after outfit. I took very few items to the dressing room that were returned to the racks. I knew what they were doing and they were doing it well. The first rule of survival says, when you have a laid back sponsor, you shop until you have absolutely everything you want, even some things you really don't. Those are the things you either wear in a crunch or take back to the store later to exchange.

Phillip fit my description of laid back perfectly. He appeared to be bored, as if he'd done this shopping thing a hundred times over. Even when Bridgette and Charla came out of the dressing room, to ask his opinion, he didn't seem interested. He simply nodded, sipped more champagne and went back to his CODE magazine.

I made another trip to the dressing room, to check on the ladies. When I pulled back the curtain, Bridgette was standing in front of the mirror, tracing her bare nipple, and I overheard her whisper to Charla.

"You two better be ready for me tonight," she warned, "cause it's on." She looked up and noticed me and she and Charla laughed. I pulled the curtain back and walked away. I needed a break, a moment to gather my thoughts. A cigarette, and I don't even smoke. While I was walking away, I glanced at my watch, I realized it was time to call my sitter and check on Kahlil. That's when Phillip finally spoke.

"They're so crazy, aren't they?"

"No, no, not at all," I answered.

"So, your name is Kelly, right?"

I nodded, trying to edge toward the counter, "Yeah,

that's me."

"Nice to meet you. And I do mean that," he said quietly.

"Thanks. Nice to meet you, too," I said. "Excuse me for a minute?"

I needed to talk to the sitter, talk to my son, get back to reality. Seeing Bridgette and Charla buying all those clothes was definitely taking me back. Deric and I were saving as much as possible, coming close to having enough money for the down payment on a duplex or a Brownstone. Seeing the girls inside the store getting laced up for the next few months, was tearing me up inside.

Nancy, my sitter, brought my attention back to the real world, away from the extensive shopping spree going on right under my nose. Nancy took care of Kahlil and three other children and all three were close to four years old. Kahlil was the baby of the group and the other youngsters weren't allowed to touch him for any reason. Kahlil realized he was untouchable and was taking advantage of it and, Nancy told me, having a very good time at it. She told me Kahlil would walk up to the other little boys and take their toys away from them, knowing there would be no consequences. Nancy thought it was funny, his figuring out his safe status. But before we could talk further about his antics, Bridgette and Charla strutted up to the counter, fully dressed.

"We're going to go, Kelly," Bridgette announced, winking at me. "I want to checkout the jewelry store down the block. You know how it is, don't you?"

I smiled.

"We had so much fun," Charla purred.

"Well, I'm glad. Make sure you two come back and

173

see a sista', okay?"

"Oh, we will," Bridgette assured me.

Phillip finished the last of his champagne, then joined us at the counter. "Ready to go?" he asked.

"We want to make one more stop Phillip, okay?" Bridgette said.

He smiled, "I told you I was taking you shopping, right?"

"You sure did!" Bridgette reached up and kissed his cheek.

"Well, let's go," he directed.

"Okay, next stop is up the block. It's a jewelry shop," Charla announced.

Phillip waved towards the door. "You two go ahead. I'll pay for this and put your things in the car, then meet you there."

The ladies took off. I could feel Phillip's stare, as I rang up the collection they'd amassed. Damn, he was a serious baller and I could smell his Cool Water cologne.

"So, you like your job?" His voice was strong and deep.

"Ummm...hmm, yes I do."

"I can tell."

My eye's widened at his attentiveness, "How so?" I asked.

"You're really into it. That's how. And you really know what looks good on a person."

"Thank you."

"If I might add, you're very fashionable yourself."

"Thanks. Now, may I ask you a question?" I said.

"Sure?" Phillip leaned against the counter.

"You didn't seem to be enjoying yourself. Why is that?"

"Just tired, that's all."

"Tired of shopping?" I wanted to know.

He nudged his head towards the door. "No. Tired of those two."

One thing about running every day--it allowed me to get a slice of pizza on my lunch break anytime I wanted to. I was craving one of Al's tomato slices real bad and headed out of the plant for the pizzeria, as if I was in the finals of the Olympic walk race. I was trying to beat the lunch rush.

I knew it was Trent as soon as I heard his voice. "Yo, where you headed, Money'?"

I slowed and turned around, "Down to the pizzeria. Come'on, break bread with a brother."

A couple of minutes later, we were sitting in Al's Pizzeria waiting on our lunch and enjoying the break. Al's was very small. In fact, he only had six tables inside. Most of his business was done over the counter and people took their slices to the park or back to work with them.

"How's everything?" Trent asked.

"I'm straight. What about you?"

"Aww', man, the wife is upset with me again."

I chuckled, "For what?"

"I didn't tell you?"

"Tell me what?"

"Sometimes, she gets into these funky moods about me cheating on her and making my two youngest behind her back." Trent sighed, wiped his brow and looked around the diner.

"So, wifey' has decided to go back down memory lane?" I asked.

"Yeah. It never fails. Sometimes it happens every six months or so. But here lately, something has been pissing her off and it's like a brother is getting to a point where he hates walking through the door after work."

"That bad?"

"Worse."

Trent was quiet for a second, thinking. "Yo, Money', what about you?"

"What about me?"

"You said your wife stepped out, right?"

"That's right."

"I'm just wondering, Yo'. Do you from time to time, get frustrated and scream and holler and just disrupt shit because of it?"

"Nah' man. I used to, back in the day. But my girl's changed and all that hollerin' and screamin' don't do any good."

"Well shit, you need to tell my girl that for me 'cause I've changed too and she's getting just down right ignorant."

Trent was interrupted by the hard New York accent that I'd grown to love. This one in particular was Italian and only came with age. "Hey, Deric, your slices of pie are ready."

"Thanks, Al." I collected the pizza and returned to the table, after listening to one of Al's jokes he told me and his wife.

"So she's been bustin' your chops huh?" I clarified with Trent.

Trent took a bite of his slice. "I don't know what's

gotten into her." He hesitated for a second, "So you've never vented about what happened between you and your wife?"

"Not since we've moved here."

"That's hard to believe?"

"Why?"

"Just is. I'd think it would be harder for a man to sit around, knowing his lady was with someone else, that's all."

Trent's comments made me stop chewing for a second. I'd never really thought about the visual of what Kelly must have done with Lee and Scooter, even after I taped some of the phone conversations when she and Lee had phone sex. "Just haven't got into it, I guess," I told Trent.

"Shit, Tina talks all kind of smack. Talkin' bout', *What did you do to her. Where did you take her. Where did you two eat? What did you two eat?* Yo, Money', check this out. Guess what she asked me the other night, when I was hittin' it?"

I lifted my shoulders and shook my head, "I don't know Trent."

"Come on Money', guess?"

"You want me to guess?"

"Yeah, guess?"

"Okay, she wanted to know-- if it was in or not?"

Trent chuckled and wiped his mouth. "Remind me to see if I can get you on Def Comedy Jam nigga', when Russell Simmons starts that shit back up."

"Man, that's ya'll's business, what you do in the bed."

"Whatever--listen to this anyway. She asked me, '*Is this how you gave it to her?*' Right in the middle of me doing my best work Dog'."

"Now, that's wild, I have to admit."

"That's what I'm saying, this shit has gone mad crazy and it's driving me out my mind."

Later that day, I was stuck in traffic after work. I was only twelve miles from home, right on the outer edge of the Lincoln Tunnel. Things had changed a little, since I first began commuting. I remembered, when I first started, the homeless would stand along the road or near the tunnel, begging from the drivers in the grid-locked traffic, telling jokes with handmade cue cards, even offering to wash your windshield for whatever change you might spare. That's all changed though and I thought it was great, because I didn't have to worry about someone jumping in front of the car and scaring me half to death. The new mayor put a halt to the panhandling. It's very rare that you will encounter a window washer near the tunnel.

I glanced at the car beside me. The couple in the car was obviously not having a good day. I couldn't hear what they were saying, but it looked like they were each screaming at the top of their lungs, trying to get some point across to the other. The scene brought me back to the conversation Trent and I had shared at lunch, because it quickly made me think of Trent's wife cussing him out for creeping outside their marriage.

That's when, for the first time since making my decision to be with Kelly, I wondered why I'd taken on the commitment of marriage and raising another man's child. It wasn't an angry thought. I love Kelly and my son. Anybody who knew the changes she'd put me through would attest to that. It was interesting, the difference between Trent's wife and her continuing anger, versus our situation. Did I not care for Kelly, as much as Tina cared for Trent? Was it jealousy that enraged her? Or did she have a legitimate argument? If so, why wasn't I equally angry? Where was my rage? I really felt like a sucker, when Trent said he didn't know any man who'd look past their lady stepping out on them and continue as though nothing had ever happened. It did sound soft and it's exactly what I'd done.

I dismissed it all, cleared my head of Kelly being with other men and letting one of them swell up her stomach, while he walked away free and clear, with no commitment to the child. I ignored the fact I'd taken responsibility for a situation his sorry ass should have handled. I'd done it to uplift Kelly. She hadn't one soul in her corner and I felt sorry for her. I wanted to show her I could protect her, take care of her, even when she was wrong. Maybe I wanted to show her she should have listened to me and been only with me.

Trent was right. Being played and coming to a point of trying to deal with it was a touchy subject. In fact, all the reflection I had encountered began to bother me, while I sat in the car, so I turned on the air and the radio. Luckily, traffic started moving again and my attention was focused on the bumper-to bumper nightmare of getting through the tunnel.

Kelly and Kahlil were waiting for me, when I finally got home. I stopped at Pathmart for some orange juice and a pack of Topps Football Cards for Kahlil. He didn't know much about the cards yet, but I wanted to start a collection for him. I still had mine, from when I was a young. While Kahlil played with the cards, throwing them in the air, I moved to the kitchen, where Kelly was balancing her checkbook.

"What's happening?"

"Nothin much. Just trying to decide what I'm going to do with the extra money I made this pay period." She looked up, "Remember those girls I told you about, Charla and Bridgette. The ones who came in and spent all that money?"

"Yeah, I guess so."

"Well, my commission came to almost five hundred dollars. Plus, there was a lady who came in just before they did and I made three hundred off her stuff," Kelly smiled. "I think I'm going to go shopping myself."

I frowned, "Shopping?"

"Um..hmm. Go and buy me a few things."

"You think that's wise, Kelly?"

"Sure do, don't you?"

"It's just that we've been saving everything we can for a down payment on our new place. You know, the more we have, the better."

Kelly looked at me strangely, as if she was tired of hearing about money and saving money for the house. She sighed. "Yeah, you're right. Wouldn't want to take money away from the down payment, would I."

A couple of days afterwards, it was slow at the boutique. There was a nasty drizzling rain coming down nonstop. The delivery trucks, with new pieces we'd ordered, were also nonstop. Taking inventory was the only thing keeping me busy. My mind kept focusing on my conversation with Deric. I couldn't shake it, like all of the other times he'd asked me to go over and beyond for saving for the down payment of our house. The money I made was extra and that's the key word, extra. I agreed on saving money, in order to become home owners and stop paying rent. Most of my paycheck went into that fund, while his checks still paid the bills.

But this was extra money, money we hadn't budgeted or planned on. I'd already put the agreed upon amount of money towards the house account. I couldn't understand why Deric was having a problem with me spending the extra money on a little something for myself. Was it that hard for him to understand that, after all this time, I still loved to dress nice, look nice?

I'd changed a lot over the last couple of years, but not in that aspect. I was still the Kelly who loved to look good, smell good and be sharp and attractive, wherever I went. I was still the Kelly whose confidence ran on what I wore on a daily basis. The Kelly who used to raid her mother's closet, because my friends had already seen everything I had in mine.

Besides, this wasn't just about me. Working at the boutique required me to look nice and on a certain level. How in the world could I convince someone to buy something, if my appearance didn't prove I knew how to dress well?

I decided to let this issue slide. Again. I didn't want to get into a confrontation with Deric. I decided to just grin and bear it, the same way I've done for years. But my decision didn't sit well. If I could have stopped the replays of Bridgette's and Charla's comments and the memories of their recent shopping spree, I might have been able to deal with it a lot better. But I couldn't. I wanted my day too.

I kept remembering Phillip, the way he stayed all up in my grill for about twenty minutes after Charla and Bridgette left. He worked hard to convince me he was really tired of hanging out with them. When he asked if he could leave his number, I told him to put it on the counter and after he left, I studied the card. It had his name and telephone number. No company, no title, no hint of who he was or what he did. I shrugged it off and tucked the card in a drawer. He'd called several times, but always when I was out of the boutique.

That same rainy afternoon, while I was taking inventory, which had become a shade or two darker, Philllip strutted into the boutique with a smile plastered on his face. He was undimmed by the cool, rainy day.

"Hello," he called out as he shook off the rain.

"Hello," I said, stunned to see him again.

"We have to stop meeting this way," he grinned.

When I didn't say anything, he frowned.

"Relax, Kelly. Haven't you been getting my messages? I needed to set up an appointment to do a little shopping."

"Really?"

"Yes, really. Can you spare me some time?"

"That's my job," I told him.

Phillip pulled a small paper bag from behind his back. "I brought tea. What do you like? Strawberry Patch or Raspberry?"

He got me good with that one. "Rasperry," I told him. "How did you know I enjoyed tea?" I tried to calm myself, when I realized I sounded excited.

"Intuition, that's all. Intuition."

I moved toward the couch and Phillip followed me.

"So, who are you shopping for? Charla, Bridgette or both? You know, we have a lot of new stuff in that I know they'll like."

He placed the tea on the table. "I'm not shopping for Charla or Bridgette this time," he let me know.

"Mother, Sister?"

He shook his head no, "I have another friend and thought I would surprise her with a few things."

"That's nice of you. I'm sure she'll be pleased."

I took the top off my tea and blew into it, all the while wondering how many friends Phillip had and what he really did for a living. "So, tell me, what does your friend look like, so I can get a feel for what she might like."

He sighed and thought about my question. "Well, she's a little taller than you, just a smidgen' though. She's a slender build, long hair, brown eyes. I don't know. She's a model. Does that help?"

"A model, huh?"

"Yeah, she's with one of these big agencies. I met her a while ago and I think it's time I surprise her with something so she'll realize I'm interested."

"Well, what does she like? I mean what colors, type of style, materials?"

Philllip shook his head. "I don't know, haven't even sat down and talked about those things yet." He took a sip of his tea and sat back.

I looked around the store, considering various styles for his friend. "Wow. This is not going to be easy, Phillip. Shopping for a woman is really somewhat of an art."

"That's why I came to you. Charla and Bridgette have been raving about you, since they left this place."

"I thought you said you were tired of those two?" I blurted out of remembrance.

"Well, I didn't mean to sound difficult. I'm kind of frustrated with them. Guess I need a break or something."

"So, this model friend is exactly the break you need huh?"

He thought for a moment. "Yeah, I think she is."

Once again, I considered what we had in the store for his friend. "Well, lets see.." I stood up and pulled a dark blue Richard Tyler Couture, pairing the single button jacket with matching trousers, and held it up. "You think she'll like this? It's comfortable, the fabric is beautiful and she can dress it up or down, depending on the accessories she wears with it."

Philllip studied the outfit. "I don't know. I can't really tell what that looks like on the hanger." He thought for a moment longer, twisting and tuning his head. Then he sighed.

"What's wrong?"

"I can't picture what it would look like on her."

I held it closer to my body. Phillip sat up.

"I know. Why don't you try it on for me?"

"Me?"

"Sure, why not?"

Well, selling clothes was my job and it was a slow day. Besides, it's not like I'd never tried on clothes to model for husbands who came in wanting something for their wives. And I enjoyed wearing the Couture designs, even if only for a few minutes. Before I knew it, I'd tried on and displayed fifteen outfits. Dazzling pieces, even some of FUBU's new female line. Everything I put on was guaranteed to make any woman melt and appreciate Philllip's hard work. He was pleased and decided to buy all fifteen. He laid his Platinum American Express card on the counter. "Thanks for your help, Kelly."

"You're welcome. I'm sure she's going to be really happy with these pieces."

"You think so?"

"Without a doubt. Everything here is exactly what I would wear, without hesitation."

"Really?"

"Yes, everything here is top notch."

Phillip looked down at the clothes on the counter. "Well they're all yours," he said, without hesitating.

I looked away from the cash register then back at him. "Excuse me?"

"You take them. I've changed my mind. Forget that fake ass artificial woman I was going to give them to. She has nothing but clothes anyway. I want you to have them instead."

"I can't take these. Be serious?"

"Why not?"

"Because it wouldn't be right."

"You don't think so?"

"Noo." I chuckled, unable to believe what he was trying to do.

"Who's to say it isn't right? If I were you, I'd jump on it. Hell, you get the commission off the sales, plus new clothes at the same time. I would say that makes for a very good day?"

I looked at all the clothes, then calculated what the commission would be. '*He ain't lying about that,*' I thought.

"So, you'll take them?" He smiled.

I began to study this overly neat brutha' on the other side of the counter like I never had before, thinking about how he'd try to play me. "Look, it's not like I don't know what you're about, Phillip." I told him.

He brought his hand to his chest, nice and slow. "You know what I'm about?"

"Yeah, I know. I'm not saying you're not smooth or anything like that, but I do know what you're trying to do."

He tilted his head to one side. "Tell me, then. What am I trying to do?"

"It's plain as day. You're trying to get with me and you're using all this to do it."

He tilted his head towards the other side. "Wrong," he answered, sounding like a device on a TV game show. "You have me all wrong, Kelly."

"Well, tell me, what this is all about then. What are you trying to do?"

Phillip looked out towards the street through the window and then stepped to the door. "Stay put, I'll be right back," he said.

I began folding the clothes as he left the boutique, but he was back in a couple minutes, with two more cups of tea. He motioned me over to the couch. Phillip was either the smoothest man I've ever met or so full of bull that my radar couldn't get through it all. He was my age, but as smooth as a fifty-year-old man who'd been around a time or two. He insisted he just wanted to sit down and talk. Hell, this was Kelly he was trying to convince. I wasn't falling for that. I wanted to know what he really wanted from me?

"So, I'm still waiting to hear what this is all about," I reminded him.

"You're so sharp on your toes, aren't you?"

"Like I said, I've been around. So, what's up?"

Phillip sipped his tea, "Would you believe absolutely nothing?"

I was stunned for a moment. "Nothin'? What do you mean?"

"Just what I said. Nothing." He smiled at my expression. "Look, it's like this. When I came in shopping with Bridgette and Charla, I watched you work. I enjoyed your personality and ...this is going to sound corny as hell."

"Tell me?"

"While I was sitting here, I said to myself, I wouldn't mind being friends with her. She seems like nice peeps. That's the honest to God truth." Phillip took his balled fist and gently pounded his heart.

I laughed. I thought I'd heard it all.

"See, I knew you'd clown me. I'm serious. That's all my intentions were, when I came back in here to see you."

"And the clothes? Were you really buying them for someone else?"

"Yes, I was buying them for....."

I interrupted him. "For another friend?"

"Now, see, you've got me all wrong, Kelly."

"Well, tell me then, Phillip. How many friends do you have anyway?"

"Oh my goodness," he blurted. "Well, lets start off with Charla and Bridgette."

"I'm listening."

"It's like this. I can be up front with you, right?"

I nodded.

"We're all friends and we go and do things together."

"Like what?" I knew he didn't have to tell me. But I

started to have fun with it.

"I'm not too proud about my relationship with those two. But hey, every man experiments a time or two."

"I think I know already, anyway," I told him.

He smiled and seemed relieved. "So that's what we do."

"I understand."

"Now, my friend for whom I was buying for today. She's a little bit more serious, but the truth of the matter is, I ain't really feeling anybody right now. You ever been there?"

More then he ever knew. "So, you want to be friends with me, huh?"

His eyes widened. "I mean, I would like to. Hey, New York City is a great place to have a friend or two."

I recalled Deric saying the same thing about his friend, Trent. "Yeah, they're important. But you know I'm married, don't you?"

"I figured that," he looked at my finger.

"I don't wear it all the time."

"It's so traditional," he said. "I understand."

We chatted another half hour. Phillip did most of the talking, trying to convince me all he wanted was friendship. He left the boutique, fully aware that I didn't trust him, nor did I jump headfirst into friendships. And there was the issue of the clothes he'd paid for and told me to enjoy. Shoot, I had to decide what to do? I stood at the counter, my hand caressing the clothing, and thought about my choices. I couldn't take them home with me and tell Deric the owner of the largest hip-hop and style magazine in the country bought them from me, for me. No, not hardly. But, I could have taken them home and told Deric the owner, Marco, let us have some pieces because he had too many in inventory. But Deric knew the mentality of New Yorker's doing business and it would have never flown. I finally decided to leave them in my locker at work and take them home, one at a time, over the next couple of months, so I wouldn't draw any attention to them.

Months Later

We were at the park with lil'Kahlil. While Kelly pushed him in the swing, I sat down on a park bench and thought about the nerve she had, asking me such a crazy question the night before. I'd been watching "*Law and Order,*" my eyes glued to the screen, as the homicide trial was begining.
"Deric?"
"Hmmmm?"
"Deric, can I ask you something?"
"Go'head."
"Are you sure?"
"Kelly? Come on now, I'm tryin' to watch this."
"Okay, I want to know if it's all right for me to have a male friend?"
Kelly's question came at the same time the prosecutor began questioning his witness. I only heard what came out of the television. "What did you say?"
"I want to know if it's okay to have a male friend?"
She didn't have to say it again. I looked over at her and her head was bowed just a bit and her eyes were slanted upward like she was waiting for me to blow. "A male friend?"

189

She nodded.

"Kelly, what are you talking about?"

"Just what I said, would you mind?"

"Yes, I would mind." I turned off the television, "Okay, what's the deal and who is he?"

Kelly's answers weren't what I wanted to hear. In the span of an hour, my life turned, once more, into drama. Drama created in my mind by our past, by Kelly's past and by her insistence that she explore her new found friendship despite my objections. Kelly insisted her new found friend was just that. A friend. But I wasn't having it. There was no way I was going to sit back, while Kelly, with her wild-ass past, had a so-called friendship at my expense. She kept trying to convince me there was nothing more going on with this man she finally decided to tell me about.

"We're just friends, Deric. I barely talk to him. He calls to see how I'm doing. Sometimes, when I get a rare break, I might call him. Aren't you the one who said we needed friends here?"

"I said it. But I didn't mean with the opposite sex. And I'm not trying to hear this friendship bull anyway. A man and a woman can't be strictly friends, without some kind of other thoughts running through one of their heads."

"You're wrong. Deric, and I'm going to show you. And I know that's not the only reason why you don't want Phillip and I to be friends."

"Tell me why Kelly?"

"You don't trust me, that's the reason."

I thought about it for a minute, "You're damn right, I don't. Now what?"

Kelly stared at me, tapping her foot, not saying a word. I knew she was upset and I didn't care. She never did answer my question and the confrontation had been eating at me ever since.

What we began to go through was getting really complicated and I could tell lil'Kahlil began to sense something wasn't right between Kelly and me. We weren't speaking like we would normally do and our walks around the corner to the park had become quiet. The laughter and excitement, we used to take along with us, became a thing of the past. Even our family hug at the end of the day turned into becoming fake as hell. I didn't realize what I had done until afterwards, when I kissed him on the side of his little fat cheek one night, before Kelly tucked him in the bed, then walked away, leaving Kelly with no love at all for the first time in his life. But, damn it, I wasn't going through any more nonsense with Kelly. If she thought I was going to stand by, while she did whatever she wanted with her so called friend behind my back, she had another thing coming. I even talked to Trent about it.

"I thought about seeing a lawyer today," I told him over lunch.

"Damn, you getting serious, huh?"

"Hell, yes. Been serious."

"Your wife has balls, man," Trent said.

"What do you mean?"

"I'm just sayin', if I approached my wife with some story about, *do you mind if I have a female friend*, with my past, you'd be talking to me in a hospital bed because sista' girl would shoot me on the spot. And that's for real."

At first, I wasn't going to bother Deric with the friendship question. I was going to keep it a secret. I could have done it. Where there's a will, there's a way, as the cliché goes. But I was trying to do the right thing, tell my spouse what I thought he might want to know. I really trusted Phillip by now and thought Deric would trust me. If I'd known he was going to get all protective and shit, I'd never would've said anything, husband or not.

The tension and drama in our house was something we'd not faced since leaving Detroit.

Phillip was serious and honest about being friends. He hadn't once come on to me. If I hadn't known about Charla and Bridgette, I would've thought he was gay. All he ever wanted was conversation. There was no kissing, no romantic dates, no intimate dinners. Just two people, getting to know each other and being friends. It must have been sort of like some kind of New York thing, because his honesty about being friends and his actions to support it surprised me at first as well. But Phillip talked to me about several other people who were his friends. Some were even married, and Phillip even mentioned meeting Deric when we got our situation settled. But Deric made it clear the he refused to believe in what I intended out of the friendship with Phillip.

"Kelly, have you ever in your life had a male friend you didn't fuck?" he asked me one day, when I was washing the dishes.

"Dang, Deric. Why do you have to come at me like that?"

He shrugged, "Just answer the question."

"No," I snapped.

"See? That's what I mean. I don't see how you think this whole friendship thing can work- it just can't."

"You're just going to have to trust me," I told him. It was obvious he didn't.

The next morning, during our run through Central Park, I just had to tell Trent what Kelly said to me. It was bugging me like crazy.

"Trust!" Trent shouted. He stopped and began to run in place. I ran a small circle around him and listened. "So, do you?"

"Trust her?"

"Yeah, trust her?"

"To a certain extent."

"And what's that?"

"To where I can see her, that's about it."

"Smart man, Deric," Trent said.

And we were off and running again.

Trust. That was the whole issue. Deric didn't trust me to have a male friend, because of my past, and there was nothing I could do about it. After a while my friendship with Phillip became a project just to show Deric he was wrong about me. My past in Detroit was the past, over. Yet still, Deric's lack of trust burned inside me. I wanted to prove to him that I could have a male friend, regardless of what he thought.

I considered dropping the whole thing and being what he wanted me to be. It was clear he wanted a wife to come home to. He wanted to believe he had all of my affairs and bad times with him and he was going to hold everything I've ever done against me as long as he could, reminding me that I owed him something, for marrying me and helping with Kahlil. Of course, I was grateful to Deric. He'd stepped in like I would never have imagined when I got pregnant. I've told him how grateful I was, time and time again. What else did he want from me?

That's what I wanted to know. All I could give him was my thanks. I couldn't take back or undo one thing I'd done. If I could, I don't know if I even would, because it's made me who I am. Without my past, I don't know if I would've been able to think about what was going on and I wouldn't have my baby boy. If Deric had told me to get the hell away from him three years ago, I would've been okay. I'd have taken care of Kahlil somehow. I would've managed. That's just how I am.

I refused to give up my friendship with Phillip, despite Deric's demands. Our relationship was getting worse every day, every week. He refused to accept the fact that I'd changed and he had nothing to worry about. I remembered all the reasons I'd originally had for not marrying Deric in the first place. It seemed I'd been right, back then, when I'd seriously considered going on my own, avoiding marriage because of my observation of the whole institution. Instead, I'd run for the protection marriage could give me and my son. It was one of the reasons I always talked to Cece about. Now, I was paying the price. I didn't want to experience the things I saw my parents go through, the fights and bitterness. At least, Phillip saw it my way.

"You sure you're okay?" he asked, as we sat at the Green Kitchen Restaurant on the East Side of Manhattan.

I'll be okay," I said. Then I tried to brighten up my mood. "So, how's the magazine business going?"

"Still number one. There's another copy cat coming out next month. But, after a few months of seeing what this business is all about, I'm sure they'll fold, just like the others."

"You're so confident."

"Not in a bad way, I hope."

"No, just about your business dealings."

"Yeah, have to be. But it gets boring sometime, you know."

"Boring?"

Yes, boring. Dreadful. After a couple of years, things always seem to get boring to me," Phillip admitted.

"I know the feeling," I said.

"Yeah?"

"More than you know."

We both seemed to drift for a moment.

Phillip cleared his throat, drawing my attention back to the moment. "He doesn't know you're here, does he?"

I shook my head no and took a sip of my water.

"What are you two going to do, Kelly? I didn't mean for any of this to happen. Getting in the middle of marriages, is not my type of thing."

"Don't worry about it, Phillip. This is our problem. He's just going to have to begin to trust me again."

Phillip smiled at me, almost laughing.

"What? What is it?"

"Still kind of hard imagining you out there, like you

195

say you were. It doesn't seem like it could be, that's all."

"Really?"

"Truly."

"Believe, me. I was."

"Everybody has their times," Phillip commented.

"What about you? Did you have your times?"

"I was having my time, the first time you saw me. I still have my times and wish that I didn't."

Phillip took a sip of his tea and seemed to give his statement some thought. We both went back into our daze.

"That's the problem with Deric," I said.

"What's that?"

"He doesn't have any times."

"That he'll admit to," Phillip rushed to say. "And I'm not talking down on him, either. Everyone has times in their lives, we're all human. So really, who's being truthful in your situation? I want you to think about that."

"So, you still think I'm being too hard on myself, don't you?"

"I always have. We're friends, Kelly. Nothing but friends."

It was drizzling rain when we left the restaurant. Any second the rain would begin to come down at a much quicker and harder pace.

"You sure you're going to be all right?" Phillip asked me.

"I'll be okay." He made sure my scarf was covering all of my hair. "Thank you," I told him.

"No problem. You're going to call me, right?"

"Umm..hmmm, soon as I can," I answered.

He gave me a concerned look. "Be safe. I'll talk to you later," Phillip said and he stood still, as I turned and walked away.

I began my journey back to the boutique. As I crossed the street to the next block, I felt someone much too close to me. I looked up and noticed Deric. His face was dripping wet.

"I see you decided to keep seeing him?"

"Just lunch, Deric. That's all it was." We stopped as soon as we crossed the block.

"I don't like it, Kelly."

"Sorry, Deric, but you just saw for yourself, nothing is going on between us, that should make you happy?"

"You probably mean, nothing went on between you two today, right." Deric wiped the drizzle from his face.

"Look, I'm not standing out here and going through this with you. I told you, nothing's going on. Now, I have to get back to work I'll see you at home."

An hour later, Phillip was in the police station, answering questions, while trying to understand what he'd just witnessed.

"So Phillip, are you sure he's the man?"

"That's him," Phillip told the police officer, as they scanned the police line-up.

"And you saw him take her by the arm, and throw her into the street, in front of oncoming traffic?"

"Look damn it! I'm not going over it again. I saw the whole fuckin' thing okay? Oh boy-just snapped."

"Okay, okay. Try to calm yourself," the officer soothed.

"Do you know if they have any realatives in the area?"

"Nah', I don't think so. All I know is, they have a little boy and he stays with the sitter, next door to where they live in Jersey. That's all I know."

Later in Detroit

Kahlil and Cece were in the kitchen, kissing, while they waited for their pasta to finish cooking on the stove. When the phone rang.

"Hello?"

"Mrs. Richardson?"

"Yes? This is she," Cece said.

"My name is Officer Bennet, from New York City Police homicide unit."

"New York City, homicide…?"

"That's correct and I'm sorry, but I have some bad news."

"From New York City?"

"What is it, baby?" Kahlil asked.

"The police from New York City? Here, you talk to them."

Kahlil took the phone, "Yes..this is Kahlil Richardson, how can I help you?"

"Mr. Richardson, as I told your wife, my name is Detective Bennet from NYC police homicide."

"What can I do for you?"

"Well, Mr. Richardson, I'm sorry to inform you but Kelly Thomas was killed by her husband earlier today."

"Kelly Thomas?" Kahlil repeated.

Cece looked up at Kahlil, "That's Deric's last name. What's wrong with Kelly?"

Kahlil put his arm around Cece.

"Are you still there?" the Detective asked.

"Yes, yes. I'm here."

"I'm calling to inform you of her death, because of the last will and testimony we located at her place of residence. Mrs. Thomas requested that you and your wife be responsible for her son, Kahlil, if she or her husband were ever unable to do so."

"She has a son named Kahlil?" Cece inhaled sharply as Kahlil looked down at her in surprise.

"Yes sir, his name is Kahlil. And we need to get him to you as soon as possible, so we can try to prevent additional trauma to him, of losing his mother and father in this truly untimely, gruesome incident."

Kahlil stood stunned and Cece noticed the look on his face. It was the same expression he had, when Sid was led off to prison and she knew something was terribly wrong. Cece began to cry. Kahlil dropped the phone and held Cece close.

"Hello? Mr. Richardson, hello? Mr. Richardson, is everything okay?...Hello?" The detective called out.

Switchin' Ain't Easy

Both Rick and Teresa were as hyped as five cups of coffee could get anybody, but they hadn't a sip of the java jive. They were bouncing and excited, running on pure adrenaline, energized from the truism of the sacred moment they were encountering. Good weather, perfect traffic, a brand new sparkling car for all in Baltimore to see combined with new attitudes were the sources of their galvanized souls. Rick smiled over at Teresa, when she plopped in some more traveling music in her attempt to keep the party alive. Oh yeah... Tupac! At the first sound of the beat, she joined "Pac" and his everlasting, distinct diction.

"Picture me rolling!" Teresa sang. She put her hands above her head, her long slim fingers fully extended, grooving to the beat, as her newly shaped behind wiggled in her seat, which was barely giving her enough room to get loose like she would have liked. But she made do and began twisting and bending as far as her seat belt would allow. Rick looked over at her. His eyes traveled down her "Nu South" jeans. The sight of them only made Rick wish they were out dancing, so he could see the excellent fit which was hugging her sculptured body.

Teresa's body looked magnificent. It was the product of seven months of daily gruesome workouts, relentless aerobic and weight training, along with tuna fish and grapefruit juice diet.

Progression at its best, is what it definitely was, for Rick and Teresa. Not long ago, two years to be exact—they were in Baltimore, living in the projects, without the proper mindset to realize their lives could be better. Then they received a letter from the government, notifying them their welfare would be discontinued. They'd done nothing for the last fifteen years, since graduating from high school, but sit at home, twirling their thumbs and living day-by-day off of the state.

"What's that in your hand?" Rick had asked, as he sat in the small kitchen, smelling the strong scent from the fish being cooked next door. Smells leaked profusely through the worn out project walls. The fish was so strong it almost took over the smell of bud' that was seeping from Ricks clothing.

"A letter from the welfare office," Teresa said, "talkin' 'bout they goin' to stop sending us checks in three months."

Rick didn't react. He went on with his business, like he usually did, when any talk of change rang through his ears. He picked up a deck of cards and began to shuffle. "Did you go get those food stamps from D.J.?" Rick wanted to know.

Teresa was still reading the letter and ignored his

question. "Ricky, I don't think they playin' this time. I think we got to figure out what we goin' to do, because in three months, we ain't goin' to be getting no money to live."

Ricky lit a cigarette. "Whatever….how they goin' to put everybody who's on welfare off of it? That's bullshit. It don't matter no way. I can get us at least two month's living here, without paying anything at all, if they do take our checks. I told you, cuttin' the landlord in on my food stamp scam would do us some good down the road."

"And after that…what we goin' to do?" Teresa asked.

Ricky rubbed his face and lightly stomped his foot on the floor. The conversation was definitely bringing down his high. He shrugged his shoulders and shook his head. "I don't know, but we goin' to survive," Ricky said with certainty.

His answer wasn't what Teresa wanted to hear. Ricky may not have known what he was going to do, but Teresa decided she wasn't going to be ass out in the streets. The very next day, Teresa decided to get herself ready to go see what her letter was all about, starting at dawn. Getting dressed and ready for the day was much different from what Teresa usually did so early in the morning. For years, she'd sat in her chair, looking down through the window at Ricky, serving as a lookout from their fifteenth floor apartment, while he hustled, trying to make a dollar. Ricky would do just about anything to reach his goal—come back after the night, with a dollar more than he walked out the door with.

Teresa started getting ready at dawn. She had to boil the water, to get it hot before washing. The water heater hadn't worked for weeks and there was no way she was washing her ass in the rusty, cold water that ran through the pipes. The building was beyond repair. It smelled of squalor. Like piles of horse shit, combined with garbage cans of pissy diapers, pissy hallways and malt liquor. During the day, everyone who hustled to make a dollar at night slept and the building was surprisingly quiet. But from seven in the evening, until about eight in the morning? Forget about it. The building was so loud, one dare not look at the bed and think they were going to get eight hours sleep to get ready for the next day, like normal folk. It wasn't happening.

The letter from the government was as eye-opening as an Iyanla Vanzant book. At precisely eight in the morning, Teresa was standing tall at the job training center, to get herself some skills. She'd been thinking about seeing what they offered for months anyway. The letter was just the extra push that got her past the "pondering" stage. Teresa would sometimes dream of a better life. She was getting tired of looking down through the window at Ricky. She had become exhausted from all the scheming and games she was involved in, just to keep her head above water.

Her first step towards improving herself was not a difficult choice at all. Looking at all of the circumstances, Teresa was lucky. She didn't have kids, like many of the other women in the projects. She was living in the projects because she always had. She grew up there and, until she received her letter of "do right," she more than likely would have just kept on dreaming and lived with her circumstances the rest of her life.

Teresa was relieved she'd decided to attend. Her name was on a list of possible attendees and she saw Ricky's name, too. The social workers asked her what she would like to do, then showed her a list of jobs she could be trained for.

"I want to become a secretary, at least for now," Teresa answered. They set her up for classes and gave her two weeks advance pay for her training. She rushed home and told Ricky that the computer classes—the ones he always complained were never offered for brothers in the hood—were for the taking. Ricky still went out to the corner to hustle that night, but when he looked up at the window and didn't see his love's eyes watching his back as she had done for years, he called it an early night. The next morning, Ricky followed her down to the job training office and began his transformation as well.

Now, two years later, and after a whole lot of soul searching, praying and hard work, Ricky and Teresa were on their way back to the old projects, riding in their brand new Honda Acura, eager to see their friends. Ricky was smiling ear to ear in his new car, even though he wanted to purchase a Lexus, but it wasn't in their financial plans. He and Teresa were not only working hard, they were reading everything in print about saving money and living within their means. The Lexus was definitely out. They'd read everything from the state of the New World Order to stocks and bonds. The knowledge they obtained made them realize their new combined income of fifty-thousand a year was going to be tight for what they had in mind. But they knew with careful planning their dreams were attainable. They wanted future college for themselves and the children they were planning, not to mention retirement. Plus, they'd just moved into a house. Three bedrooms, one and a half baths. They were happy with what they had accomplished in the short time they'd set their minds to become better people.

"I can't wait to see Leelee and D.J.!" Teresa said with a big ol'smile on her face. "I can't believe it's been two whole years since we even sat down and talked!"

"It doesn't seem like it though...as busy as we've been," Ricky said.

"I know, baby...We've been some working souls and it feels good!" Teresa said.

Ricky pointed to the projects. He could see them from the expressway. Four tarnished, brown brick buildings, all the same height, standing in a semi-circle. "Well, here we are!" Ricky announced.

Teresa fixed her eyes on the dwelling and just stared. It was hard to believe she'd lived in such a terrible looking place for so long. She even turned up her lip, unknowingly. The building looked worse than it had when they lived there. Most of the windows had been broken out, raggedy curtains were blowing from the openings, the basketball courts were full of debris and the basketball rims were bent and hanging from all the daily abuse. Teresa shook her head, as her high from her new life came down drastically. "Yeah, here we are...here we are," she mumbled to herself.

The whole crew met Ricky and Teresa, when they pulled up in front of the projects. It seemed as though everybody in their old building came out. There hadn't been a brand new vehicle pull up to the building in a good while. Ricky and Teresa jumped out of the car with open arms.

"What up, Black!" D.J. said sharply as he reached out to Ricky. They embraced and D.J. could barely look Ricky in the eyes, because he was so busy looking at the car. Ricky looked over at Teresa. She and Leelee were hugging and screaming at the top of their lungs, as they spun around in circles with one another. Friends, together, at last.

"Gurrrl, look atch'you!" Leelee said, sizing up Teresa. "Gurrrl, you done lost some weight......you look like you at least ten years younger."

Teresa looked Leelee over. "I see you still keeping your hair fly!" It was all Teresa could muster as a compliment. Leele had gained at least thirty pounds on her already thick body and she was beginning to look like many of the women they used to rank on, while sitting in the window together.

"Thank you! I'm still puttin' dat' peroxide in it to keep the color gold," Leelee assured Teresa, as she patted down the sides of her short haircut. Everyone stood around the car. Ricky had a huge smile on his face and looked around.

"Who do I need to pay, to watch my car?" Ricky asked the young boys and drunks who were watching the reunion. No one answered. "What? Don't nobody want to make a couple of dollars?" They all looked at Ricky like he'd brought up a very bad subject—work.

A young dark-skinned boy walked up to Ricky wearing jeans, sneakers and a tee shirt, "I'll do it."

Ricky sized him up, "How much you going to charge me?" Ricky wanted to know. D.J. gave Ricky a surprising look. The Ricky he'd always known had never offered to pay anybody for anything.

"I dunno'," the boy said, as he looked at the car and put his hands in his pockets.

"Young brother, always know your price. You understand?"

The young boy moved his hands around in his pockets and nodded yes.

"Well, you think about it, while I go visit my peeps, okay?"

"The keys in it?" little man asked, peeping through the windows. Everyone laughed.

"Boy, you must be crazy!" Rick said, playfully punching him in the stomach.

"Come on, nigga's, let's go up to the crib!" D.J. said to everyone.

Teresa slyly looked at Ricky, as the elevator door struggled to shut to take them up to D.J.'s and Leelee's apartment. The smell of piss and all of its daily combinations almost knocked them both to their knees. Ricky covered his nose the best he could and wished the chugging elevator would hurry up and get to where they were going. When they finally made it, Teresa thought to herself, "*I'm taking the steps back down...forget that!*"

D.J. opened the door to the apartment and everyone followed in. Ricky squinted his eyes. It seemed a lot darker inside than he remembered.

"All right now! Everybody take ya' seats like back in the day. You know how we do! Just don't sit in my chair. I got to have my lucky chair, 'cause we goin' to bust dat' ass in spades today!" he said in a joyful mood.

"Still talking shit I see!" Ricky pointed out.

Teresa and Leelee sat down, smiling at each other, still looking like small girls who hadn't seen their best friends over the whole summer break.

Ricky looked up at the ceiling in the apartment.

"Damn, D.J...why don't you get Terron to get his ass in here to fix the ceiling, before it falls in?"

"Man, that shit ain't goin' nowhere," D.J. confirmed. "It been like dat' almost since you left. Ain't it, Leelee?" Leelee nodded her head yes. "I told Terron about it...when it first happened. Only thing he did was tell the muthafuckas upstairs to move to another apartment, so the whole damn floor wouldn't fall through. Ain't nobody even up in dat' one no more, Ricky, so I guess dat' shit will be all right." Ricky shook his head, as D.J. sat down and opened a fresh pack of cards and began to shuffle them. Then there was a knock at the door.

"Come on!" D.J. screamed. He wasn't about to get up from his chair. He never did. He'd grown up in this same building and knew everybody that lived in every apartment in all the buildings. He was cool with all the young gang bangers who patrolled the lobby—he'd fucked most of their mothers, so wasn't anybody getting in the building who wasn't supposed to be. And those who lived there knew not to approach him with any bullshit, because he always had heat on him. So everyone felt comfortable, as their guest opened the door and their eyes were wide, waiting to see who it was.

"I should've known!" Leelee shouted, as everyone else expressed surprise to see who walked in. Quickly it became loud inside the apartment with greetings and small talk.

"Should have known what! Should have known what! Tell a nigga' what you should've known?" Peanut joked, as he walked over to Teresa, then Ricky, and gave them hugs, Vita followed him, giving out hugs as well.

"I should've known it was yo' ass!" Leelee scolded,

smiling ear to ear. "Anytime anybody sit down to play cards, who got's to bring dae' asses over to talk shit?" Leelee asked over the earsplitting welcomes and greetings.

"That's right. That's right, I do!" Peanut joked. Then he put his hands on his hips, as he stood over the card table. Peanut was dark skin and skinny and really needed to get his teeth cleaned. "Look at Ricky and Teresa, looking all fly and shit!"

Ricky and Teresa smiled. Ricky felt a little funny. It was odd, looking different than everyone else. He didn't wear his hair in a barely combed afro anymore. He had cut it down several inches and made sure it stayed rounded. He had on a v-neck and jeans, not something his friends would be used to seeing him in. His sneakers seemed to be barely worn at all, instead of the ones he used to wear years ago, almost like house shoes.

"Where's Jess and Retha?" Teresa asked, referring to Vita's man and Peanut's lady. D.J. started to deal the cards while his cigarette hung from his mouth.

"Oh, you haven't heard?" Peanut asked.

"Heard what?" Teresa asked surprised.

Ricky squinted his eyes through D.J.'s cigarette smoke and looked at Peanut. Leelee sat still and watched D.J. deal. They already knew what was happening with the two.

Peanut looked around. "Shit...me and Retha. We ain't together no more."

Vita ran her hand through her weave and put her hand on her hip. "And me and Jess split up too!" Vita said, with much attitude.

"Me and Vita stay together now," Peanut informed.

"Ain't that right, baby?"

Vita switched weight from her left leg to the right. Everyone could tell she thought she was looking good in her tight jeans. "Ummm-hmmm, that's right. And Jess and Retha together now, too," Vita explained.

The surprise was enough to make Ricky open his mouth again, "Are you serious?"

"Hell, yeah...dat' ain't no joke, you heard? One night, we was playin' cards and shit and Vita was looking good to me. I mean look at that body--do you blame me for peepin' game? And I guess Retha was looking good to Jess, 'cause the next day, she moved out and baby girl moved in," Peanut said, pointing to Vita.

"Man, ya'll crazy as hell!" Ricky said, as Teresa started to laugh.

"What, nigga? Why stay wit' somebody you don't want to be wit?" Peanut asked.

Ricky had never been the one to bite his tongue. "It's just that, ya'll was with each other for a long, long time. And Vita and Jess, too? I just don't know many peeps' who say they going to break up, in one night, and the shit happens. Damn, that shit is surprising, that's all."

"Man, don't nobody stay together no mo'," Peanut explained.

"Well, why ya'll split up?" Ricky wanted to know.

"'Cause, nigga, she said she wanted to live upstairs wit' Jess. So I said, take yo' ass on, 'cause I want to get wit' Vita."

"Just like that?" Teresa asked.

"Umm-hmmm. Dat damn simple!" Vita said, then blew

a kiss to Peanut.

"Word, and I bet ya'll don't stay together forever your damn self," Peanut proclaimed looking at Ricky then Teresa.

"Somebody done told you wrong Peanut, 'cause we staying together, and that's the bottom line. It's called commitment, and that's what we made to each other," Ricky promised. "See you need to understand, me and Teresa, we work with each other, and for each other, that's how it's supposed to be. So I can tell you right here in your face, I'm going to be with my Boo, until the day I die."

Teresa smiled and told Leelee, "That's why I give it to him anyway he want it, you know what I mean?" Leelee chuckled.

Ricky turned his eyes to D.J., then Leelee, "At least Leelee and D.J. know what I'm talking about?" D.J. peeked over at Leelee. "Look, they still together, handling they business and ......"

D.J. cut Ricky off and his eyes tightened, "For now," he said sharply. "Let's play cards, niggas!" D.J. instructed, then he picked up his hand and without looking Leelee in the eyes asked, "What you biddin', Leelee?"

Leelee pushed her back into her chair in surprise of her man's slick comment and caught her breath, "I'm bettin' you don't want to fuck with me!" she said back to D.J.

And the card game was on.

Just Different

Michelle moved the strands of her silky black hair dangling on the side of her face away and tucked them behind her ear. Anthony loved the way she looked when she did that.

"Do you remember the first time we did this?" Michelle asked quietly.

Anthony waited until Michelle was comfortably laying in his arms, before he answered. "Yes. I sure do."

Michelle moved closer to his chest. She was really enjoying the DOLCE & GABBANA lingering on his body. Michelle smiled as she cuddled and took Anthony's strong black hand and cupped it in-between both of her small hands. She enjoyed the way his black skin matched perfectly against her tan color. "When? When was the first time?"

Anthony didn't hesitate. "Exactly four years ago." His eyes shifted down to Michelle. "Why, did you think I'd forgotten or something?"

"No, I've just been traveling down memory lane and

remembered its been years since we did this for the first time and I wanted to let you know, I still enjoy it and I'm already looking forward to the next time we get together."

Anthony looked up at the ceiling. He and Michelle both agreed that the Ritz Carlton was their favorite place to meet. Everything about the Ritz was very close to what they were used to in their own homes.

"Michelle?" Anthony called out.

"Yes, baby?"

"Do you still feel the same about what we're doing after all this time?"

Michelle put her hand on Anthony's chest and pushed herself up, so she could look directly in his eyes when she answered, "Yes, I do. I feel even stronger about it, because its real." As soon as she answered, the palm of her hand felt the concern leave Anthony's body. "Why, don't you?"

"I do, but I haven't gotten over the guilty part of being away from my wife during these few hours, as long as we've been doing this."

"You probably think the worst about me, because I can, don't you?" Michelle asked.

"No, no that's not it, Michelle. Its just, if we're ever caught, who's going to believe we've never done anything but lay in the bed together, fully dressed." Anthony chuckled, "Definitely not my wife."

Michelle slid back into the shell of Anthony's strong hold, "Well, it's true and I feel good about it. We're friends, as close as friends can get."

"But is it right? I enjoy every single second of laying in this bed with you, talking and gently caressing your body.

But are we friends or lovers-and why don't I enjoy this with my wife, as much as I do you?"

"Because we're friends, and I don't have anymore expectations from you," Michelle answered.

Anthony smiled, "That's too easy of an answer Michelle. Do you think it's because I don't love her anymore? Do you think I'm tired of her? What about you, how do you feel about being with me and away from James?"

"I feel relieved. I still love him, love him with all my heart. Love him to death- we've been together for sixteen years. But everyone needs to relax every now and then. When I see him after I'm with you, I'm rejuvenated."

"Tell me something. How would you feel if he was doing the same thing with a friend, as we speak?"

"The very same thing we're doing?"

"Yes."

"Every time they meet?"

"Yes."

"Well, I would hope he was enjoying the moment as well. To me, this is nothing more than a great massage that I can't get anywhere else."

"So you're saying this is better than anything you've experienced?"

Michelle looked up at Anthony and thought, "No, just different. Just different. Now, listen to the music and hold me okay?"

His & Her Journal's

Sunday afternoon

Today, I thought I'd lay in bed in front of the fireplace, watch television and relax. It's entirely too cold outside to do much of anything else. Earlier this morning, I went outside and shoveled the snow and put down salt on the driveway leading to the front door. I didn't want to have to struggle, getting out of the driveway, before I had to fight with all my brethren heading to work tomorrow on the roadway. Besides, more than likely, there's going to be a lot of children in the emergency room with frostbite that we're going to have to treat, because they'll probably be out in the snow all day today enjoying the first snow fall of the year. A doctor's work never slows.

It took me about an hour and a half to finish with the snow outside. When I went into the kitchen, Rachel had a hot cup of coffee waiting for me and a nice smile. I really appreciated that. She was in the kitchen, placing a pot roast and vegetables in the crock-pot and keeping an eye on the seven-up cake that was in the oven.

Now the game is on and the 49er's are playing the Lions. Rachel has the entire house smelling so good with that pot-roast. I really want to go down and check everything out, but I know she'd run me out of there, like she always does.

I'm so fortunate to have Rachel. She knows how much I like to relax on Sunday and enjoy a good meal.

The snow kept us both inside from going to church today and it was her idea that I come on up and get into the bed and watch the game. The logs in the fireplace really have things cozy in here and the game is really good. I miss watching Barry Sanders though. He really meant a lot to our city of Detroit. I hope his retirement isn't final, the Lion's could really use him now.

216

Well the game is over. Looks like it's been over for about two hours because there's a entirely different game on now, between Dallas and Green Bay and they're well into the fourth quarter. Talk about a powerful slumber. One of the best I can remember in a long time on a Sunday aftertnoon. I wasn't planning on going to sleep, but Rachel came in the room with nothing on but her birthday suit and totally took me by surprise. Rachel knows how much I love to see her entirely naked and, when she pranced into the room and crawled into bed next to me, she really made a good day much better. She didn't even say anything to me, when I said hello to her, but "what's the score?" I told her and we started to watch the game together and before I knew it, Rachel realized I was excited about her showing up like she did and she put her head under the blanket and took her time satisfying me, until I couldn't take it anymore and put me into the deepest sleep, which I've just recovered from.

Well, what do you know? Here comes dinner. Um, Um, Um, it smells good and Rachel still looks good. Who would've guessed I would be writing all this in my journal. what a good idea for reflection by our counselor.

Monday- Rachel at lunch

I'll start today's entry with last night's activities, because it's really the only thing that's been on my mind all day. I just hope my client and the judge didn't noticed me drifting away during the prosecution's cross. I really hadn't expected Lou to join me in the tub last night. It was a pleasant surprise. I can't remember the last time we both sat together in our garden tub. I remember, years ago, that's why we bought it. So we could spend quality time together and relax. But that wasn't all that happened in the tub, because Lou brought a bottle of wine with him and Barry White's, *I Got Staying Power*, was playing through our intercom speakers and instantly the mood was set.

I have a secret too. After the first couple of minutes in the tub, Lou had me. It surprised me when he started to talk to me, because I was ready to reach out for him and get things underway. He was sooooo cool and patient! I just melted when he told me I meant everything in the world to him. Then he told me how proud he was of me, because of everything we had attained, we'd gotten it together. I started crying, when he told me he couldn't have picked a better woman in the world to have his children. He gave me all the credit in the world for making sure all four of our boys were now off and into college, about to make an impact on the world. Then he leaned over and kissed me on the lips and picked me up and carried me to the bed. And it gets better.

The music was still playing and he took a towel and dried me off then placed me on my stomach and began to give me a massage with oil. I didn't even know he had erotic oil. Then he stopped and just looked at me. Then I felt his tongue trickle all the way down my back...down to my behind –just everywhere down there. Then he turned me over and paid attention to my breasts and ask me if I was ready. All I did was smile, because he knew I was-- I already had three orgasms without him inside of me. Imagine two fifty-four year old's, carrying on like it was their first time together? Lou made me realize, he was serious about making sure these were going to be the best years of our lives. Then it happened. Lou entered me and I swear, it wasn't thirty seconds before I was satisfied. And he was proud and didn't struggle or worry about his own needs. He just scooped me up beside him in the bed and the music ended and I fell asleep in his arms. I never slept so good in my life. I really love that man.

Monday night

I almost forgot to say, I'm so glad we didn't decide to separate after our boys left the house. I finally realized that we just needed to talk things out and get an understanding. Being married is a lot of work.

Please Listen

I was not feeling the crew who came into the restaurant and was shown a table in my section. They were all about my age, late twenties, and wide-eyed about the time they were having on the town. Los Angeles really brings it out of people. I counted six heads and filled as many glasses of ice water. I knew this would be my last table for the day, because it was already quarter past five. Another forty-five minutes and my shift was over and I was going home to soak my aching feet, which were ready to go home three hours before. I took a deep refreshing breath and psyched myself up, then walked over to the table and greeted my customers.

"Welcome to Leon's," I said to everyone, as I placed their glasses on the table. The guy sitting even with my right breast glanced up at me, then for a brief moment took his mental picture, as he looked closer and closer. It wasn't an unusual reaction and I was trying my best to grin and bear it, as I always did. Finally, thank God, he shook his head dismissing his thoughts, and looked down at his menu.

"I'll give you all a chance to look at the menus and come back to take your orders in a minute or two."

They all agreed and, as I turned away, another young woman joined the group, sliding into the booth beside the guy who'd taken the mental picture of me earlier.

"'Scuse me? Don't I get any water?"

"She didn't know you were here, Kim," the guy beside her pointed out.

"Shut up Byron," she told him.

I glanced back at the group and noticed the light brown skinned girl, who called me out. She was looking wide-eyed at me, and what little hair she had, was pulled into a pony tail and her sleeveless shirt, was way too tight. My eyes, couldn't help but to travel down to her short shorts, which had already ridden up in-between her thick legs, which she continually tried to pull down as she sat. She looked like she was on a POGO stick, up and down, up and down pulling those shorts away. But I answered her politely,

"No problem. I'll have you something to drink as soon as I can," I told her. I turned back around and began to walk away.

"'Scuse me? 'Scuse me!" Kim squealed, snapping her fingers at me. "Aren't you the actress that played Kelly in that movie, *Fed Up with the Fanny*?"

I turned to answer her, but Byron opened his mouth first. "Nooooo, that ain't her," he said. "I thought she was, too, at first."

I smiled, "No, she's right. It's me," I told them.

"What....get out?" Byron said, looking around the

table with a grin.

"No, it's really me," I assured him.

"That was the bomb movie!" Byron exclaimed, "You played the hell out of that girl, Kelly." Everyone around the table agreed.

"She did all right," Kim sang out, then she rolled her eyes at me and tossed a wicked look towards Byron. Everyone was shocked. I know I was. "I didn't like how you weren't able to get Khalil in bed. Now, if that was me, and I wanted that man, I could've had him," she boasted.

I chuckled inside, "That was the director's decision. Besides, it's the way the book was written."

"Well, I don't care. I still would've got with his fine ass," she claimed. She looked at Byron, who was taking another picture of me. This time, he had the zoom lens all over me and I felt him. "Dang, Byron, you don't have to stare. She ain't all that! Think about it. If she was, she wouldn't be in here, about to get me a glass of water, with TWO straws, would she?"

Right then it seemed to me the entire restaurant became ridiculously quiet and her words echoed off the walls. I can't stand to be loud talked. Her thick-ass didn't know me well enough to be making any personal comments about my life. Way too many people assume that right, just because they've seen you on the movie screen. Gary, my husband, says it's the price of being in a movie which grossed over forty-five-million-dollars and only cost five million to make. But I don't share his attitude about it. All I got for the movie was union scale, no percentage of the big bucks, and now I was waiting on tables and serving fools like Ms. Kim. It was driving me crazy and my temper got the best of me.

"Listen, bitch," I screamed, "you don't know me like that and if you don't shut up, I'm going to whoop your wide ass all over this floor!"

"Bitch?" Kim looked around her table of friends. "Who she calling bitch?"

"You!" Everyone at the table chorused in unison.

"That's right, you! You thick-ass, loud mouth!" I called out.

My boss, Leon, heard the commotion and came out of the kitchen, wiping his hands on his apron, with a frown covering his wrinkled face. "What's the problem?" he asked.

"Your food-serving, table wiping, wanna-be actress is the problem," Kim shouted.

"No, you're the problem, coming in here, disrespecting somebody, like you don't have any damn sense," I said back.

Leon turned to me. "Same problem again?" He asked under his breath. When I nodded my head, while I kept my eyes on Ms. Big Mouth, Leon sighed. "DeeDee, don't let it get you down. Just go with the flow. She's not worth it."

"Go with the flow?" I cut my eyes at Leon.

He nodded towards them, "Now these are my customers DeeDee and if they don't eat, I don't make any money and you don't get paid," he said.

"That's right," Kim smirked. "You better listen, bitch, before they move your non-acting ass into the kitchen to wash the dirty-ass dishes!"

My hands moved to the back of my apron. I didn't have to take her stuff, I thought, as I stiffened ready to go to blows. I didn't care if it was the only source of income me and

Gary had coming in. I'd been at Leon's for a little over six months and this wasn't the first time someone had gotten ignorant with me, and it wouldn't be the last, I was sure. People were recognizing me from the movie, then harping on the fact that, after playing in such a successful film, I was now waiting on tables.

Kim was the final straw, sitting at her table, pointing her finger and shouting at me. Apparently, she was delighted with the idea that she could dispel her man's fantasies about me, but I still wasn't about to take any more abuse. I untied my apron, then turned around and walked away, dropping it on the floor behind me.

Gary was on the phone when I got home. As soon as he hung up, I told him I was through at Leon's.

"You're what?"

"You heard me. I quit."

Gary stood up from the cluttered couch, which served as his desk and work space. He picked up the phone. "I have to talk to Leon. We're going to need that money, DeeDee."

I shook my head, "Uh..uh, put down the phone, Gary," I said, with my hand over his on the receiver. "What part didn't you understand? I don't want to work at his restaurant anymore. There are too many people who come through there who've seen the movie, not just once, but several times."

"What do you expect, we're in L.A.?" Gary shrugged.

"You don't understand how embarrassing it is, waiting on tables, hearing their comments and nasty attitudes. I could do without the comments. I'm not to proud too work, waiting on tables, but no one has the right to comment on what I do for a living." I sighed, "I don't know what I was thinking when I took that job."

"You were thinking about us paying the bills around here." Gary's voice was low as he released the phone, but I heard his comment.

"Why don't you go back to work then? Matter of fact, why don't you go back to your job? You said they would take you back in a heartbeat, right? Then we can go back to the way things were around here, before you decided to become my business-manager-slash-producer and forgetting all about your damn job at the law firm. I'll be happy to sit home and get back to studying my craft and getting back in top shape for a role."

"DeeDee, I've got too much going on right now," he snapped. "I told you before, I'm going to get you the role you want, in somebody's picture. It's just that, this business is built on relationships and I'm building as we speak." Gary stood up and walked towards the door. "Oh, by the way, Angie called."

"What did she say?"

"For you to call her."

"That's it?"

"That's it." He glared at me. "I'm gonna' go try to get your job back. Those tips at that place are just too good to pass up," he said, as he opened the door. Our apartment walls rattled when he slammed the door shut behind him.

"You're wasting your time! I'm not going back!" I shouted out.

I collapsed on the couch, amid the array of newspapers,

entertainment magazines, trade magazines and clutter that Gary had been working with. Where had it all gone wrong? Two years ago, the world had been our oyster. Lately, pearls and joyful times were few and far between.

I met Gary the night of the premier of "Fanny." Elated with our success and early reviews, the entire cast went to a nearby club to celebrate. Gary had been there with a group of men. Later, I found out they were lawyers, too. He came over to our table and asked me to dance. We spent most of the evening on the dance floor. I introduced him to the other cast members and was surprised he didn't recognize any of them, because we had been on the cover of all of the major black magazines. Later, we joined his friends for a drink. Still, none of them recognized us. Gary wasn't into the celebrity circles, as near as I could tell. The simple acceptance of me as a person, not an actress was heart warming after some of my more recent encounters with men, wanting to date me just because I was on the big screen.

Gary and I clicked from the first moment. He was fun to talk to and treated me like an ordinary person, which I enjoyed the most. He was a successful attorney, on his way in a mid-sized law firm. We went to dinner at the best restaurants, quiet places, which was fine with me. We met the other lawyers and their wives at a jazz bar, near his office, most Friday evenings. After a while, I knew I was falling in love with this man and I sensed he felt the same. We were getting really serious and I felt it was time to tell him what I did for a living, because he still, never actually knew. After all, everyone in L.A. is an actress.

Gary admitted he rarely went to the movies, but agreed

to take me to see "Fanny." It was at the dollar-fifty movies close to my place. We settled into our seats and he enthusiastically dug into his box of popcorn. Gary didn't react to the first scene featuring my character it was real quick. He just smiled, apparently noting the resemblance. A few minutes later, the screen was filled with me, my brown eyes, my dark skin, my short hair cut and my 125 pound body that I wanted back so much, sitting on a couch with my legs crossed talking to my best friend in the movie Cece.

"Gary bolted upright in his seat, dumping his popcorn into my lap, as he turned to stare at me. "Why didn't you tell me?" People around us hissed at his shout and I smiled and kissed him on the cheek. "Why didn't you tell me you were in this movie? I almost had a heart attack," he whispered.

I put my fingers to his lips. "Hush. People are trying to hear. Just enjoy." Gary sat back, but kept looking at me, after all of my scenes. Even after seeing the movie and realizing I was an working actress, Gary's attitude toward me didn't change. I could've been a police officer for all the difference it made. I was relieved to discover that knowing who I was didn't change his attitude. That's when I began to fall deeply in love, knowing I'd found a man I could trust and admire and who loved me for me. We were married four months later. There was no point in waiting. We were right for each other. I related to Gary, I liked what he was about. We had long, lingering conversations, we could discuss issues, without disagreeing, and if we didn't see eye to eye, it didn't matter. And the sex. Um...um...um. Gary was warm, loving and real.

After a year of marriage, Gary had begun to express

an interest in my career, what I was doing, the roles I was reading for. It was wonderful to share my interests and my dreams with him. Our only bone of contention was my agent, Angie. I'd met her five years earlier. After doing a nationwide car commercial, a friend in Denver introduced us. Angie convinced me to move out to Los Angeles, to pursue my acting career. Angie and I were friends, as well as actress and agent.

Gary was against our relationship though. When he started to question the parts I was reading for, he began to urge me to sever my connection with Angie, contending our friendship was keeping me from obtaining the status we all believed I could attain in the movie industry. Gary started to insist our association wasn't based on business, that we let our emotions get in the way of sound, professional decisions. He was furious when Angie and I turned down the opportunity for me to appear in one of those booty shaking, breast baring, foul-mouthed movies with no substance or element. We knew it was a marginal film, when the producers assured us I didn't have to audition, saying the part was mine if I wanted it. After reading the slimy script, I figured the part was anybody's who'd agree to it. There were three scenes which were total nudes, four others were bare breasts and one required me to go down on a guy in his car, just because he had a Lexus with nice rims. We immediately declined the offer, realizing the film would typecast me for the rest of my acting career. Plus, it was just a plain old nasty movie that made women look like hoes. Gary was not pleased and he and Angie had engaged in a shouting match in our living room, because he thought I should do it, to let people know I was still alive.

A week later, Gary came home from work in high

spirits. Dropping his jacket on the back of the couch, he brushed a kiss across my cheek and settled onto a chair.

"So, how was your day?" he wanted to know.

"Okay, I worked out. Studied for the upcoming role in Spike's new movie." I rolled my eyes. "You know everybody and their mama is going be out for those roles. But I'm planning to be at the top of my game." I raised an eyebrow, when I noticed the unfamiliar gaze in Gary's eyes. "What about you? How was your day?"

Gary grinned. "Mine? Oh, fine. Great." He hesitated, then leaned forward in the chair. "Look, DeeDee, I know I probably should have discussed this with you, but...."

"Discussed what?"

"My job. I quit my job."

Gary told me he felt that Angie couldn't take care of my best interests anymore and that he'd been studying the industry on his own for months. He told me if I wouldn't drop her as an agent, he thought he should be my manager, to protect and promote me. I didn't think it was a big deal. I knew how much we had in the bank, to keep us going for a while, plus, Gary said the firm would take him back, whenever he was ready. So I was game. You hear about it all the time in this business, close friends or family members handling the business interests of those in the business. There's a trust factor that's not evident in other relationships. Besides, Gary had a great gift of gab. His background as an attorney gave him the drive and push he said I was lacking in my search for roles. I figured we'd be a good team. Unfortunately, he and Angie were constantly at each other's throats.

Gary went with me to the audition for Spike's film.

This was a new experience for him and I could tell he was amazed by what an actess goes through, what I go through, every time I try for a part. Looking around, it was hard to believe the number of black actresses present, many of whom I would see at other auditions year round that called for a black face. Yet, here they were, plus many more, all gathered together like starving vultures, waiting, hyping themselves for a supporting role in one film. I became frustrated and left the audition in tears. I knew there wasn't a chance I'd get a call back. There were way too many big names at the audition, who were all sitting in a back office, actresses who'd played staring roles in successful films and had the inside track. It was that bad.

"Let's talk, baby," Gary said, gently caressing my arm. "What's wrong?"

"This whole system is wrong," I said. "There aren't enough roles for all of us. Whenever there's a casting call, everybody who's anybody shows up. I don't know if I even want to do this anymore," I admitted through my tears.

"No...no, baby," Gary soothed. "You want to do it. You were born to do it."

"But how am I supposed to get work? It's like what I did in 'Fanny' doesn't mean a damn thing anymore."

"Look, I'm going to make this work for you. I'm going to change hats and become a producer. I'll get you all types of roles, because they'll be ones that I help create. How's that sound?"

"Gary, you don't know anything about producing!"

He snorted. "Neither do those fools producing all these sorry ass movies. If they did, you'd be in the starring roles.

Right?"

Later that same week, I learned that a potential television role on a new sitcom that I had the inside track in had been dropped. Angie was clearly disappointed when she called.

"DeeDee, I just got a call from the TV network. They decided to drop the black girlfriend in the show, keep all the friends white."

"Why? Why would they change the script?"

"I don't know. They said it has something to do with the marketing scheme of the program."

"Oh, I get it. They're going to be advertising to an all-white audience and there's no need to take a chance on a black girl in the show, because there won't be a single black person in any of the commercials, right?"

"Dee, come on. You're starting to sound like Gary."

"It's true, Angie. And how many nights did I spend rehearsing those contrite-ass lines? How long did it take me to prepare to come off as an uppity, brash black bitch, one who didn't know any blacks, including her mother and father? Untold hours, I spent, Angie. I have a right to be upset, damn it!"

Fortunately, Angie was willing to let me talk through my frustrations and I was off on a tangent. I yelled about the industry and how screwed up the whole system was. I yelled about the unfairness toward blacks. I was delighted to have an agent, but the truth is, a black agent in this business is good, if you want a shot at being in the two or three movies a year made for black audiences. It's the way the game is played and it's never going to change. Black director, black producers and all black cast is called a "black movie," and black agents have a chance to get you into them, plus they still compete with white agents who have black clients. But when it comes to getting you in and actually signed to do a mainstream movie, things get sticky. Black agents are treated as bad as black actors in this business. I told Angie that white agents...white agents can get you in the door. Sad and unfair. But true. They have the contacts and they can get their calls returned and can convince their friends they won't even know their client is black. Angie knew what I was saying was true, because she has said the same thing to me, more than once. There was finally a moment of silence after I wound down.

"DeeDee, do you want to look for another agent? A white agent?" Angie asked me. "I'll understand."

I did think about letting Angie go and seeing if a white agent could get me better work. But I couldn't do it. Our friendship was important to me and the trust and loyalty we shared was sacred, something that I wasn't going to get with anyone else.

"No, Angie. I just needed to get it all out of my system. That's all. Call it venting."

Meantime, Gary was busy wheeling and dealing. As he spent more time on the streets, trying to build relationships with producers and directors and anyone else who could provide a boost for my career, I found myself pulling away, withdrawing from him.

Discussing business with him had gotten one-sided. His side. Don't get me wrong. I was proud of what Gary had done in the short time he'd called himself a producer. And I honestly believe most of what he'd done, was for me. All my moaning and groaning about the industry is what gave him the idea of getting into the business in the first place. But Gary doesn't just listen. He's a fixer-upper. Any problem in the world, Gary feels the need to jump in and fix it for me, even if I'm capable of handling it myself or am willing to just let it go. He started fixing things for me the day he became my manager and it seemed to get worse as time went on.

I came home one day in tears, after being told by a producer that I wasn't black enough for a part we all felt certain I'd get. Gary held me in his arms and assured me it would be okay, that I wasn't to let this kind of thing upset me. The next night, Gary came in seething.

"I saw Tom today," he announced.

"Tom who?"

The producer, the one who said you weren't black enough for the part."

"You saw....him? Why? For what?"

"To talk to him. See if I could change his mind."

I shook my head, I didn't appreciate it. "So, what did he say?"

"Not much. He's full of shit."

"Full of....Gary, what do you mean?"

He shrugged. "I met him for lunch. Told him I thought he was making a mistake. I reminded him of the recognition you get from your first movie and the fact it's still playing in theaters after two years and selling like hell on tape. Told him black audiences don't forget stellar performances by a black face." Gary cleared his throat and sat forward on the chair. "He told me, you weren't black enough. I asked him if he could explain that to me." Gary frowned. "He said you weren't 'hoochiefied' enough, that he needed a woman with the demeanor of a hoe, someone out of the ghetto, who's been with lot's of Zulu brothers. So, I explained to him that you came out of the projects in Denver, that you knew the environment all too well. And you know what he said? Are you ready for this? He said, he didn't get that vibe from you, that he could've sworn you were from the Valley. Can you believe that shit?"

I could believe it. Gary didn't wait for an answer.

"Anyway, I said he ought to reconsider and he said he'd already evaluated you and I asked how many blacks he had working on the film and how many had helped in that evaluation of you and he said none...and none. And then he said it didn't matter, because the film wasn't about black life, it was about money and gritty nasty black hoes on screen make money. He had the nerve to ask me, '*Don't you watch the music videos? That's what people want to see. That exact image.*' And that's when I flipped the table over on him," Gary ended in disgust.

"You did what?" I stared at him. "Gary...Gary, you had no right..."

"I was just trying to help," he shouted.

"Help? Help do what? Get me blackballed?"

"No, damn it, help you get the role. That's all, the role. I could tell you were upset about it, so I went to see what I could do."

"Upset? Yes, I was upset. And I'm even more upset now!"

Gary frowned. "Why?"

"Gary, I didn't tell you about the role so you'd go

hunt the man down. I told you because I felt like talking. Talking about my disappointment. Just talking, Gary."

"Well, I didn't like how you were feeling. I wanted to do what I could to make it better."

"And as you see, there's nothing you can do."

"I tried."

"But no one asked you to, Gary," I said, with a sigh.

He didn't get it. He didn't think he'd done anything wrong. He couldn't understand my anger or my being upset. That's when I stopped talking with him about my business. I kept everything bottled up inside, despite days when I felt I might burst with disappointment or frustration. I thought about going to Angie, but she was battling the same issues I was, being black and a woman in the film industry. It wasn't easy for any of us.

Inevitably, the damn broke after a while and Angie called me with good news. I made a very romantic dinner for me and Gary, but still I'd planned on keeping my business to myself and my mouth shut. We enjoyed the quiet dinner with wine, and music and I have to admit I was finally feeling good about myself and career again. After dinner, we made love and I laid curled up in Gary's arms.

He kissed my forehead, then asked quietly, "How're things going, baby? You haven't talked much about the auditions or anything else lately. You know I'm still your manager and working hard everyday for you." He ran his index finger across my nipples. Still perky and sensitive, they responded instantly and I felt a shiver ripple through my body. "Are things okay?" he asked, brushing my nipples a second time, then a third. I smiled, my body responding to his attention, and I wanted him to share this moment with me concerning my latest news. Besides it was already a done deal.

"Baby, I've been asked to co-host the Awards."

Gary raised up on his elbow, at attention. "The Awards?"

"Umm hmm."

"Baby, this is great. Do you know what this means? This means you're being recognized for your work."

I blushed. "Finally."

Gary grinned. "How much are they paying?"

"Nothing," I told him.

"Nothin'....Nothin'?" He repeated.

"Nothing, Gary."

"Nah'.., baby, they should be paying, he said. "See, that's what I mean about Angie."

"Gary, don't start. Not tonight. It's a done deal and it'll be good for my career."

He studied my face for a moment and noticed how happy I was. "You're right, baby," he said.

'*He's finally learned,*' I said to myself, after he didn't say anything more. He just continued to hold me tight through the rest of the night.

I was pulled out of my thoughts by the shrill ringing of the phone. I thought it was Angie, being impatient about my not returning her page during my workout time. I caught the phone on the third ring.

"Hey, Angie, what's up?"

"DeeDee?"

It wasn't Angie.

"Yes, speaking."

"DeeDee, this is Ron."

I gasped, recognizing the voice of the man who headed up the Awards. "Hello, Ron. This is such a surprise?"

"I'm calling about the Awards show," he said.

"Yes, rehearsals start tomorrow night. I'm so excited, I can hardly wait. I was going to thank you tomorrow, but I guess now will do!"

"No need. Tomorrow is what I'm calling about DeeDee."

"Rehearsal?"

"Not exactly." Ron cleared his throat. "Your manager paid me a visit today."

"My who?"

"Your manager. Gary. Isn't Gary your manager?"

"Well...yes."

"He came to see me today. He made some demands I can't meet. I honestly thought you understood that, after I squared things with Angie."

"Ron, there must be some misunderstanding. I..."

Ron cut in. "I'm disappointed. But you know how I work. I don't hide behind assistants or agents. I wanted to call you personally, to let you know I've decided to go with another co-host for the show."

My heart plummeted and my hands shook. "Ron, there must be a misunderstanding," I repeated. "I never sent anyone to talk to you about any demands. Angie and I agreed to do the show under the terms we discussed. Look, let me clear this up. Can I get back to you in an hour or so?"

"Sorry, DeeDee. Decision's made. Good luck in the future."

I heard a click, then a dial tone. I sat there, listening to the annoying buzz and staring at the entertainment magazines scattered across the floor that seemed like I would never get a chance to be in. Slowly, I replaced the receiver. I stood up and walked to the bedroom, dazed. I packed my bags. I was leaving. I had to leave. Maybe, my leaving would help Gary understand. I wanted him to realize the importance of talking and listening. Just listening. That's all I ever wanted Gary to do, just listen to me.

Happy

"Not mine, not mine, hell no, not mine."

Barry looked over at his roomate, Joe, when he heard the ruffle of pages. "What the hell you doin', Joe?"

Joe continued. "Not mine, this is not mine and this one is definitely not mine." Joe looked up. "I'm going over my credit report, that's what. I have to show the judge what accounts were actually mine and actually Dawn's."

"Ohh, so you guys are at the stage of splitting things up now?"

"Yeah, and it's nonsense, because most of things she's trying to hold me responsible for, she had way before I met her." Joe got a charge when he noticed another entry. "Look at this shit! Lacy's, I ain't never shopped at no damn Lacy's. How and the hell, did this get on my report?"

Barry smiled. "Cause you two were married. It's a joint account, I bet?"

Joe made sure. "Yep, sure is. Shit, I never approved

this."

"You don't have to. When your married, they assume wife and husband talk about those type of things. Are you telling me, you two didn't talk?" Barry wanted to know.

Joe pasted a sarcastic look on his face. "If we did, we wouldn't be in the middle of talking to a judge and splitting all our stuff up. Secondly, I wouldn't be your roomate and I would be in my own damn house, sleeping in that king size bed that I bought and miss so dearly. Marriage is crazy man, down right crazy."

Barry looked up from his sports page as he sat at the kitchen table. "That's exactly what I've been thinking," Barry admitted."

Joe set aside his report and picked up his cup of coffee. "Don't tell me you're having second thoughts about getting married, Barry?" Joe laughed. "That's a damn shame, because just this morning I was thinking how nice it was going to feel, for the first time in my life having a bachelor pad at my age of thirty-six. You better not fuck this up for me, man?"

"I'm just being straight up about the situation, Joe. That's all, straight up truthful and don't forget this is still my place, until I leave."

"Well, you don't have to be straight up with me. You need to be straight up with Stephanie because she's your wife to be."

"Be serious. If I tell her what's on my mind it will mess up the marriage before it even gets started."

"Are you crazy? Take it from somebody who knows. Don't go into a marriage with doubt, if you do, you're doomed. Doomed. So tell me, what's on your mind?"

Joe and Barry faced off at the table. Joe was trying to read his mind.

"Well, I don't know how to tell her, but I have a problem with her already being married before." Joe began to laugh. "What?" Barry wanted to know. "What?"

"What type of damn problem is that? That's not a problem."

"It is to me."

"Why?"

"Because I always wanted to be the first to do things to my wife."

"First to do what?" Joe read his eyes. "Oh hell no...man there aren't no more virgins, negro. The last one was Mary and God hit that."

"You-are-so-mentally challenged, Joe."

"What, what I say? God did get Mary pregnant."

"Yeah, but not the way you and I would. I'm for real with this, man. I always wanted to be the first one to do everything with my wife."

"Negro like what, take her to the zoo or something?"

"No, hell no. In the bed, in-between the sheets. I know most married men have the same outlook as I do--as to being first--and since she's already been married that leaves me out in the cold. Weren't you like that?"

"Hell no, man, I never thought of no craziness like that. Who cares?"

"I do. More than likely, since she's already been married, she's probably done everything, you know what I mean? Had it here and there."

"Well, nigga, it's good that she has-- now you don't

have to teach her. Damn the instruction, just get it and enjoy!"

"See, but that's not how I think."

"Well, you don't want to get married then, cause that's the way it got to be. Okay, let's twist this around. You two haven't had sex yet. Am I right?"

Barry rubbed his hands together. "You're right," Barry confirmed.

"And, you ain't never been married, right?"

"You know I haven't."

"Now, when you two get on the honeymoon and are about to set it off, what if Stephanie asks you to eat her stuff?"

Barry smiled, "Negro are you crazy. Bon appetite!"

"Hold on, Mr. Eat'em up."

"What?"

"Now, right before you began to take care of business, what if Stephanie asks you. If you've ever put your tongue on another woman before--I mean right before you start working on her. What you going to tell her? Because I know you have, I know-your nasty ass has, Barry. And I know you'll tell her the truth and she might look at you like you're the nastiest negro on the planet, 'cause the stuff you was enjoying wasn't even all yours. So who needs to be worrying about who did what? You do. So I suggest you take your lady go get married and have fun 'cause ain't nothing promised one way or the other anyway. The name of the game is making your partner happy. Making'em and keepin'em happy. You got that?"

Barry gave Joe a glance. "That's pretty good, man. I never thought about it like that, and I damn sure don't want her questioning me."

Joe looked down at his report again. "I know you don't

your ass would be in all types of trouble."

"Tell me, what's the reason you and Dawn split up?" Barry wanted to know.

Joe shrugged his shoulders. "Just wasn't making each other happy, that's all, that's all it was." Joe picked up his credit report again. "Now look at us. This is crazy man. Mine...not mine...not mine, not mine, mine, not mine."

Before I Go

Jamell's entire being recognized that all engines were go. Every movement of her lanky dark skin body corresponded beautifully with the music, blaring in the dance studio, and looked precisely the way her dance instructor, Juliad, had envisioned for months. The sight of her elegantly flowing, left then right, then upwards and backwards, was splendid, graceful, timeless, instantly a gratifiying joy.

"Fabulous, wonderful...absolutely vibrant, gang! Jamell, you're destined to make us all famous. You're at the top of your game, Sweetheart. Keep it up, keep it up! Okay, let's call it a night!" Juliad shouted.

Jamell's supporting cast also felt the beauty of their craft and rushed over to Jamell, to congratulate her collectively, as she sat on the floor, wiping the dripping sweat from her body. She thanked them, too. Her smile was wide, radiant and loving. She always recognized that she was only as good as they made her to be.

Juliad watched the joyful gathering for a while. He

honored his dancers camaraderie and believed it was very important. Then he called out, "Jamell, Sweetheart. Can I have a second of your time, please?"

"I'll be back ya'll," Jamell told her ensemble. "The Great Ju-li-ad is calling."

Juilad released himself from stretching, his back when he noticed Jamell standing in front of him.

"What's up?" Jamell asked.

"Just wanted to conversate for a moment, Darling."

"About?" Jamell wanted to know.

Juliad thought for a beat, his arms now crossed and his chin resting on the ball of his glinched fist. Jamell kind of smiled at him. She'd always been in awe of how well he kept his body. Juliad was in his fifties, but looked as though he wasn't a day over thirty-five. His five foot-nine frame, and perfectly toned body, went well with his dark skin, narrow eyes and bald head. Dancing all his life had been good to him. "Tell me something," Juliad questioned.

"Anything," Jamell answered.

"How long have we known each other?"

"Oh...boy, here we go. Put it like this, long enough to know you're trying to bullshit me already, Juliad? Out with it?"

Juliad released his arms, and motioned to Jamell with his hand as he bent at the waist. "Come on, stretch your calf muscles with me. It's going to be a long show run and you don't want to get injured."

"You called me over to stretch?"

"Not exactly," Juliad strained as he felt the tension through his legs.

"Well, what then?" Jamell bent at the waist.

"Since I'm shutting down rehearsal two hours early today, so you can make your appointment, I hope you won't mind telling me what this doctor's call is all about. Is everything okay?"

"Oh, that's it? It's my yearly, that's all. Why you askin'"

Juliad clutched his heart. "Good, I thought you and Terrel done made a little one."

"Who? Wha'..?"

"Not that I have anything against you blessing our world with offspring, and of course having children is what married people do. Especially when you've been married for five years and dating longer than that. What can I say. Call it an educated guess?"

"Pull up, Juliad. Ohh, no...A little one isn't in our plans. Not right now, anyway. Look, the studio is finally at the point where we can bring back some of the glory from the Renaissance and you know that's been my goal all along. It's all of our goals or we wouldn't be here. I still have time left, before Terrel and I need to have a child but right now, it's all about this right here. Believe me, there's nothing to worry about." Jamell gave Juliad a glimpse of her heart-warming smile. "Now, will there be any more crazy ass off the wall questions from you today?"

"Aww, be nice. I was just concerned. I know things happen and I've long prepared myself for the day you walk in here and tell me you need to take a break, because of my God-baby. "

"Trust me, there's no need to worry, Juliad. I promise you that." Jamell began to stretch her biceps. "Hey, what are you doing tonight?"

"Tonight?"

"Yeah, what's on your schedule?"

"Well, Charles called and said he wanted to give me a rub down. And you know I love to have it rubbed."

"You're so triflin'."

"Why, what's up?"

"Have you forgotten? Ice is coming home today!"

"Oh, that's right! This is wonderful news, Jamell."

"No doubt about it, my baby brother's coming home. A mandatory forty-year sentence, reduced without any warning at all. I'm telling you, it's nothing but a blessing from God."

"Well, what do you all have planned?" Juliad asked.

"Me, Terrel and Valarie are planning on taking him out tonight. Do some dancing, just a little celebration, that's all."

"I really wish I could, but you know Charles and dance clubs? He likes the more intimate settings, plus I wasn't kidding I need a massage like you wouldn't believe. I'll give Ice some time to get acclimated again but tell him we'll all do lunch together when he's ready."

"Okay, I'll tell him."

Juliad shook his finger at Jamell. "And not too much dancing for you, young lady. I want you back in here at seven in the morning. We have work to do." Juliad turned around and looked at his dancers, who were still assembled in their gathering. "And that goes for all of you I'll see you back here at seven in the morning, so go home and get some rest!"

IN HARLEM IN ROUTE TO HER DOCTOR'S

APPOINTMENT, Jamell listened intently to her best friend and publicist as they ride in Jeep.

"And every paper in the city is already gearing up for the opening of the show. Jamell. I have friends of friends cashing in on favors, Sweetheart. If you think New York City loves you and your husband now. Just wait until they see these articles and attend the show! By the way, did I mention *Ebony* wants to do a spread on you and Terrel?"

"*Ebony!*" Jamell squealed.

"Yes *Ebony.* They called and said they're interested in doing a piece on the sexiest couple in New York City. Of course, I told them you had to think about it and I would get back to them, as soon as I had a definite answer from you guys."

"Valarie, are you crazy! Yes we'll do it! Hell yes! *Ebony?* There's no question."

"Damn right you will, but I like to make people wait. That's why I'm good at what I do. Now, how long do you think you'll be in the doctor's office, because I have to run down to the boutique and get me some lingerie?"

"I don't know, hour tops. Dr. Grayson has been kind enough for me to take this physical in parts, because of my schedule, and it usually doesn't take any longer than that. So, pick me up in a hour. Wait a minute, Valarie. Who are you buying lingerie for?"

"Huh?"

"You heard me, damn it. Who are the new draws' for?"

"They're for me, that's who. You can never have enough."

"You think I'm stupid, don't you?"

"I never said that?"

"But you're playin' me, girl. Don't think for one minute I don't know about the mail you and Ice have been sending back and forth, over the last couple of months."

"He told you?"

"He's my baby brother, he tells me everything. So, the draws' are for him, aren't they?"

"So....?"

"I knew it! Girl, you-are-soo-nasty!"

"Excuse me?"

"Valarie, you're planning to seduce my brother, aren't you!"

"Girl, think about it. Your brother has been locked up for ten years. Count'em, ten lonely secluded years. It's not going to take much to get it done anyway, I mean really-look at me?" Jamell ran her eyes up and down her friend and smiled. Valarie was nice looking. She was five-five, dark brown skinned and built like a stack of pancakes with the most precious thick body and rounded booty that girls from Harlem were known for. "Look, I just thought I would give Ice something a little special to look at tonight, it's not a big deal."

"Valerie, Ice is too young for you."

"No he's not and I'm just what he needs in his life right about now."

"What, an over-sexed freak of the week?"

"No, a seasoned companion. Plus it's only a seven year age difference, so get out my business, okay?"

AS USUAL, THE WATER RUNNING FROM THE RUSTY PIPES IN RIKERS was ice cold accompanied by its bland rustic color. But this time Ice didn't care one bit. His face was foamed up with shaving cream on the right side and he went on about his business of shaving, while he looked into his very small piece of a mirror. Ice couldn't see as well as he wanted but he could tell that he hadn't changed much in the ten years he'd been locked up. He still had the tight jaw bones and arching eye brows on his brown face. His eyes were red and tired but it was only a matter of time before they would become rested. He cut himself when he heard a sudden heavy voice echo, throughout his cell block.

"Another muthafuka' is free!" A big black guard, with rippling muscles and gold teeth, snarled throughout the cell block. His voice was strong, like Paul Robeson. Ice turned all the way around. It was D.C. He was finally going home. Ice didn't know him to well D.C. was a quiet brother and he was made that way. There was talk that his cell-mates had him in check and took turns going up in him from behind every other night. It was his punishment for ratting out their ex-cell mate and leader, for selling drugs inside. Ice knew he got a fucked up deal. Rumor was, the guards told him privately if he gave them the information they wanted, he would do four years of easy time. D.C. fell for their offer and, after spilling his guts about everything he knew about the convicts drug operation, they threw his black ass in the cell with the drug dealers best friends and told them who ratted on their leader.

No one ever forgets what happens in the pen. But D.C. took his sentence by the convicts like a man, even though he became the cell bitch as he served the rest of his time. He was responsible for keeping the cell clean, cooking and servicing the other three inmates on a daily basis. D.C. was always strong, even though he was always tired and weary. But for his courage, the convicts respected him.

"Be cool, D.C.!" an inmate on the cell block shouted. "You're all right with me!" Then, in unison, those who'd known about his tough time, including his own cell mates who filtered out the pain night after night, began to chant his name. D.C.! D.C.! D.C.! D.C.! until he was no longer in sight of their cells and mirrors that were used to glance down the prison block aisle.

When the noise subsided an octave, Ice wiped his cut face with a towel that dangled on his shoulder, then looked down. His eyes focused on his unlaced sneakers. He bent down and grabbed both ends of his laces and attempted to tie them. His first attempt was all wrong. He had problems remembering how to do something so basic. He tried again and, as his third attempt surfaced, he tilted up his head, almost wanting to holler out for directions. He did the best he could and stood up straight to put on his crisp white t-shirt. The shirt was different from the uncomfortable polyester which had occupied his frame for the last ten years. Then he brushed off his new jeans and was startled, when he heard the electric current beginning to jolt open his cell.

"Openin' up number seven and lettin' another muthafucka' go free!" The same guard's voice echoed for all to hear, as he approached Ice's cell. Ice didn't move. He could tell it was Big Bub, the big ugly guard. He waited until Bub was completely standing in front of his cell before he moved. It's the way he'd been trained.

"Let's go, nigga', or you want to spend another night in this bitch?"

"Nah, man," Ice told him

"Well, get your shit and let's go," Bub told him.

Ice picked up his bag. It was an army green laundry bag. Not much in it, except the letters he'd received from Jamell, who made a point to write him once a week, like clock work. He only had one or two of the letters he'd received from Valarie. They were so hot and nasty that, during a cell sweep earlier in the month, the guards took them away from him and sold them to other inmates for cash.

Ice stepped out of his cell.

"Ain't this a bitch, two within ten minutes," Bub mumbled, then he nodded down the cell block, leading Ice on his way. "Let's go, nigga'."

Ice began to walk down the aisle of the cell block and the entire block became unusually quiet.

"Another muthafuka' going free!" Bub shouted, as they walked. "I said another muthafuka' goin' free!"

Bub smiled and silently chuckled while he walked behind Ice. He knew the cell block hadn't forgotten and let Ice know with their silence they thought he was a pussy bitch they all wanted to take care of. "You muthafucka's ain't goin' to show no love for your boy, huh?" Bub wanted to know, as he clearly agitated the violent vibe that filled the inmate's eyes for Ice. "This muthafuka' leavin' ya'll. Ain't nobody got nuthin' to say?" he punched.

Ice could care less. He thought what he did was for the best. Best for himself and the other inmates as well, they just didn't understand. Ice was steps away from the main door that would clear him from his cell block.

"Yo, Ice?" An inmate called out.

253

Ice kept walking.

"A muthafuka', did you hear Shorty call you?" Bub asked.

Ice stopped and turned to his right side. "Yeah, sup?" He stepped towards the cell of one of the younger cats, who hadn't even been in the joint a week.

"Man, I don't give a fuck what they say about you around here. You cool with me," the inmate said, then he reached out to shake hands with Ice. Ice kind of eased and looked down the cell block and could see the out stretched arms, of some of the inmates observing what was going on, with thier small mirror's. Ice took a couple more steps towards the convict's cell and reached out to shake his hand. With lightening speed, the convict spit in Ice's face, igniting a forceful jeer and banging all over the cell block, that could be heard throughout the prison. Ice tried his best to grab the arm of the young punk and was quick enough to grab his wrist, then pull his arm out in-between the hard metal bars of the cell. Ice began turning it upward against the unwavering metal. He pushed upward with all his might, attempting to break the convicts arm, through the rowdy cheers of the inmates, and a plea from the young convict to let his arm be. Bub finally wiped the smile from his face, and stepped in to break up the commotion.

"Let him go, muthafucka'! Let him go!" Big Bub instructed, as he whisked Ice out of the cell block.

"Get off me, bitch!" Ice told Bub, as he wiped his face with his brand new shirt, while they stood in a safe zone.

"Don't start with me, nigga'. You better calm down, 'cause the Warden wants to see you."

"For what?"

"They don't pay me around here to know, muthafucka'. All they pay me for, is to do my job. So bring your ass on," Bub told him.

THE WARDEN'S OFFICE WAS NOTHING NEW to Ice. It had been where his deal went down. Normally, when a convict entered the office, inmates who worked there instantly made it known to those on the cell-blocks, but this time it was different. When they noticed Ice, with his civees' on, they knew he was on his way out and didn't want to waste their time running the useless info, even though the Warden very rarely saw convicts before they were released.

Big Bub pushed Ice into the office. "Sit down, muthafucka'. Here he is, Warden, just like you asked," Bub bootlicked to his boss.

"Thank you, Bub."

"Is there anything else I can do for you, boss?"

Warden Neri finally turned around from looking out onto the prison grounds. He was a lean white man with snow white hair. His thirty year stint in the military did him good. Even through his prison top brass uniform, you could see the power he enjoyed, all through his being.

"Yes, Bub, would you go down and bring me up a pitcher of ice cold tea?"

Ice puckered his lips and shook his head at Big Bub. The Warden's request instantly broke Bub's power down to house nigger.

"Would you like anything......Ice, isn't it?" The

warden asked.

"Yeah, that's my name. Thanks, but no, thanks."

It took the Warden all but five seconds to began talking to Ice after Bub went out for his tea.

"So, this is the big day, huh?"

Ice didn't respond. He kept his head straight and eyes on the Warden.

"I know you must be ready to bust out those new britches to get out of here, son. But the State Of New York wanted me to be sure I thanked you, personally, on their behalf for doing the right thing by us and cooperating with the State in the murder of Jason Byrd. 'New York' as he was called." Warden Neri walked over to Ice, then reached back on his desk and gave him a picture frame with a citation inside.

"What's this for?"

"It's a certificate of gratification, son from the State. Not a pardon, which would have been a lot better for you. But your drug priors were just too heavy. But I'm sure, if you get that thing copied and shown around to employers, they might even give you a break and give you a job washing dishes or something. But as I said, the State really appreciates your understanding in the untimely death of your cell mate."

"Look, anything I did, I did it for me."

"Is that the way you look at this, son?"

"My name is Ice and, hell yes, it's the way I see it. Your punk ass guards busted in our cell and raped and beat 'New York' and before you knew it, he was dead. That's what happened, that's what I saw, that's what I know."

"Well, that's not what you told the review board...Ice."

"Do I look like I'm stupid? If I would have told. I

would've been next. That's the only reason why I didn't."

The Warden paused and smiled. "You're smart. Very smart. But we did do right by you, didn't we? We kept you away from the other inmates. You know, if we would have placed you back with the general population, after you sided with us, you would've been dead in less than an hour." The Warden paused. "You know, I thought about putting you back out there, Ice? But I decided to take care of you, just the same."

"You call having me in solitary confinement for nine months taking care of me?"

"It saved your life."

"Fuck you," Ice said, to himself right before Bub walked in with the Warden's drink.

"Thanks, Bub, you can take him away now. Be careful out there....son."

ICE HAD BEEN OUTSIDE MANY TIMES DURING his stint in Rikers. But something about being on the other side of those walls made it seem like he'd never breathed fresh air before. Bub was still standing behind him, while he stood right outside of the gate, but he didn't give a fuck. He wanted to get as much good, clean air into his lungs as he could take.

"You leavin' or what, muthafuka'?"

Ice turned towards the massive hunk. "Man, fuck you. You better go back inside, to see if your master needs you to wipe his ass for him."

"You don't want to fuck with me, Ice. You know I can't leave until I see your black ass drive away. So step, muthafuka'.''

Ice and Bub exchanged cold stares. "Lata', you bitch ass nigga'," Ice told Big Bub. Ice took about four steps and realized he was finally free. Then he squinted his eyes and noticed Terrel signing autographs, as he leaned on the hood of his car.

"Thank you, Terrel!" one of two girls shouted as she walked back to her car. "My man gets out in another hour and you can best believe we'll be listening to you spin the love songs tonight! It's been seven years!"

"No problem, baby. You just make sure you do your man right tonight. He deserves it. Ya'll take care," Terrel shouted as they walked away. Terrel noticed a piece of lint on his cotton shirt and began to pick it off. Terrel was a very neat man who stood close to six-feet, dark skin with a slight afro. Terrel looked at his watch then glanced up towards the gate and noticed Ice walking towards him. "My, my my. Who and the hell left the gate open?" Terrel moved closer to Ice. "Glad to see you, my brother. You're looking good."

"Thanks, man, so are you," Ice said.

"Thanks. You know your sister, she's going to keep a brother right. She always has and I stopped worrying about shit I can't control years ago. So I'm feeling good."

Ice looked down at his new jeans and sneakers. "Look Terrel, let me thank you for the new gear. You didn't have to."

"Don't sweat it, it's cool. So you ready to put all this shit behind you, Ice?"

"Like you never knew, I'm ready to jet the fuck up out of here."

"Well, you see this right here?" Terrel ran his hand over the hood of his car.

"Yeah, yeah can't help but to."

"This is my new Beemer'. Check it out, 350 horses and if you want to get the fuck out of here, that's exactly what we going to do with this machine right here."

Terrel placed his hands on Ice's shoulders and turned him around until they both were facing the prison. "But first, I want you to stand here and defeat that shit you just walked out of, Black. I want you to leave all that shit that's been in your space right here and think about the life you have ahead of you."

Ice looked at Terrel. Then he looked at the ugly prison walls and noticed Big Bub, still staring down from the gate at them.

"That's right. Take a minute and defeat that shit, so we can get out of here," Terrel told Ice.

Ice stood without motion. He couldn't feel Terrel looking at him from the corner of his eye. Suddenly, Ice began to move his arm and he raised his middle finger up to Bub and held it still. Big Bub squinted his eyes, when he noticed his communication. Ice and Bub's eyes locked. Terrel's hand on his shoulder brought Ice out of his trance and deep hateful stare with Big Bub.

"Come on, let's get out of here," Terrel said.

BROTHER AND SISTER NEVER DREAMED sitting down and sharing a drink together would even become a possibility, until they were old and gray. Indeed, it was a joyful reunion that was totally unsuspected.

"You okay?" Ice asked Jamell, over the blaring music in the nite-club.

"Yes, Ice, I'm fine. Its just been one hell of a day that's all."

"You haven't stopped crying since you laid eyes on me, Jamell. Come on, cut it out. It's really me and I'm okay."

"Like I said, its been a hell of a day."

The next record the D.J. began to spin on the turntables startled Ice, because of the reaction of the dancers on the dance floor. "Damn, I have to get used to this shit again. It's really changed out here. Look at how these women are dressed!"

Jamell was blunt. "You better forget about all the women in here and get yourself ready for Val!"

Ice and Jamell turned their attention to the dance floor and smiled over at Terrel and Valarie getting their groove on.

"Yeah....she has it in for you tonight, baby brother."

Ice looked Valarie up and down. "She's hot, that's for sure."

"So come on, tell me why they let you out?" Val asked.

"I really don't know why."

"You don't know?"

"Not really, they said some shit about good behavior. That's all I know."

"Well, I'm proud of you. Now, it's time to get your life back in order. No more drugs, Ice, okay?"

"Oh, I ain't never going back."

"Did Terrel fill you in on the job he set up for you, at the station?" Jamell asked.

"Yeah, told me all about it. Thanks, sis' I know you

had something to do with the job and the clothes."

"Don't worry about it. It all was Terrel's idea, anyway. You know how active he is, when it comes to the prison system. Every since his father was beat and killed by guards, he's always tried to give a helping hand to anybody locked up. It's like it's a passion to him. You'll see."

Terrel and Valarie were all smiles, when they finished on the dance floor.

"Come on, Ice! You ready to dance, baby?" Valarie shouted.

"Watch yourself out there now, she's on a mission," Terrel told him.

"You want to dance with me?" Ice asked.

Valarie put her hand on her hip. "Yes, I do. And don't be out there doing the Runnin'man and shit 'cause that's played out and I have a reputation. Now come on, so I can put it on you!" They were off onto the dance floor.

Terrel kissed Jamell on the cheek. "So you okay, now that your baby brother's home, safe and sound?"

Jamell's smile wasn't full. "Yeah....I'm fine."

"What's wrong, baby?"

"I don't know. You know how it is. After you get through something, there's always something else waiting at the door to put you through something else."

"Well, not to worry, we're on a roll. You're getting ready to open on Broadway, my radio show is number one in New York City and we're about to be in *Ebony*! We're on our way, Sweetheart, so enjoy the ride with me."

"I guess."

"Hey, you sure you're okay, Jamell?"

"Yes, baby, I'm fine. Come on, let's dance the night away. You know you only live once, Terrel."

"True, true. But I have to work tonight, Sweetheart. Plus, don't you have rehearsal in the morning?"

"Sure do. But like I said, you only live once."

Terrel gave Jamell a concerned look and glanced at his watch. "Okay, now give me a kiss. 'Cause the lovers of New York are expecting me to do what I do best in exactly forty-five minutes."

"Do you have to go, baby?" Jamell wanted to know.

"You know I do. But do me a favor and listen to the show tonight, okay."

"I alway's do."

"Good, because I'll dedicate something to you. Something slow and sexy okay?"

JAMELL WAS PLEASED SHE HAD, AT LEAST for the moment, been able to distract her love ones. It was becoming increasingly difficult for her to stop hearing her doctors voice.

"I'm sorry to have to tell you this......" The words rang through Jamell's head three times over and louder than the music when she finally had a chance to sit alone. The words were the beginning of change for her and she knew the continued pounding words, blaring over and over in her mind, were going to cause great surprise and pain for everyone. She placed her hand on the bubbly sitting on the table and began to pour, while she watched Valarie and Ice on the dance floor for what seemed like hours.

"Care to dance?" A pudgy cheeked, overweight Latino

man came over to Jamell and asked.

Jamell didn't even turn around to look him in the face before she said, "Yes, I do."

In no time at all, they were on the dance floor and Jamell begin to work her body wild, hard and nasty, giving away to the rugged beat pounding the dance floor. It didn't take long for her dance partner to begin touching. He moved in cautiously, at first. He made his move when Jamell wasn't facing him. His eyes had fixed upon her ass in her tight black dress and his pelvis was drawn to her like a magnet. Jamell and the bubbly felt him, but she didn't seem to mind. She threw her hands into the air and her partner believed it was a green light to do as he pleased.

"I know that isn't Jamell." Valarie said.

Ice was so into the beat of the music himself, he didn't interrupt his dancing assult and first night of freedom to stop and look at what Valarie was talking about.

"Ice, would you stop it?"

"What? What's wrong? I thought you said you wanted to party."

"I did." Ice continued dancing and put his hands on Val's hips, to get her bouncing back to the music. "I mean I do. But look at your sister, Ice? What the hell is she over there doing?"

Ice stopped dancing. "Over where?"

Valerie put her hand on her hip and pointed. "Right there."

Jamell was in a zone. She was throwing her body at her dance partner and he was picking up all the pieces. She had turned to face him. After a few wild humps and grinds, she felt his hands on her waist, pushing her down to her knees, as if he wanted her to simulate giving him head, or even worse.

"What the fuck?" Ice mumbled to Valarie. "No, he ain't tryin' to get my sister on her knees out there. Fuck that!"

"YA'LL ARE WAY TOO PROTECIVE!" Jamell said to Ice and Valerie, as soon as they walked through the door of her place. All of them were tipsy from their drinks at the club. Jamell sat down on the couch. Valarie plopped herself in a chair and Ice sat on the floor, in-between her legs.

"What were you trying to do to me, Jamell, have me up all weekend, fielding questions as to why the lead dancer on the first black Broadway show in years was down on her knees in a dance club, without a care in the world?"

"It wasn't even like that I was just having a little fun," Jamell said.

"Well, it looked to me like he was about to pull out his dick and have some fun himself in your mouth. If you could have seen his eyes, you'd know what I'm talking about," Valarie told her.

"We're supposed to have fun before we die, aren't we? It doesn't matter anymore, anyway." Jamell said.

"Yes it does matter. You have an image. And why do you keep talking about things like they don't matter anyway? Things are taking off for you!"

"She's drunk, that's why," Ice slurred.

Valarie nodded. "I think she is, I really do."

"No, I'm sick," Jamell made clear.

"What?" Valarie questioned, as Ice sat up from rubbing Valarie's legs.

"Ya'll heard me right, I'm sick and the doctor said I only have a couple of months to live. Now, any more questions?"

Jamell stood and looked at their stunned faces, then walked slowly back into her room and turned on the radio and heard Terrel's silky smooth voice.

"And this one is going out to the lady in my life. Jamell, this one's for you," Terrel told his listening audience. "I love you so much."

Jamell stood by the radio and began to cry, as she listened to one of her all time favorites, "*Am I Dreaming*".

IT SEEMED LIKE IT WAS ONLY FIFTEEN MINUTES, before Terrel was in the Brownstone, asking questions, trying to find out what was going on. Valerie was no help at all. She was- entirely too hysterical. She spoke to Terrel in scattered phrases. Ice was so fucked up, hearing Jamell's words, that he began drinking some more. He had at least five shots of cognac straight. When Terrel approached him, he was too trashed to say anything at all.

Terrel walked into their bedroom. It was dark and very still. The radio in the room was still on and the reel to reel that Terrel had his engineer que up, which he specifically taped for emergencies, was doing just fine over the airwaves. Terrel stopped short of the bed and listened for a second. At the same time he tried to look down at Jamell, to see if she was sleep. He couldn't tell.

"Baby," he whispered. "Baby....is everything okay?" She was still. Something wasn't right and Terrel knew it.

Jamell would usually awaken at the faintest sound of his voice.
But not this time. She remained still, more than likely out from
the champagne. She had drank more than she ever had in her
life. Terrel could hear her breathing heavily. He pulled up a
chair to the side of their bed and listened to her sleep and only
hoped he could handle what was ahead.

When Jamell woke up, Terrel was sleeping in the chair.
She managed to slip out the other side of the bed, unnoticed
and unheard. She was fully clothed and wreaked of alcohol
and cigarette smoke. She made her way into the bathroom,
turned on the shower and stood with her face completely under
the water. She kept her head submerged, while she tried to
see if all of her newfound problems were a dream. It was what
she did all the time in college, when she would work to hard,
then dream that her counselor called her into his office to tell
her she didn't have enough credits to graduate in the eleventh
hour. She finally realized it wasn't going to work this time.
She had to face what her doctor revealed. She had terminal
cancer and would die, the same way her mother did four years
ago.

"Jamell? Jamell, you okay in there?" Terrel said into
the steam coming from the shower.

"Yes, I'm fine," Jamell said back. She opened her eyes
and could see Terrel standing outside of the shower.

"What's going on, baby? Valarie called me last night
and told me I needed to get home right away. When I got
home, you were asleep, so I didn't wake you."

"Thank you."

"So what's happening. You okay?"

Jamell finally picked up the bar of soap. "I don't think

this is a good time to talk about it Terrel, I have to go to rehearsal."

"What?"

"I said it's not..."

Terrel opened the shower door and stepped into the shower, fully clothed. "Is it a good time now?"

Jamell tried not to look directly at Terrel.

"Jamell, would you mind telling me what's going on, please? What's going on with the dejected face and red eyes?"

"Nothing, nothing we can't work out."

"What's to work out? I'm not clear about what you're saying to me."

Jamell starting washing her body and Terrel stopped her. Jamell began to cry.

"Jamell, what's wrong?"

"My doctor says I have terminal cancer and there's nothing anyone can do about it. They say I only have two months to live, Terrel. Two months."

Terrel and Jamell dried off and shared a long cry together. Somehow through the pain, Jamell refreshed herself and was able to put the same strong smile and positive attitude she used on everyone at the club the night before. Her strength soothed and encouraged Terrel. He tried to put things in perspective and was surprised when Jamell told him that she was off to rehearsal. She thought it was what she needed to do and there was no way, after all these years, working and sweating to obtain top billing on Broadway with her dance company, she could let them down. Terrel understood a little better, when Jamell told him she wanted this situation to be a part of her legacy and she was going to continue dancing, without anyone knowing her condition.

Terrel knew he needed to be supportive. Their entire relationship was built on support. When he didn't have a job, even before they were married, and went into deep depression, Jamell never once doubted his ability of getting an on-air personality job in the Big Apple. Even when ownership of the station changed hands and his job and livelihood seemed to be in jeopardy, Jamell gave him inspiration and support. So he knew he wanted to return the favor to his wife.

While Jamell was away at rehearsal, Terrel attempted to research cancer on the internet. What a fucking mess. It was maximum information overload. There was no way he was going to find out what the hell was going on inside of her body. He needed laymen term answers, so he could deal with what was going on with his wife. Terrel made a phone call.

"Doctor Grayson?"

"Yes, speaking."

"This is Terrel Holmes, Jamell's husband?"

"Yes, yes. How are you sir?"

"Well, actually not too good at all. Jamell broke the news to me she was diagnosed with terminal cancer and I need some questions answered. I mean, she looks to be doing so well and I don't know how to take all of this."

"Yes, she was diagnosed with terminal cervical cancer. To be honest with you, I've never seen it appear so soon, within a year's time of a check up. But I'm aware of Jamell's famiy history of cancer and I suspect it has a lot to do with her condition."

"But two months? What, can be done for her in two months? That's no time at all."

"At this point, not very much. I'm sorry. But I do think, a support group would be the best thing for both of you at this time. I'll have my nurse follow up with a call and let you know what's being offered for you and your wife. I'm very sorry about this, Terrel."

Part Two

"I COULDN'T IMAGINE BEING in Jamell's shoe's," Valerie admitted to Ice while driving in the car.

"Now I truly know how she must have felt when mom told her she was dying, when I was doing time."

"Has she said anything to you, yet?"

"Not a word. She's acting the same way she told me mom did when she found out. Strong, with a smile on her face, every single time I see her. I think the smile is a way to keep the questions away. So I haven't pushed. Who knows, maybe those group therapy sessions are helping out. What about you? Has she mentioned this at all? You're her best friend in the world."

"Not a word, every time we talk. I think she can see me about to cry. Me and Jamell have cried over a lot of shit. But not this. She won't let herself cry anymore. She's talked about how concerned she is about Terrel, though. She's starting to really worry about him."

"No doubt, he's still in shock. I'm surprised though."

"Why's that?"

"Because he's always talking positive and saying motivating things all the time. Defeating shit."

"Yeah, but--Jamell's been Terrel's love for a hell of a long time. I mean, they were seeing each other before you even went to prison."

"I remember."

"And it's going to be hard for Terrel."

"Tell me about it. Last night, I had to spin two hours of music for him non-stop, because he was deep into his thoughts, thinking about everything. He had fans calling, wondering why he wasn't talking on the air waves as usual. Shit, I didn't know what to tell them, I'm hurtin' too."

"Maybe the doctor was wrong Ice. They've been wrong before?"

"Nope. Terrel told me the doctors ran some more test and the cancer is there and spreading exactly how they said it would."

"And Jamell doesn't want to go through chemo?"

"You know how she likes to appear in public. And that would take every ounce of strength she has. Besides, chemo won't work."

"Well, I can say this. She's been very fortunate the media hasn't picked up on this. Ice, if they found out, it would be a fiasco around this place."

"I'm just happy she's at least bringing in the dollars for the show and letting people know about the talent still in Harlem, because that's what she always wanted."

Valarie stopped the car. "Well, here we are."

"Thanks for the ride, Val. Let's hope Terrel is doing better tonight."

"Yes, let's."

"What are you doing tonight?" Ice wanted to know.

"I don't know. Probably go home and do some soul searching."

"Val, do me a favor when you get in. Give Jamell a call. She should be up from her nap by now. You know, we have to keep her smiling."

THERE WAS A MAN STANDING IN THE CONTROL ROOM, talking to Terrel, when Ice entered the studio.

"Yeah, man, so that's the type of nonsense still going on at Rikers," the man said.

Instantly, his words drew the attention of Ice. Ice began to size up the guy who was talking to Terrel. He was light skinned with wavy hair and seemed like he was going out of his way to dress really, really black. Afrocentric even, to let people know what color he was. He had on a light brown, short sleeve shirt that hung long on his body and faded blue jeans and sandals. The beads on his necklace, Ice thought would probably be enough for anyone to tell what he was all about.

"So, brother, we really need your help with this one. It's bad enough the system is designed to make sure they keep the place filled to capacity with brothers. But when they start to kill our brothers, and nobody seems to give a damn, that's when we have to take a stand and let them know enough is enough."

Terrel stood up and extended his hand. "Okay, Fumaay. I'm down."

"My...brother," Fumaay acknowledged.

271

"Be listening tonight. I'll began to fill my listeners in about the situation. Just make sure you fax the rest of the info to me in the next hour, so I'll have all my ducks lined up properly, when I talk to my peeps in the streets." Terrel made clear.

"No doubt. I'll send them to you, as soon as I get home. I thank you, as well as the brothers locked up without any way to defend themselves," Fumaay said.

"No problem, no problem," Terrel answered.

Ice quickly put on his head sets and pretended to que up the night's advertisements for the show, as Fumaay walked behind him. Ice took off the head phones as soon as he shut the door. Then he called out.

"Sup', Terrel?"

"Happenin', brutha in-law?" Terrel said back.

"Chillin' man. You doin' alright?"

"Yeah I'm cool. Little tired, but I'm all right. Oh, yeah, thanks about last night, I just couldn't seem to get it going."

"I'm surprised you're able to make it in here at all. Like I told you, for me, this right here is therapy. But I know exactly how you feel."

"You're right. I don't want to be here. Told Jamell the same thing, but she pleaded with me to keep working and you know I don't want to upset her."

"True, we have to keep her smiling."

"That's all I want to do," Terrel assured.

"So, who was the brother that just left?"

"Oh, that's Fumaay. He's one of New York's finest civil right's leaders. I always call him the next Al Sharpton."

"Damn, he's got that kind of influence?"

"Oh yeah, he's a part of all the struggles for the brothers. Has been for as long as I can remember. This very moment he's trying to get some attention over at Rikers."

"My old home?"

"Yep. There's been three murders last month and the prisoners are crying out, blaming the deaths on the guards. But the administration constantly blames what's going on strictly on the inmates."

"So he came to you, huh?"

"Yep', he knows how I feel about prison, man. Don't forget, my father was killed inside. And to this day, they've never told us what happened. So every chance I get, I do what I can."

"Same old shit, happening in that hell hoe, I see," Ice said.

"Yep, nothing's changed. Wait a minute? Shit happened when you were in?"

Ice nodded and he began pulling music for the show.

"What happened?"

"Man, I don't like talking about it."

"Any and all info that I get always helps, though."

Ice took a deep breath. "It was my cell-mate." Just those few words took Ice back to the moment, like he was watching it at the drive-in movies. "They called him 'New York', because at one time he ran the biggest drug operation in the state and was sent up on manslaughter charges. One night, after the lights had been out for about three hours, and I know for sure it was three hours, because that's how long it always took for me to fall asleep in that bitch. I was just about off to sleep. Anyway, three guards opened our cell and dragged

'New York' from the top bunk. I didn't know what the hell was going on and neither did 'New York', because he was already in a deep sleep from the blunt he had smoked before lights out. So he was dazed when they snatched him down. I thought they had found out about the weed and were about to drag him out the cell, but one of the guards hit him over the head with his night-stick and knocked him on the ground. Shit, 'New York' was my boy, so I jumped up and the other two guards held me so I couldn't stop what was about to happen. And right before my eyes they raped him, all three of them, beat him, then laid him back into his bunk. The next day, the doctor came in and said he was dead. And those muthafucka's said he hung himself."

"That's bull shit," Terrel acknowledged.

"That's what I know."

"Did you tell anyone about it?"

"Couldn't. The guards told me, if I did, they would do the same thing to me. So I had to live with that shit on my conscience, plus watch my back from the other inmates. They all thought I was lite', because I didn't tell the investigators who came down what happened. It got to a point where they had me in solitary confinement. The inmates wanted me dead."

Terrel looked across at Ice. Then figured it out. "So, that's how you got out?"

"Shit, I guess."

"What you mean, you guess? You watched those punk ass guards kill a man and said nothing? Hell yes, that's why you got out."

"What? You got a problem with what I did, Terrel?"

"Yeah, I do. The same shit happened to my pops. I

even talked to the guy who saw how he was killed and the punk wouldn't tell me shit. So yeah, I got a problem with it."

"Tell, me. What I was supposed to do then? End up dead, too? Because either way, I was goin' to be a dead muthafucka'. Believe that."

JUST AS ICE SAID, JAMELL WAS UP AND IT WAS A GOOD thing Valarie called, because Jamell was on her way to focus her mind on the situation she couldn't change.

"So how are you, Doll?" Valarie questioned.

"Fine, I guess. All things considered."

"I know, I know."

There was a brief lull.

"Jamell?" Valarie called out.

"Yes?"

"Girl, I really do love you, you know that, don't you?"

Jamell got a charge and Valarie could hear it on the other end. "Yeah, I know, and I love you, too!"

"Ahh, you're so.....sweet. Let me tell you something, and this is the only thing I'm going to say about the situation."

"What, what is it?"

"Well, I wanted you to know that I think you should be commended on how strong you are. I mean, I don't think I could be as strong as you."

"Thank you Valarie....But it's only one way for me to be. You know how I've lived my life. No need turning into a little punk sissy now," Jamell chuckled.

"Yeah, those are the words I was looking for, because

that's exactly what I would be."

"Naww, no you wouldn't, that's why....." Jamell stopped her thought.

"Why, what, hun'?"

"We need to really talk, Valarie," Jamell said.

"That's why I'm here and it's what we've always done, right?"

"You're right. You're right. But we really have to talk about something," Jamell repeated.

"Fine with me."

"Well, you know me and Terrel have been going to group therapy about my condition, right?"

"Yes, I remember you telling me that."

"Well the group counselor--and I have to agree with her--is really emphatic about making sure our spouses have everything they need before we pass on."

Valarie didn't answer right back. It was the first time she heard Jamell speak of death and it gave her a queasy feeling.

"Valarie? You with me?"

"Yes, yes right here."

"So, what I think Terrel should have when I go, is you. Wow, I don't believe I said it," Jamell said.

Valarie heard Jamell, but she didn't respond.

"Val?" Jamell chuckled through the phone. "I don't expect you to say, Oh hell yes, I'll fuck your man when you die." She chuckled again. "But say something?"

"Jamell, girl, have you gone crazy? There is no...."

"Before you answer, hear me out."

"No, because......"

"Just listen to me for a second. No matter how you

feel about it right now, please, just think about what I'm saying. It's a no brainier that I'm dying. By now, everyone who knows has come to grips with that. At least I have and I need to leave my man with someone I know, who can take care of him mentally and physically. Someone who would never try to get him to forget me. You understand?"

"You guys talked about this with the counselor, Jamell?"

"I talked to her by myself a couple of days ago. And she told me if you're the person I want for Terrel, when I move on, then I should ask you. And she was right."

"Right about what?"

"About the way you would react. I expected you to be surprised."

"Well, yes, I'm surprised. There's no way I could do this."

"Why?"

"Because I couldn't. It wouldn't be right. You're my best friend in the world, for one, and how and the hell would that look to people that know us?"

"I've seen worse things happen in this city," Jamell affirmed. "Plus, this is the Big Apple! Nothing is surprising here anymore."

"This is not funny, Jamell. How could you ask me to do something like that? Are you okay?"

"I'm fine. I just think you're the perfect woman for him. Besides me."

"Would you stop that?"

"I'm serious. How long have you known Terrel?"

"I don't know, since junior high, I think."

"See, that's years before he and I ever met."

"So?"

"So, it means you two are friends. And that's exactly what he's going to need, when I go. Come to think of it, so are you, Sweetheart."

A MONTH LATER

"How you feeling baby?" Terrel asked Jamell. They'd been reflecting on her next to last dance performance, which had been a few hours earlier.

"I'm fine, I'm just happy that I'm going to be able to finish up the last show tomorrow. You know that means so much to me."

"I know, baby, and I'm happy, too."

" I told Juliad tonight."

"You did?"

"Yes, and when I left the dressing room he was still there, sitting by himself in the corner, in a daze. I'll give him some time, then call to see how he's doing later. He promised he wouldn't tell any of the other dancers, until after our last show."

"Baby, I don't know how you're doing this."

"Doing what?"

"Being so strong. It's unbelievable."

"I don't know. Maybe seeing my mother go through this is helping me. She was very strong, you know?"

"Yeah, I remember."

"But I've cried. Believe me, I've cried my eyes out,

because I still can't believe I'm dying."

"Don't say that, baby girl…"

"Well, it's true. I've already accepted there's nothing I can do."

Terrel put his arm around Jamell like he was never going to let go. "You know?"

"What's that."

"When you're sometimes sitting alone, and thinking about what you'd do in certain situations, difficult situations pertaining to your life. I've always said, that if I ran into a difficult situation, I would take it like it came and just call it life. Because that's exactly what it is."

"Yes, this is life, baby. And I would never wish this cancer on my worst enemy, Terrel."

Terrel was at least able to mumble, "I know, I know."

"It's just so unpredictable. But so far, I've been able to beat the doctor's predictions. He thought I would be restricted to the bed by now. I really enjoy going in to see him on my own and seeing the look on his face, when he sees that I'm still standing and strong."

"Please just keep doing whatever you're doing, baby. Please, for me, keep it up."

"I'm just having a good time and living and dancing like I've never done before and praying to God every chance I get."

"And you're shocking the world with your performance, I might add."

"I hope we'll still be able to do *Ebony* together. I asked Valarie to see if they could speed up the interview."

"Who cares? I just want to spend every damn second

I can with you."

Terrel put his arm around Jamell as they snuggled on the couch for about forty-five minutes.

"So, how's Ice working out? You never talk about him any more." Jamell wanted to know.

"He's cool."

"Cool?"

"Yeah, he's all right."

"Is that all you can say about my brother?"

Terrel huffed. "Jamell, do you know how Ice got out of prison?"

"Yeah, for good behavior. Why?"

"Please..."

"What?"

"That's not even half of it."

"What are you talking about, Terrel?"

"Well you know Fumaay right?"

"Yeah, you worked with him to get donations to some of the prisoners in county during the holidays."

"Well, he came to see me about some of the foul shit going on in Rikers."

"Like what?"

"Killings, by the guards, and no one seems to care about it."

"So, what's it have to do with Ice?"

"Come to find out, your brother had the chance to blow the whistle on a couple of guards he witnessed kill his cell-mate and didn't do it."

"Are you sure?"

"He told me himself. For his silence, they let him go

free."

"Doesn't sound like Ice. But you're upset with him over that?"

"Pissed."

"Why?"

"I know prison is rough and I know Riker's is the last place anyone could ever want to be, but I just don't think it was right for him to keep his mouth shut about a murder. Especially seeing they're still doing the same damn thing up there."

"Wait a minute."

"What?"

"This has to do more with the way your father was killed, than Ice, doesn't it?"

"I just think he could have gone another route, without keeping his mouth shut and helping the ones inside doing all the killing."

"Well, he's out now. And I'm happy about it. Very much so. That's all I can say and I hope you don't hold what he did against him."

THE NIGHT WAS FULL OF MIXED EMOTIONS. The Broadway show had been a huge success and Juliad and his troops with Jamell leading the charge, had accomplished what they'd set out to do. Once again, Harlem was on its way to being recognized as the premier location of the arts. But it all was bitter-sweet. It was Jamell's last performance and she was being bothered by a headache and intense body pain and fever. Terrel didn't want her to take the stage and Dr. Grayson was highly against it. But Jamell was adamant about doing the last show. Then it happened. Immediately after the show, Jamell sat in her chair in the dressing room and collapsed.

"HI BABY..." JAMELL MUMBLED to Terrel, as she felt him standing next to the bed, where she laid with her eyes closed.

"How you feeling?" Terrel asked.

"I'm just here, baby. I can't even explain it."

"Don't worry about it. I brought you some water."

"Thank you."

Terrel leaned over into the bed and raised Jamell up, as she drank from a straw.

"So how long have I been laid up in this bed?"

"It doesn't matter. The longer the better."

"I'm serious, Terrel, how long?"

"Fourteen...Fourteen weeks, Jamell."

"That's a long time for someone to have to wait to die, don't you think?"

"Come on, baby girl. Don't start."

"So how you doing, Terrel? You holding up okay?"

Terrel took a deep breath. "I'm fine."

"I guess this is a good time to tell you what's been on my mind for the last couple of months, Terrel."

Terrel sat down. "What is it?"

"Well, you remember you promised to keep me smiling until my very last day, right?"

"I sure do. And haven't I?"

"Yes, you have and I love you very much for it."

"So, what's this all about then?"

"Well, we've never talked about what you're going to

do when I go."

"Aww, come on, Jamell?"

"No, we have to talk about this, Terrel. Believe me, it's not easy for me, either."

"Okay, go ahead, baby."

"I wanted to know if you have anyone in mind to be with, after I'm gone?"

"What? No way, Jamell."

"I'm just saying if you do, it's okay. Look at me, I've been laid up in this bed for months, and I can tell you're miserable as hell. I even hear your pain over the radio at night."

"It's not about that. All I'm worried about is you. That's all that matters to me right now."

"Well, I'm worried about you."

"No need to be, I'll be okay."

"I am, Terrel, and I want you to do something for me."

"Like what?"

"This is not easy for me, but I want you and Valarie to be together."

"Ha', you're funny. Come on get some rest."

"No, I'm serious, Terrel."

"You couldn't be."

"Yes I am. I would really like to see you two together before I die. Think about it. She's perfect for you. You've known her for the longest, you're great friends and you both have something in common."

"Like what?"

"Me."

THE NEXT FEW WEEKS WERE FULL OF persistence and push by Jamell to get Terrel and Valarie together. Jamell was becoming weak, and was weaker than she led everyone to believe. She had lost most of her strength, lots of weight and was coming close to sleeping the entire day through. When she did awake, either Terrel or Valarie were in the room with her, along with her nurse. Ice couldn't stand to see his sister suffer and only came in to see her early in the morning and before dinner.

"I don't know why I'm doing this," Valarie told Terrel.

Terrel took a sip of his water. "Don't fool yourself. You're doing it, so we can get Jamell's mind off of getting us together. That's why we're both sitting down here about to eat this. What is this anyway?"

"It's tuna casserole. You've never had it before?"

"Yeah, but it never looked like this?"

"Whatever, Terrel. Let's just get through this, okay?"

JAMELL WAS CURIOUS. She'd finally pushed enough to have Terrel and Valarie have dinner downstairs. She felt different than she thought she would. She was empty, instead of being happy that there would be a possibility of someone taking care of her husband, after she passed away. Terrel and Valarie were right downstairs in the dining room. It was the only way Terrel would go along with her request. The only time he would leave the house would be to go to work and, even then, he called home every thirty minutes to see how Jamell was doing. The nurse was sitting with Jamell and, after she finished helping her drink a glass of water, Jamell told her that she wanted to be alone for a while and asked her to leave the door open. It was difficult for Jamell to hear what was going on downstairs, but she tried as best as she could to hear what was being said.

"Seconds, huh'? I see you don't have any problems with the way my casserole tastes." Valarie boasted.

"I'm hungry, that's why."

"See, this is already affecting our friendship."

"Why you say that?"

"'Cause I've known you all my damn life and already don't know what to talk to you about."

"I know. It's crazy but I promised Jamell I would keep her smiling and that's what I'm going to do."

Valerie took a sip of water. "You're right. So how's work?"

"It's tough. You know I've joined forces with Fumaay. He's trying to get down to the bottom of all the murders going down at Rikers."

"Yeah, Jamell told me about it."

"She did?"

"Umm,hmm. She said you were holding some type of grudge with Ice, too."

"No, I'm not."

"Well what's the problem then?"

"It's not a grudge. The man had to do what he had to do in order to get out of prison. I just don't think what he did was right, that's all."

"One thing about Ice though," Valarie admitted.

"What's that?"

"He won't talk about what happened in there, that's for sure."

"You've asked him?" Terrel wanted to know.

"Well, not about the situation you're talking about, but life inside, in general. He's very closed mouthed about it."

"So what's up with you two? I thought everything was a go."

"We were going to try things out. But after Jamell became sick, neither one of us has even mentioned a thing about it. What? What are you smiling about, Terrel?"

"You know what?"

"No what?"

"I wouldn't be surprised, one day down the road, they'll be three or four little 'Ice cubes' running around."

"Me and Ice and children?"

"That's what I said."

Terrel and Valarie both began to laugh and were startled as they noticed Ice standing in the doorway.

"Hey, Ice," Valarie said.

"Sup man?" Terrel wanted to know.

Ice was surprised to see Terrel and Valarie eating dinner together. "So, how's Jamell?" Ice asked.

"She's fine," Terrel and Valarie answered as Ice walked upstairs to see his sister.

JAMELL ONLY HEARD, Terrel's laughter, for the first time in months, as she tried to listen. She began to cry and decided to no longer fight the pain shooting through her body. She prayed, then closed her eyes and passed away. It was at least thirty minutes before anyone knew. Ice was sitting next to her. When he realized she wasn't breathing, his cries alerted everyone else in the house.

TERREL, VALARIE AND ICE were still under the tent at the grave site, after the funeral. They told Juliad they'd be over to the dance studio, where everyone was gathering to eat and drink and celebrate Jamell's home coming. Valarie couldn't take her pain any longer and stood just outside the tent, while Terrel and Ice were sitting in chairs, but rows away from one another in prayer. Suddenly, Ice stood up.

"You ain't shit, Terrel!"

Terrel raised his head and wiped his eyes. "What?"

"You heard me." Then Ice looked over to Valarie. "And Val, you ain't nuthin' but a damn hoe bitch!" Ice rushed over to Terrel and grabbed him from his chair.

"What's your problem, Ice?"

"My problem?"

"That's right, what's your problem?" Terrel asked as he looked at Ice's hands on his body. Valarie ran over to the commotion.

"How the hell you goin' to be sitting down having dinner with this bitch, while your wife and my sister and Val supposedly your best friend, was upstairs dying, that's what I want to know? Muthafucka, explain that too me?"

Terrel looked at Valarie, who was crying. "It's what she wanted, Ice." Terrel told him. "It's exactly what she wanted."

"What?" Ice asked.

"He's right Ice, Valarie talked to me months ago about taking care of Terrel, when she passed away."

Terrel then Ice turned their heads to Valarie to gain a better understanding of what Val knew.

"You know how Jamell was, Ice? She loved Terrel, she loved you, she even loved me. And we all loved her." Valarie began to cry uncontrollably. "Now stop it, Ice. Stop it, cause it's exactly what she wanted. Ice looked at Terrel as he continued his hold, then outside the tent at his sister's grave site then back at Terrel.

Terrel shook his head at Ice and whispered. "It's what she wanted Ice. Jamell just wanted me to be taken care of, that's just how she was."

Terrel and Ice locked their eyes on one another. They both gained an understanding from their pain. At the same time, they noticed tears forming in each others eyes. One teardrop each, fell down onto their faces. Ice was no longer fighting against what he thought was true. No way it could be true. He knew how much Terrel loved his sister, and Valarie too. Ice fell exhausted into Terrel's arms, then Terrel reached out for Val, and all three stood tightly clinched together, as they cried away their pain, for a woman who only wanted the best, for her man, brother, and best friend.

A Thought

Does death really do us part?
Or is it concealed and intrusive through the night and acted
upon to where the commitment we make is demoted to a
play ground pact?
Does death really do us part?
Separation within living bodies. Together or not.
Willing or not.
Does death really do us part?
Words of honor, words of meaning
Really?
Does death really do us part?
Sitting together...
Laying together...
Breathing together..
Does it mean we're together

Does death really do us part?

Acknowledgments

As always I want to thank the Creator for giving me the opportunity and patience to make my third work a success. Everyone should know that GOD is a wonderful shield and stepping out on faith is never a problem when you believe.

My parents Ann Griffin and Carl White for always letting me know-there's nothing I can't achieve! Always in my thoughts and prayers you've done a wonderful job!
Thanks go out to Miea Allen and my whole crew ☺ Thanks for the support twenty–four seven. S.B.L.Y.B.

To DanaRae Pomeroy, thank you so very much! Get ready to go at it again!
The entire family! Family know who they be ☺. Trey, Sandy, Brea Karla, Bidea, Qleo.Bidea Reva Walker, Emma Moore, Deenne, Erika, Aron. Also to my cousin Jeff White-doing great things in Philly! Danny, Tyke, Phil, Jerry, Amos and all of our family members

striving to make a difference.

Richard Griffin, Sue White, Chaka & Julie Chandler, Clarretta Allen, Uncle Warner Parsons

Thanks to my advance readers Anne Killcrease, Tabitha Floyd, Mary Melson

Number one fan—Rhonda Whitfield--Special thanks to Mary D. Roker, and all the book clubs around the nation. Specail thanks to Marsilina Eikerenkoetter, Dawn Godbold, Robin Augustine, Tracy Booth, Robin Clark, Helen Jackson, Minnyette Williams, Kimberly Bennett of Friends in Spirit- Denora Watts, Diva Book Club-Jeanette Wallington-Motown Review Book Club, Carla Newsome McManus-Sisters and Brothers Book Club of Hotlanta, Black Men Advocating Reading, Journey's End Literary Club-Authors on Tour President and Founder Vanessa Woodward, Mofee@aol.com for keeping my site tight! Not to forget Theresa, Dianna, and Tina who run the TNT Driving Service in Dallas--sorry I missed you last time but a brutha' was seriously out of action-next time though without a doubt. Tracy Roberts-for the interviews-keep doing your thang! Gerrie E. Summers and all black media and websites who help promote our writers.

Much love goes out to Terry Poindexter and entire family! Thanks for the phone calls brutha' you are still crazy! Remember this remember that☺. Mark and Latina Anthony and family, Darryle Melson, Carol Brown and family, Lisa Durroh and family, Rosita Page, Frank Tatum, Debbie and Donna Turner, Sandy Jackson, Lee Craft and family, Deborah L. Payton, Lamonte Waugh, Randy Clarkson, Alvin Dent, Maricruz E. Andeme, Ronald Steward, Mark Stinson, Kaloa Hearne, Garland Williams, David Dungy, Rick Carter, Michael Washington and family, Toni Jones and family, Nate

Beach, Joy Eubanks, Karen Wilson, Lisa Starks, Teresa House, Richale Watkins, Kim Mills, <<<stay strong-Waydis Boxton and family.

Big ups to my New York City Connection-Reggie English, Bill Bolden, Sheryl Jones, Ernestine Callender, Tonya Anderson, Wilton Cedeno, Vaughn Graham, Pam Mason, Joann Christian.

James Parham, Roy Johnson. <<<true soilders
Be on the look out for my first non-fiction piece with Dr. Arthur Thomas- Coming soon!......

I'm sure I missed a few but you know I have nothing but love for ya!

All the writers I've met along the way. Keep doing what you do-and don't let up! Walter Mosley, Sheneska Jackson, Victoria Christopher Murry, Yolanda Joe, Timm McCann, Thomas Green, Sister Souljah, Snoop Dog, Colin Channer, Lolita Files, Eric Jerome Dickey, <<don't forget my tickets to the premier! Can't wait to see ya' work on the big screen! Linda Dominique Grosvenor, Tonya Marie Evans, Brian C. Egeston, Teretha G. Houston, Michael Baisden, Sharon Mitchell, Patricia Haley-Brown

Support our black booksellers! I'm going to say it again. Support our black establishments because they push the books! All day, everyday! Believe me, there's a black bookseller in a city near you......

One more thing--don't forget to vote! We need to get out and vote.

Check out my website-www.Franklinwhite.com and let them know about it on Amazon.com and B&N.com

Peace. Courage.